The Triumph
of Frankenstein

BY THE SAME AUTHOR

The Quest of Frankenstein

The Triumph of Frankenstein

by
Frank Schildiner

A Black Coat Press Book

Acknowledgements: Mary Shelley and Jean-Claude Carrière.

Visit our website at www.blackcoatpress.com

ISBN 978-1-61227-594-9. First Printing. March 2017. Published by Black Coat Press, an imprint of Hollywood Comics.com, LLC, P.O. Box 17270, Encino, CA 91416. All rights reserved. Except for review purposes, no part of this book may be reproduced or transmitted in any form or by any means, electronic or mechanical, including photocopying, recording, or by any information storage and retrieval system, without permission in writing from the publisher. The stories and characters depicted in this novel are entirely fictional. Printed in the United States of America.

CHAPTER I

The night birds were hushed and the insects barely rustled. This was a bad sign, a portent of horror that old Moraika the wise woman was awaiting. She sensed it coming, knew that, when the blanco woman took the old slaver mansion, the darkness would enter the land. When even the animals who ruled the night were silent and frightened, the land was warning all to beware…to hide or be consumed.

Shaking her gourd, a medicine object she only used to frighten away the jaguars, serpents and other animals, she summoned the tribe to the long house. They came, obedient despite the youngsters' desire to refute the ancient beliefs of the old crone. But they all sensed something in Moraika. She was old when their grandparents were young and knew secrets that she only imparted in hushed whispers in the night.

As tiny as Khuno the hunter's young daughter of ten summers, and as withered as a flower denied water, the ancient crone seemed to grow in size and power as they squatted within in the long house. Nobody in the small tribe could mistake Moraika for some elder who lived beyond her years. She had knowledge, inner power, and could see the invisible forces that lived in the world. When she called and demanded attention, all obeyed without murmur or question.

This small tribe was named in their primordial and nearly forgotten tongue, "The Living." They were a small collection of huts and one long house on the shore of a mighty lake in the country known to the world as San Pedro. This nearly uninhabited region of that country was called *Corazon Negro*, the Black Heart. Few tribes resided in this harsh rainforest, a forbidding land with a terrible history.

The Living possessed a simple, yet surprisingly deep, view of the universe. Humanity was divided into three distinct parts: the first was the Living, their folk, never large but very tightly knit; the second group was the jungle dwellers, other tribes of humans who kept to themselves, rarely dealing with the Living. There was a harmony between both groups; the jungle dwellers kept to the deep rainforest; the hunters of the Living stayed on the outskirts.

The final group was the outsiders, men and women from across the lake. They possessed no respect for the land, the Living, or the jungle folk. They viewed all as obstacles to be defeated, with fire, metal and powders which exploded. The Living possessed no true respect for these humans; they were missing an essential element of life.

This element was the nature of life and death. The spirit of life, called Allpa, embodied the air, the sky, the jungle, the waters of the lake, the plants, the animals and humanity. You embraced Allpa, who was part of all living beings. To deny this spirit was to oppose the entire natural world, a path that resulted in a bad end.

Death was known as Supay, but this spirit was neither feared, nor embraced. To the Living, death was an inevitability for all. Even ancient trees, ones with branches larger than the long house, fell one day and became part of the earth. It was a cycle: Allpa created life; Supay brought them back to the dust. A cycle, one the Living understood and respected.

But outsiders, they seemed to believe this simple, yet complex, way of life was to be opposed, to be defeated. They attempted to destroy parts of the jungle to seize metals or stones from the ground. Or they tinkered with the body, believing they could live as long as the mountains one day. Foolish. In the end, no beings could deny the power of Allpa and Supay. But the outsiders did come to the *Corazon Negro* with this battle in mind.

The first outsider to come was a seeker of gold and other metals and jewels. Known as Hortado, the man died from the bite of a yellow snake two days after arriving. His followers all fell to a fever, their bodies quickly consumed by the creatures of the jungle.

The next of the whites to arrive was Hortado's brother, who sought the remains of his dead sibling. Heartier and stronger of body, this Hortado survived the land, but slowly went mad. Declaring himself a king, and later the son of God, he brutally murdered many of his followers before killing himself by leaping into a fire.

It was many years before another arrived, this one a fat, jolly man called Father Pupo. The Living knew he was as insane as Hortado, but in a different way. Where the former howled, screamed and attacked with his sword and blade, Pupo giggled and used a long black whip on the bodies of his followers and The Living. With the help of outsiders from his land, he built a house, larger than the long house with a second floor. The Living hid from him, hiding in the jungle, knowing he wished to enslave them and send them across the lake and into the hands of other whites. Pupo also died badly; his mangled corpse was one day found to be missing eyes, hands, tongue, feet and testicles.

Three more came to live in the large house on the top of the hill over the years. And they all died in terrible ways. One declared to all one day that he was God, sounding like the ancient dead Hortado. He stepped off the balcony on his house and crashed to the ground, breaking his neck and dying instantly. The second went into the jungle with a hunting party and vanished without a trace. Nothing, not even the metal rifles he and his men carried were ever found. And the last was killed by his wife, maddened that she found him in the bed of one of the slaves. The slave himself died as well and the wife ran into the lake, screaming and wailing. Old Moraika, who claimed to have known both Hortado brothers, once told that the screaming white wife was eaten by a giant snapping turtle. None questioned her word, but all who fished the river made certain they did so quietly, fearful of waking the terrible turtle.

And none of The Living questioned the tales of Moraika on the history of *Corazon Negro*. There was something fearful and abysmal about the land they called their home. The air was always heavy, humid and difficult to breathe by all but those native to the expanse. The days were short, with harsh sunlight that beat down upon all with startling intensity. And the nights were stygian, terrifying and filled with the cries of animals, the chirps of thousands of insects, and the calls of creatures unknown to all but The Living.

But the true horror to outsiders were the scents, the many smells that the jungle released which wafted into the nostrils of all. There was an overwhelming pungent sweetness that hung over everything, a noxious odor that was, at first, pleasurable. But within time, the corruption of that spoor became paralyzing, intoxicating and nauseating. To The Living, this was the aroma of life and death, birth and decay. But to the whites and others from beyond the lake, this was the essence of the very monstrous nature of the *Corazon Negro*.

Old Moraika declared that this was the jungle's method of protecting itself from those who sought to despoil the land and the people. Few could argue. She used the thighbone of Hortado as her walking stick, and many said her medicine gourd was filled with the finger bones of other whites who died in the land of The Living. Even Ayar the Fisherman, strongest in the village and one of its leaders, dared not argue with to the ancient wise woman. She was Allpa and Supay in one body, life and death, a terrible being who the tribe respected above all.

And the ancient crone was most fearful of the newest outsider, the pale-skinned woman and her companion. They appeared two moons ago, taking the old Pupo dwelling. A large team of men appeared with them, working day and night and carrying in many boxes brought from boats. But the workers left as soon as their duties were completed. These men, all strong, large workers with rough hands and loud voices, left with their heads low and their words hushed. The *Corazon Negro* was, to them, a fearful place full of terrible creatures. Escape was their choice, happily and without a second thought.

But the woman stayed, her male following her like an obedient pet. She met briefly with Moraika and The Living, giving them metal knives, leather pouches, food and medicines that the wise woman deemed acceptable. She gave these items as payment for privacy, requesting she never be interrupted in her work.

This request was met with amusement by all of The Living. None wished to enter the stone and wooden long house created by Father Pupo many years ago. The tribe didn't have a word in their language, but they felt an inner revulsion for the house. There was a wrongness about the dwelling on the hill… a violation of the natural order that they respected so fully. None would step a foot in that place, even if threatened with a horrible, lingering death. The closest they could come to referring to that fearful locale was to call it, "not part of Allpa or Supay." To The Living, nothing was more dreadful than that pronouncement.

But this woman's presence caused the old wise woman to become fearful and restless. And this was alarming to The Living, since nothing seemed to break the powerful calm of ancient Moraika. She stared at the jungle, the lake, and the horrible house on the hill for hours without moving. At these times, she resembled a statue, a carving made from a hoary piece of wood from one of the massive trees in the jungle. And when she emerged from these trances, her words were harsh, guttural and chilling. Old Moraika hinted at fearful times coming, events of monumental magnitude. None scoffed, though some, such as the gossipy Killa the Gatherer, or the dour Pacha the Lame, wondered if the crone's mind was finally losing its grip upon life. But even this, they contemplated only in their hearts, never daring to utter such a thought out loud.

When all were assembled in the long house, Moraika pointed her thighbone cane at the fire and whispered, "No fire. No sounds. None speak."

Pacha, who limped because of a jaguar bite had left him in charge of the fires and long house, put out the fire. And The Living sat in silence, staring up at Moraika. Even the babes, unnamed yet, and in their parent's arms, went silent. The wise woman had a strange ability to bring quiet to even the youngest of the tribe, often with a soft word. The children were not fearful at these times; they just obeyed without understanding why. Just as their parents and siblings did at the command of the ancient crone.

The twisted hag stood at the head of the gathering, her eyes scanning left and right. Jungle and lake. Her head moved back and forth in odd, jerky movements. To many present, she resembled a bird, a tiny creature that lived in fear of dozens of predators who dogged their steps on land, water and air. The Living knew something bad was coming, none having ever seen the wise woman behaving in such an odd manner. But Moraika's calm was broken, and her tribe squatted at her feet, fearful at the portents.

Then her ancient form froze, her eyes locking upon the lake. A visible shudder filled her body and she closed her eyes. The Living all tensed, watching her and feeling the dread cover them like a dark mist. Something was coming, something loathsome and rank, a transgression against the natural order that caused Moraika to quake in terror.

A low sloshing sound broke the apprehensive stillness, a wet sound of movement that was peculiar to their ears. It sounded as if a giant being was stepping from the depths of the lake, streaming with water and weighed down. The discord grew in volume, approaching the long house with long, heavy strides. Instinctively, the children hid their eyes, the young pressing their faces into the arms of a nearby adult, the older hiding their heads in their arms. They knew, without understanding, the truth of the situation. Something unnatural had arrived in their world, something fearsome and dangerous.

Then the being arrived, standing framed in the doorway of the long house. The creature was shaped like a man, but was like no being The Living had ever viewed. He was tall; two of The Living standing on each

11

other would not reach this creature's head. And his skin, visible in the bare light, was the pale gray of an ancient corpse. His hair, as dark as that of the tribe, was long, wild and framed his head like the pelt of a jungle cat. A giant, terrifying figure. Its clothes were a collection of tattered rags, the remnants of the odd coverings outsiders used to hide their bodies.

But it was the eyes, the unnatural yellow orbs that scanned them with deliberation, that they would remember to their dying day. They were large, luminescent and strange to view. They were neither the golden optics of the jungle cat, nor the faceted jewels of the larger insects. There was an almost reptilian coldness within these eyes, a perverse alien intensity that tore into the tribe with a glance.

This was no common outsider, this was a bizarre being too terrible to contemplate. The Living huddled before the creature shaped like a man, none daring the utter a sound or move a muscle. They were as frozen as a sparrow before a serpent, incapable of even the natural reactions of fight or flight. For they all knew, in their heart of hearts that either would result in an instant and painful demise.

The colossal fiend then smiled, causing all of the tribe to instinctively recoil. Razor sharp teeth glinted in the bare light, the fangs of a predator in the maw of a man-shaped monstrosity. They could be nothing more perverse, a more contorted parody of Allpa and Supay. The Living quaked with fright, waiting for the eldritch beast to strike.

But then the creature turned away, heading towards the house on the hill. Its stride was long and water shed from the miscreation's odd clothes. It fell as if Allpa's water wished to flee the form of this evil organism.

The monster vanished from view within seconds, no trace of a passage visible. But all knew the fiend's target: the outsider woman in the horrible house on the hill.

Finally, it was Moraika who spoke, her watery eyes meeting all of the tribe in a glance, "It begins again."

"What begins?" Khuno was the only who dared to ask, and even that was done in a voice that shook.

"The destroyers of Allpa, the deniers of Supay. They return. And they seek to change the order of all." Moraika's voice was a harsh croak, a rasp as fearful as that of the being who had just left them in peace.

"Do we run? Hide?" Killa huddled next to Pacha and looked at the crone with a tear streaked face.

Moraika shook her head slowly, deliberately, "No. We prepare. I will tell you. First, we sleep. Then, the work begins. For the outsider in the house on the hill is now an enemy to all life. And we must be ready when she acts to destroy Allpa and Supay. Go! Go to your homes and sleep. We have much to do."

The Living filed out, but few would sleep that night. All remembered the ghastly yellow eyes and the terrible teeth of the creature. And all remembered he had gone to the home of the outsider.

The outsider known by the odd name of Frankenstein.

CHAPTER II

Martin Mars examined the desiccated corpse Hans laid out on the metal table. Its yellow and brown fangs glinted in the harsh electric light, casting an unearthly light upon the chamber. The harsh antiseptic smell of alcohol barely hid the underlying stench of blood, mold, dust, excrement, and decay. This was a room where corpses lay, sometimes for longer than was hygienic. But each carcass released a piece of itself into the atmosphere, placing a permanent trace upon it for all time.

"Excellent, Hans. Truly excellent. How did you find such a... unique specimen?" Mars's voice was a soft purr, the insinuating tones of a cat as it puts its victim at ease before the death strike.

Mars was a man of medium height, with a balding head of dark hair and narrow, brown eyes. He possessed a clear complexion, a fit body and a bright, if slightly crooked, toothed smile, which was engaging. To any who viewed him, Mars would be a moderately successful businessman, probably a regular churchgoer with a wife, two children and a pet dog,

And they would be wrong on all counts. Martin Mars, real name Henry Toole, despised churches, women, children and pet animals. Despite an outward appearance of geniality, Martin Mars was a cold-blooded man, a calculating creature capable of doing anything to further his cause.

And that cause was Martin Mars. The son of a Midwestern farmer, he had discovered at an early age that he despised farm life and anything related to it in any way. Commerce was even less interesting. The kids at school who would wheel and deal for baseball cigar cards, marbles and cash were fools in his young mind. What young Henry Toole a.k.a. the future Martin Mars craved was adulation. He wanted people to worship the very ground he walked on, to give him all he demanded willingly and happily. The path to that route appeared difficult, until the day he killed the ghoul that murdered old Mrs. Wilson.

How the creature arrived at Two Forks, Iowa, nobody ever found out. But there were rumors of something strange inhabiting the old graveyard just outside town. Most of the folk in town didn't have any kin in that graveyard; it had been filled up shortly after the Civil War. But old Mrs. Wilson, the widow of the late Colonel Paul Wilson, whose family helped build Twin Fork, had family in that boneyard. Dutifully, each Sunday, rain, snow or shine, she walked the two miles to the graveyard and paid her respects to her and her husband's many relatives buried there.

And young Henry Toole lay in wait, hoping to see something terrible happen. He didn't give a give a damn what happened to the old biddy. She was a nasty woman, a harsh gossip, and critic to all in town. Even at 11, Henry Toole witnessed how many men and women flinched when she walked into a room. He knew, without comprehending why, that they were all frightened of becoming the old woman's next target. In a way, she reminded him of Dennis Sweeny, the butcher's boy. Dennis was big, loud, stupid, but terrifyingly strong. His idea of fun was stealing lunches from smaller kids. His dad, who was a larger copy of the son, taught Dennis how to box and wrestle, and encouraged him to bully anyone weaker.

Old lady Wilson was cut from the same cloth as Dennis and his oversized father, Billy. But Wilson's tactics were smarter, more insidious. As the wife of a war hero and a relation of the town fathers, she sat on many committees, civil, religious and social. And in each of these circles, Mrs. Wilson used her power to put down anyone whom she disliked, or felt didn't demonstrate the proper servile diffidence towards her. Cutting remarks, gossip and snubbing were her weapons, and she used them with the skill of a veteran prizefighter in the ring.

This was why the future Martin Mars crouched in the bushes at the north corner of the graveyard. His reasoning was sound. The wind was blowing his direction, so no predator could sense his presence. And his family's farm was north of the cemetery, a fact which would be important later.

He was well-prepared for this possible encounter. He carried his father's shotgun, loaded with slug shells, his late grandpa's old Colt Dragoon, and an old, but very sharp sickle that hung in the barn. If these weapons were too much, Henry Toole planned on hightailing it back home and pretending he'd never come to this place.

The graveyard was a small plot, about two or three acres wide, shaped like a half-moon. The tombstones were mostly falling into disrepair, many having tipped over from the twister three years back. A heavy layer of weeds and undergrowth covered the once-manicured site. There was a melancholy air about this place, not merely because this was a burial ground for loved ones from the town, but the neglect and shabbiness projected a forlorn atmosphere to the world. This place, meant to be a monument to the loss of loved ones, was little more than a dumping ground for the past. It was a human refuse heap, little better than a trash pile. But, in this case, the waste was once a living breathing person.

Precisely at noon, Mrs. Wilson appeared, stepping slowly across the crumbling stone arch that once held a large iron gate. She followed the weed-covered path to the Wilson plot, bending down to remove several leaves from her husband's headstone. Then she began to pray, her harsh voice echoing across the cemetery.

To the future Martin Mars, she sounded like a crow, caw-cawing into the air and hoping everyone heard her call. Because he knew she didn't believe in God, the Devil, or even in the goodness of her late husband. He'd watched her in church, spotting the fake manner she behaved. Mrs. Wilson tried to be better than everyone, first to speak in all prayers, loudest voice when hymns were sung. But there was always a glint in her eyes, a covetous gleam that told her true mission. She wanted to be viewed as the most God-fearing, the Lord's most faithful follower. This way Mrs. Wilson could criticize others, question their faith and fervor.

The same went for her marriage to the late Colonel Wilson. The Colonel, a veteran of the Spanish American war, was a drunk, a shell-shocked wreck of a man. Loud noises frightened him, as did silence, the neigh of horses and a host of other ailments. The rare times he could bring himself into public view, usually upon some day in which soldiers were celebrated, everyone knew he was sneaking nips of corn whiskey from a pair of flasks he kept in his hip pockets. The adults in town were publically polite to the formerly great warhorse, but spoke with amused delight at his pathetic, bedraggled figure when they thought nobody was listening.

But if one had listened to Mrs. Wilson, you would have been led to believe that the old lush was General Sherman himself. She spoke in glowing terms of his bravery, his kindness, his generosity for all to hear. For most of the people his age, her tales were history. These stories were the legends of a brave warrior who fought evil Indians and slippery Spaniards. The fact that their son William, and their daughter Lilly, had moved away from the state, Jack becoming a land surveyor in Texas and Lilly marrying a Pennsylvania lawyer, and never visited, didn't shake the Wilson legend.

This was a great lesson for Henry Toole. He learned at that young age that the truth truly mattered very little in the minds of most people. If you told a story right, with just enough truth and conviction to make it believable, the fiction became reality. This was the path he set for himself, the path to adulation like Mrs. Wilson craved and demanded. But on a larger and more successful scale.

And it all came to fruition when the ghoul moved into view. The creature was about the size of Mrs. Wilson, a shabby, low figure that appeared to slither as it crept up on the unsuspecting old woman. The ghoul's skin was an unnatural muddy brownish white, a pigmentation no creature walking the Earth would ever hold. It possessed long bony fingers, each ending in a long, sharp, black talon. And its mouth was a mass of brown and black teeth, each wickedly sharp.

The future Martin Mars originally thought of saving Mrs. Wilson, presenting himself as a heroic figure to all in town. But he dismissed the idea, remembering that the old woman would find a method to make herself the center of attention. No, best to be a young man who almost completely succeeded, arriving just after the attack. This would allow him to act modestly when compliments arrived. A modest hero was preferable at a young age.

Which was why he watched as the ghoul snarled, causing Mrs. Wilson to shriek and turn. She tumbled back as the monstrous creature pounced, the barbed claws piercing the elderly flesh without resistance. Her cries were cut off as the ghoul bit down on her exposed neck, snuffing Mrs. Wilson's life in an instant.

Waiting until the beast was beginning to feed, Henry Toole crept closer, raised the shotgun and fired twice at the quivering form. The ghoul's head exploded in a shower of yellow matter, a fleshy wave that covered a nearby tombstone. Pulling out the huge pistol, the young boy pumped bullet after bullet into the fallen monster.

But this attack proved unnecessary; the ghoul was dead. The creature's arms and legs quivered for a moment, and then it fell still and dead. The hideous form lay across the torn body of Mrs. Wilson, her red blood mixing with the ghoul's stick brown secretions. The stench that rising was horrific, a nauseating compound of copper, rotted meat and other disgusting scents.

And that was where the townspeople, roused by the sound of multiple gunshots, found Henry Toole. He was crouched by the corpse of Mrs. Wilson and her killer, the victim's blood still on the enormous orifice that was once the ghoul's mouth.

"I tried to save her. I was too late!" His voice was hollow and sad, a downcast hero who was unable to save the life of a good woman.

And that was the first step in his career, that of a showman of the oddities of the world. The people of the town celebrated his accomplishment, gave him a new shotgun of his own as a gift. Only Dennis Sweeny was unimpressed, determined to knock the town's new young hero down a few metaphorical pegs. But Henry Toole was ready, having prepared for this inevitability.

This scene took place on the baseball field. A group of eighth graders were playing a game, getting ready for tryouts for the team. No adults were present, exactly the location for a bully to make his presence felt. To make certain his plans went right, Henry made certain he was seen heading towards the outhouse back behind right field.

"Hey, you!" Dennis stepped into view as Henry exited the outhouse. He had both fists balled and he raised one with dramatic slowness.

And that was when Henry Toole struck. Pulling the hunk of lead pipe from his sleeve, secreted there when he was in the outhouse, he slammed the metal into the taller boy's stomach. Dennis wasn't even able to moan, he merely dropped and began puking his guts up on the grass. Henry pocketed the pipe and walked on, knowing it looked as if Henry Toole punched out Dennis Sweeny. The legend began to grow...

But back in the present, the former Henry Toole used a set of shiny silver forceps to peel back the lips of the dead werewolf. The mouth was enormous, the oversized fangs the largest he had ever seen in a shapeshifter. Exactly what he required for the trip to Europe to be a grand success.

On this expedition, he possessed the body of a kobold from the German Black Forest, a book bound in human skin on the worship of Satan taken from a cult started by the infamous mass murderer Gilles de Rais, the mummified eyeballs of a dead Spanish Templar, and the decorated skull of an Italian necromancer. All were obtained by hunts and theft, for Martin Mars and his assistant Hans had no compunctions about killing to obtain their chosen items. Four old Satanists were killed by his hand, with another two sliced to pieces by Hans. This had allowed them to take the disgusting book as well as all the skull vessels and the likes from the hidden dark temple. The satanic accoutrements weren't particularly interesting, but would make for good stage props for his traveling museum and radio show.

Hans slid closer to the table, a submissive smile chasing across his unlovely face. He was a tiny man, a foot shorter than Martin Mars; he possessed rounded, hunched shoulders, pasty, pale skin and the hissing sibilant voice of a servile man. His watery dark eyes were too large for his face, and his buck teeth made him look like a pathetic, weak little man. He was also a complete and utter psychopath with a love for blood.

In many ways, Hans reminded Martin Mars of a hyena, a predator who waits for the moment when something strong is weak and helpless. Then they strike with a ferocity that caused even the strongest to fear these creatures. Since rescuing the little man, Hans's talents had proved useful in Martin Mars's mission. Whether it be was an antiques dealer who didn't want to part with the mummified hand of a hanged warlock, or a newspaper editor who rejected the Mars Mysteries weekly cartoons, little Hans more than earned his keep.

"I was walking through an old graveyard and found a stone. On it was a scratching, from a knife. It read, '*May he burn in Hell*,' So I dug it up and found this in the grave. Did I do right, sir?" Hans's voice was a hissing wheeze, disagreeable on the ears, but he was as loyal as a dog to Mars.

"You did, you did." Martin Mars crossed to his leather bag and began retrieving his tools. He would take the head of this creature; the rest could be dumped into the Seine. "Did you leave the grave open?"

Hans shook his head slowly, almost bowing as he replied, "No, no. I covered it up and stamped on the dirt.

I did not want the silly Frenchies to think the Werewolf was walking about again."

Martin Mars nodded and checked the edge of the bone saw. The metal was sharp, freshly honed and polished by Hans. "Well done, well done. Did you obtain our letters and telegrams from the drop boxes?"

Hans smiled with happiness, his lips quivering as he pulled a small stack of papers from his inside jacket pocket. "I did, master. I read them, as you ordered. Shall I tell you each?"

"Yes, yes." Martin Mars began sawing at the exposed neck, watching as puffs of dust rose in the air from the dried carcass. "Summarize each, summarize each."

Hans scanned the first page. "The Kane newspapers are now carrying your weekly column. They will pay what you asked. And *The Daily Beast* in London agreed to your terms as well."

"Excellent, excellent. Continue, continue." Mars placed the head in on a metal tray and began searching for a large metal container. Formaldehyde would preserve the dry flesh, but he didn't want the skull damaged in transport. When he shipped this back his headquarters in Chicago, the curators of his traveling museum would prepare the remains as an exhibit. He would then write a tale of how he stalked the creature, chasing it through the streets of Paris... or perhaps the ancient sewer tunnels. And then the story would end with how Martin Mars had once again saved the lives of innocent men and women from a terrible supernatural monster. People would pay to gape in terrified astonishment at the heroic actions of the legendary monster hunter.

"Two hunters in a place called Lytton in Canada spotted a hairy ape creature in the woods. But the lady who sent the letter, your Miss Morse, writes that they were drinking spirits made from corn." Hans's goblin face twisted briefly at the mention of alcohol. He might be a murderer who was once sought by all of Berlin , but he didn't stoop to drunken antics!

"Toss it aside, toss it aside." Mars pushed the body of the nurse aside and opened a cabinet. A large silver container lay within, used for scientific specimens. Hans did a good job picking this laboratory for their base in France. Everything they required was available here. And it was far from any neighbors or the police.

"Three reports of vampires in London, Wallachia and Warsaw. A gray-skinned giant killed six men in a shanty town in a place called San Pedro. A giant rat is killing people in Dutch East India..." Hans continued to read, carefully shuffling each page with careful, precise efficiency.

"Hold! Hold!" Martin Mars slammed the metal canister down on the metal table and stepped close to his assistant. "Repeat what you just said!"

Hans knew his employer was very excited. His habit of repeating himself suddenly dropped off and his eyes were wide and wild. Shuffling back several pages, he began again, "Three reports of vampires in London, Wallachia and Warsaw. A gray-skinned giant killed six men in a shanty town in a place called San Pedro. A giant rat..."

"Stop! Cease speaking. The gray-skinned giant. Provide me the specifics of this assault. Leave no details out." Mars was breathing heavily, gripping the edge of the table and staring at Hans.

Hans placed the disused messages aside and scanned the page in question. "The information is from two weeks past. In the slum of a small city called Plata.

A man walked through the region. He is described as ten feet-tall with skin the color of granite. A group of men attempted to rob him and he killed them all." Hans summarized the details in a monotone voice, his eyes scanning for anything else Mars might wish to know.

"How did he kill them?" Mars leaned forward, almost vibrating as he listened.

Hans read the lines three times and made certain he wasn't making a mistake. "One with his hands, one he stomped upon, and the others..."

"Yes?" Mars whispered.

"He... bit their necks. Tore out their throats..." Hans was hesitant to state these words, they sounded so grotesque.

Martin Mars banged his fist down on the metal surface. "At last! This is the one!"

"The one... what, master?" Hans took a step back, wondering if his employer suddenly lost what was left of his reason.

"The hunt I've always dreamed of, Hans. The find of finds, the greatest treasure of the hidden world." Mars looked off in the distance, seeing the millions who would pay tribute to his bravery once he captured this prize.

"You say this is a true story, master?" Hans had learned many odd and terrible things since Martin Mars saved him from a crazed mob back home, but these statements were the oddest ones he'd heard yet.

"It is, Hans, it is! Have you ever heard of a creature called Gouroull?" Mars placed the head of the werewolf in the vessel and began making his plans. The hunt of his life was about to begin...

CHAPTER III

The arm twitched, the fingers spasming briefly before falling limp. Elizabeth Frankenstein frowned and changed the setting on the nearby dial and watched the arm again. Nothing happened. She sighed, shaking her head slowly.

"We're missing an element in the elixir. A compound that revitalizes the dead tissue." She lifted the arm, detached from the corpse of a boy involved in a bus accident, and studied the severed limb without visible interest. Stepping over to the far end of the room, Elizabeth tossed the limb out the window and watched as it fell into the jungle sward.

"We've followed every step of your ancestor's notes. I don't see what we could have missed." Hugh Larkin watched Elizabeth Frankenstein with greedy eyes, worshiping her from afar. Yet, he knew in his heart she possessed no ability to respond in kind.

They'd met in university, both medical students at the prestigious University of Edinburgh. Elizabeth, one of only ten women in the whole school, was a standout, a genius with the ability to make the best teachers appear foolish and decrepit. Her sharp tongue and flashing blue eyes caused many of the staff and student body to invent colorful nicknames at her expense. But she was disinterested in such nonsense, constantly demonstrating her brilliance in all fields of study.

Why had she chosen him, Hugh still never comprehended. He was an excellent student, but not on her level of knowledge and skill. And he had a moderate income since his parent's death, but nothing close to that of twenty or more students in their class. Yet, one day, Elizabeth stepped into his path, a powerful figure that overwhelmed him despite his greater height and strength.

"You are Hugh Larkin. I require a partner in my studies. Do you agree?" Elizabeth didn't wait for his answer. She merely thrust a slip of paper into his hand, nodded, and headed off towards the anatomy lab.

The page proved to be the townhouse she owned near the university. He arrived dutifully at noon the next day and their studies began. Besides the required work for the school, Elizabeth had a plan for advanced work, studies into the nervous system, pathology, biology, chemistry... the list was long and quite esoteric. Larkin found himself following her lead, her brilliance forging a pathway that led them both to graduate with honors.

But there was a darker side to Elizabeth's research. On four occasions, they stole unclaimed bodies from the hospital morgue, replacing the weight in the pauper's coffins with sand bags. She possessed a deep fascination with the dead; her knowledge of pathology was greater than the entire faculty of the medical college. Yet, she never revealed that to anyone, specializing in surgical studies and research throughout their time in school.

Then came the day he found her with a fresh corpse in the morgue, injecting a series of fluids in the body of a heart attack victim. The body shuddered several times before blood spurted from the cadaver's nostrils. Elizabeth watched the body with rapt fascination, her whole body vibrating with delight at the reactions.

"What are you doing?" Hugh's voice was high-pitched and terrified as he viewed the predatory gleam in her eyes.

"Changing the world," replied Elizabeth in a hushed whisper, one filled with delight. She took him back to her townhouse without another word, yanking off his clothes and pushing him into her bed.

She was a fierce lover, though to use that term was completely incorrect. This was sexual release, a biological response Elizabeth required, and undertook for her own needs. She left the bed hours later when the act was completed and never referred to their sexual congress at any time. But later, as they ate a cold collation that her maid left for her each night, Elizabeth revealed the truth of her work, of her heritage. Hugh had tried to discuss the occurrence in her bedroom, yet she clearly possessed no interest in discussing their affair.

"My great grand-uncle was a man named Victor Frankenstein. You do not know his name? Good, I thought not. His name is lost in time, an unsung hero in medical science. My uncle realized that death need not be an inevitability, that life could be brought back to the dead!" Elizabeth's face flushed as she spoke of her long-dead relative. This was the greatest emotional response she had ever demonstrated before Hugh.

"But that's not possible," he said. "Dead is dead. Once the bodily functions cease, decomposition begins and..." Hugh was cut off by a slicing motion by Elizabeth's hand.

"Don't be as foolish as those old imbeciles, Hugh! You viewed with your own eyes the brief return to life of that corpse this morning. That was the first step in recreating Victor Frankenstein's work. I have his early notes and the reactions were exactly the same!" Elizabeth stepped over to a shelf in her lab and pulled out a sheaf of notes and a battered yellowing book with a cracked leather cover.

"A few jerking motions of a nervous system is not a return to life," objected Hugh. "Cadavers often react that way. I once viewed one sit up straight when I was assigned to pathology." His reply was cold and crisp. He was experiencing mixed emotions about Elizabeth, her mania and her humiliating disinterest in any emotional connection since their sexual encounter.

"That is merely the first step. It was a brief resurrection of the nervous system. Here, read this passage. You do read German? Good! You'll find Victor illuminates every step of the creation of the compound. And the physical reaction is precise, down to the exact timing of the responses!" Elizabeth pushed the yellowing pages before his eyes, watching as he read the precisely written lines of text.

And the words were exactly as she stated. The details were as Hugh observed, the spasms, the blood and fluids appearing a short time later. Hugh looked up and handed back the diary, still disbelieving the larger story that Victor Frankenstein and his modern ancestor insisted was possible.

He was about to reply when Elizabeth slapped a large piece of parchment upon the table. The etching was monstrous, a grotesque gargoyle, a troll of myth, a penny dreadful nightmare created by an opium eater. The monstrosity was enormous, with twisted features, elongated jaws with the sharp teeth of a predatory beast. All in the form of a mockery of mankind, a horrific sight for the eyes.

She tapped the word next to the dreadful drawing, the word that would change Hugh Larkin's whole life: *Gouroull*.

"What is a Gouroull?" Hugh studied the signature at the bottom, noting that this work of horror was performed by Victor Frankenstein himself.

Elizabeth did not answer, but placed a slip of newspaper on top of the etching. The article mentioned a maniac murdering a drifter in a town in Ireland called Kanderly. The death was by a bitten throat, a terrible bite that nearly tore the victim's head from his shoulders. The police sketch was remarkably similar to the drawing by Victor Frankenstein.

"A coincidence," Hugh scoffed, still unconvinced this was little more than a bit of fiction by a madman.

"I thought that myself, until I interviewed an elderly woman who resided in that town. She referred to the attacker as *Gouroull*. I never mentioned the name. And she gave me this," Elizabeth handed him another piece of newsprint, this one in French.

The story was similar to the Irish article, though twenty years later. A giant maniac murdered a minister by tearing out his throat with his teeth, leaving the holy man's battered and violated widow behind. There was no drawing, but the description by a witness was that of a giant gray-skinned man with sharp teeth.

"Gouroull, from what I have learned in my research, is the name of my ancestor Victor Frankenstein's greatest success. A creature that was once dead, but is now living. But not merely alive, but near immortal. I will recreate and improve upon Victor's work. And you will help me, Hugh. We will defeat death and change the face of the world." Elizabeth took his hand in hers. The clasp was not a loving embrace, but a declaration of ownership similar to that one might use on a pet.

And sadly, Hugh Larkin agreed immediately. The trepidation he felt, viewing that terrifying visage from the past, was suppressed in favor of his devotion to Elizabeth Frankenstein. Somehow, she invaded his mind and spirit. Was it the constant teachings that led him to be viewed as nearly as intelligent as she by their colleagues? The random sexual encounters? This usually occurred two or three times a year, always without warning or discussion, before, during, or after an "event." Hugh relished those times, but didn't anticipate them or await their occurrences.

No, it was probably her mind. Elizabeth Frankenstein possessed a brilliance capable of transforming the world. Her recreation of Victor's legendary work bordered on mania, but the results were unquestionable. And soon, they would yield results that would place her name among the greats in scientific history.

And now, years later, he watched Elizabeth as she opened the storage locker and determined which limb to utilize for her next attempt at reanimation. She stood of medium height, with short blond hair, oddly light blue eyes, and a narrow mouth that was often down turned in annoyance. Her body was taut and athletic, gymnastically limber and full of boundless energy. Elizabeth Frankenstein wasn't beautiful, or even classically handsome, but she was striking. People looked twice when she walked past, but few men, even lascivious ones, were willing to view her in a sexual context. She resembled an ancient statue of a fierce goddess, a terrible being whose mission was based in torment and destruction rather than fertility. There was nothing gentle about Elizabeth Frankenstein, but there was greatness within her. And Hugh Larkin was determined to remain at her side to achieve those ambitions.

"Perhaps we need more Selenian vampire tongue. That is the one portion of the compound we haven't increased." Hugh lifted the metal jar and studied the label. *Pretorius Apothecary* in Ingolstadt. An odd firm that Elizabeth stated was connected to her ancestor, though further information was never provided. All Hugh knew was they supplied all of the odd requirements for the elixir she brewed in her quest to defeat death.

"I attempted that last year in Styria. Remember those results? I doubt the walls of Karnstein Castle will ever be clean again." Elizabeth chuckled and pulled out a short brown leg and studied it for a moment. "This one will serve. I think perhaps we should lessen the Deep Ones' scales. I don't believe we've tried that."

Hugh was about to answer, when the door to the lab swung open. A figure stood outlined in the threshold, a massive figure hidden in shadows. Nobody moved. Even the usually tempestuous Elizabeth appeared unable to step forward and toss out a sharp demand or a threat. Hugh found he was holding his breath, sensing some-thing terrible was about to occur.

Then the shadowy form stepped into a view, a huge gray-skinned body with hideous alien yellow eyes. Hugh's mouth dropped as he recognized the distorted, massive frame as it approached with a light, long stride.

"Gouroull." Elizabeth did not so much say the name as exhale it; this was the creature she had dreamed of since her discovery of Victor's diary.

"Frankenstein." Gouroull's voice was a deep, in-human rasp. It possessed an inhuman resonance that was formed by organs inhuman in nature. There was a de-monic, malignant alien quality to this creature who bore some resemblance to mankind.

"At last," Elizabeth said, extending her hands in welcome.

CHAPTER IV

The *Princess of San Pedro* rode smoothly across the Atlantic. The liner was an enormous steel structure, an inconceivably huge presence riding atop this body of water. Yet, it slid through the waves with an impressive ease, slicing through the upsurges without transferring the sensations to the many passengers.

Originally a ship of the White Star line, the vessel was purchased by the country of San Pedro, specifically the new junta leader, Major Jose Murillo, the grandson of the infamous "Tiger of San Pedro," General Juan Murillo. Major Murillo, later known as President-General Jose Murillo, wished a private source of income for himself and used the county's finances to ensure his future wealth. The *Princess* became a popular liner for the wealthy, as well as a low-cost means of shipping to and from Central and South America.

The ship itself was well-kept, luxurious, and a popular transport for the wealthiest classes across Europe and North America. The *Princess* traveled a simple route, touching the coasts of the United States, England, France, Spain, Portugal and back to San Pedro. Many passengers didn't complete the full circular journey, but the ship was still popular and profitable.

One of the reasons for this acclaim was the very distinct social differences within the ship. Luxury liners exist in a social stratum similar to society itself. Each level of the ship was a class unto itself, a position based on your designation in the unspoken caste that exists throughout the world.

The wealthiest classes, usually those born to money and position, rode the ship on the top levels. These people possessed private dining accommodations, exercise areas and lounges where they were served in sybaritic luxury. The servants upon that level were a silent, efficient cadre who rarely lasted more than three voyages. Some were replaced for offending their affluent patrons, others hired for their impressive skills by the people they served.

The middle level passengers were a mixed lot. New millionaires who were excluded for making their own wealth "in trade" were the norm. But also present were employees of the first class excursionists and a few well-bred yet poor nobles from various countries. The accommodations were almost as impressive as their betters in the top of the ship, though smaller. There were a vastly different lot than the ones who existed on the top of the ship. A fast talking, jolly, fun loving group, they were rarely replaced and held onto their jobs with the ferocity of a hounds upon a piece of meat. These servants were better known as the "forty thieves" by the sailors, a nickname embraced by the group secretly. They were a light-fingered lot, quick to pocket lost goods while running illegal gambling operations and the sale of illegal luxuries to anyone willing to pay.

The final class was on the lowest level, third class. These were often passengers hoping to make a new life in another country. Also within this group were men and women who were servants traveling with the employers. There were no luxuries upon this level, recreation was provided by the passengers themselves, with card and dice games as the standard. The servants in the third class were an angry, resentful cluster of men and women who did little and would jump ship at the first opportunity. The upkeep of this area was minimal, just good enough to pass inspection by the supervisors. There was a seedy, slovenly air about this level, an undercurrent of oppression that sat upon the passengers and staff like a heavy weight. People viewing these men and women often noticed the downcast eyes, rounded, hunched shoulders and melancholic demeanor. These passengers soon realized they were viewed as less important than the goods beneath their feet; they were merely a lesser form of cargo.

Hans, like his employer Martin Mars, were relegated to the second class accommodations on the *Princess*. This was a source of great distress and anger to Martin Mars, who could not accept that he was merely viewed as a curiosity. He viewed himself as a nobleman among peasants, the living embodiment of the colonial spirit. The image he wished to progress was that of a latter day H. Rider Haggard hero, the last true explorer in a world increasing oppressed by industrialization and modern societal values.

But sadly for Martin Mars, that was never meant to be. To the world, he was a showman, a collector of curiosities. Martin Mars was a semi-respectable P.T. Barnum, a purveyor of flim-flam. To most, he was merely a well-dressed carnival barker, a freak show boss. The fact that he dressed well and possessed a superficial charm allowed him occasional glimpses of the well-bred members of society. But to them, he would never be anything other than an entertainer, a clown who could be abandoned the moment he attempted to break through the distinct social barriers.

To Hans, this was to be expected. He knew that one only crossed those caste lines through the wholesale slaughter of humanity. Through the death of thousands, a pauper could rise to be a prince. A quick search through the great figures of history told that as a simple fact. Julius Caesar was a well-bred nobody who slaughtered Germans, French and his fellow Romans to become the master of the Eternal City; Genseric the Vandal king slaughtered Romans, rebel Vandals, Africans and barbaric tribes, and died an elderly king of a vast empire; Attila and Genghis Khan wiped out entire cities and their names still lived to this day. The story of mankind was that of blood, fire and death. This was the great leveler of all fictional social classes. Any other attempt to cross these lines would result in the individual being treated as a *parvenu*, a grasping climber attempting to venture into territory in which they were not invited.

Hans was content with his place, for now. He owed Mars his life and until that debt was paid, he would remain at the man's side, assisting his search into the odd and the unusual. Because if it weren't for Martin Mars, Hans knew he would be dead by either the hands of the criminals of Berlin, or the authorities.

It was a few years ago since they first met. Hans never knew why Mars was in Berlin, but Hans was there, working and... playing. He had an urge, a need, to destroy and corrupt. Children were his fixation; they were so innocent and weak. Perfect subjects for his...needs...

Eleven fell by his hands, eleven beautiful creatures. He hated himself for every single one, but he was compelled to take more... to feel their last breaths as the razor caressed their tender flesh. The police were baffled by his pleasures, even their wisest lacking comprehension as to his thirsts.

This caused the police to behave as they always did when confused, like fools. They began harassing every criminal they could find, demanding information. Hans despised all of them, the weak ineffectual foolish guardians of law and order and the despicable, selfish, cruel masters of crime. They were more monstrous than he, they chose their cruelties and selfishness. Hans knew his monstrous acts were urges within him, a terrible aspect of his inner self that he fought but could not defeat.

It was on the day he was about to lure the twelfth child away that Martin Mars appeared. Hans was about to say something to a little girl when Mars grabbed his arm and frog-marched him down the street. Hans was too stunned by this large man's bizarre actions to protest for several steps.

"Don't say a fucking word, not a fucking word." Mars's voice was an American accented hiss, a snarl with odd pronunciation.

Hans didn't speak, confused and frightened by this odd foreigner. Was he caught for his crimes? If so, why by an American? He doubted the man was like that fictional hero Nick Carter, saving lives for the sake of doing good. There was something dangerous about this man, as if he, too, possessed urges from within, ones he controlled better than Hans.

Finally, they stopped in a small bar, a tiny, dark establishment that appeared to cater to the well-dressed men and cheap-looking women. Pushing Hans into a seat in the back, Mars vanished into the gloom, returning a moment later with two glasses of thick, amber beer. Dropping in the chair opposite, he took a large drink and stared at Hans.

"You're an idiot." Mars's words were hushed but an intense snarl. "A genuine fool. Killing randomly, luring children from the streets. Idiot."

Hans opened his mouth to protest, but clamped his lips shut when he spotted a murderous glint in the man's eyes. He revised his assessment of this man. He was not merely dangerous; this American was insane.

"Good, you're smart. Then listen. I know about all the children you've butchered. You have a need, right?" Mars didn't wait for a response, but nodded as if Hans replied in the affirmative. "Good. Because I have need for a man who isn't afraid of blood."

"Tell me more." Hans took a sip of his beer, sat back and listened to Martin Mars. He became the man's loyal retainer on that day. They were bonded even closer when Mars set up a crazed beggar for Hans's crimes. They stayed in Berlin long enough to see the man captured by the local police and charged with every unsolved crime in the city.

This was why Hans sat on the *Princess*, on the second class deck. A sketchpad sat in his lap and he was working furious, whistling away as he worked. He was an excellent draftsman and weapons designer, an asset that Mars used to full advantage.

"What are you whistling?" A tiny voice piped from in front of Hans. He lowered his sketch pad and spotted the source of the inquiry. She was a tiny girl, probably no more than six or seven years-old. Dressed in a crisp white sailor suit, complete with a diminutive cap, she stared up at Hans with large, luminous brown eyes. The girl possessed dusky skin and a lovely clear complexion. She was a beautiful child, one that would be celebrated for her beauty, so long as it lasted.

That was the sad truth that only Hans appeared to comprehend. The inner light that was innocence was a fleeting presence in the world. Many children were corrupted early, the true beauty being diminished by the harsh reality that was life. But some, a rare few, still possessed this energy within them for some time. And this was what Hans sought in the children he killed, back in Berlin, Hamburg and Cologne. The razor allowed him that fleeting touch of innocence, that vitality destroyed by the depredations of society.

Hans cleared his throat. "It is *In the Hall of the Mountain King* by Edvard Greig in the play *Peer Gynt*."

The little girl smiled. "That's a pretty name for a play. What is it about?"

Hans nodded. "It is about a boy who doesn't fit in anywhere. He travels the world and sees remarkable sights."

The girl nodded and attempted to hum the tune, her tiny lips vibrating and producing a sound only slightly like the powerful song Hans habitually whistled. "You're nice. What's your name?"

"Hans. What is yours?"

"Elizabetta," the girl replied and tried again to hum the song. She didn't notice Hans's flinch and staring eyes.

It was the name, a name so close to one quite special to Hans. Elsie, she was the last of his extraordinary work. She had such a memorable, delightful ebullience, a gentle kind spirit which he feasted upon that day. Her face still floated in his mind, frightened but still unsullied and hopeful his desecrations would cease. The touch of her silken curls still caused his palms to itch as well as the warm spurt as the razor caressed her silken flesh. True bliss.

And now, on this ship, he felt the call once again. The whistle of the cold blade sang in his ears, a fleeting memory. Oh, he'd killed at Martin Mars's orders since that wonderful time with Elsie. But none received his special attention, the true, slow embrace of the knife. Hans wanted to taste this little Elizabetta, watch the light disappear from her eyes as he drank it. She would be a delight, a true banquet of innocence for his being.

But it was not meant to be. Hans sat back in his chair, the wood and canvas creaking loudly. His promise held him back from taking this little life, from reveling in her end. But the urge was so great, the desire to watch her inner light dim and fade to nothingness... Hans's mind was screaming, begging to be allowed to reach for the razor and begin the embrace of the cold steel again. But that would not happen; he had promised Martin Mars, his rescuer.

Hans knew he was a terrible creature. He accepted, with some sadness, that he was different from others. His compulsions were inner-born, not from anything in his upbringing. His father was a kind man, a lawyer who worked for the government. His mother was a decent woman, a housewife who volunteered to help the poor through their church. Good people, upstanding publically and privately. Yet, they produced a monster, a sub-human creature who many compared to something out of a Grimm's fairy tale. Hans fought the cravings for years, sensing that once he took that first life, he would be hard pressed to ever stop.

The first was in Hamburg, a child whore in a poor section. She was a petite waif, a dirty-faced Madonna in his eyes. But she was corrupted, even at a young age. But the touch of purity that still lingered in the child's soul, a speck of light if you will, was still present. And that night, Hans drank deep, feasted upon the child, before consigning her to cold embrace of the Elbe. No word of her death ever reached his ears, but four others also fell to his inner yearnings before the police began to suspect this was the work of a single man. That was when Hans moved to Cologne and began again.

Here and now, he wanted to return to his dark path, the way he despised but also coveted without question. But in agreeing to serve Mars, that path was cut off. Oh, they both still murdered in every place they resided. Martin Mars's urges were similar, yet different. For him, the knife was an ejaculation, a substitute for his non-functional sex organs. The great man desired women, but also despised them with a cold loathing. To fulfill that longing, Mars embraced clubs and knives. He was cautious, sometimes going six months before choosing a new victim, but the result was the same. A corpse for Hans to hide or destroy.

"There you are, little one!" A tall man with the same dark eyes and swarthy skin stepped up and scooped Elizabetta up in a fond embrace. The tiny child squealed with delight, her cries growing louder as the man's vast mustaches caressed her cheek.

"Papa! I learned a new song. Listen!" Elizabetta hummed her version of *In the Hall of the Mountain King* as her father looked on with a happy smile.

"My apologies, Senhor. She does love to bother strangers. Thank you for watching her." The man hugged the girl and gave her a loud kiss on the cheek.

"No bother. She is a delightful child. Cherish her." Hans's hands still itched for the razor, but the moment was lost. This young innocent would maintain her virtuous quality, at least for now. Soon the world would reduce her to another shrill, faceless fool. Another mindless cog in the machinery that was the modern world. A true loss, far greater than if she was embraced by the blade.

"You wanted her, didn't you? Didn't you?" Martin Mars stepped out from around the corner. He looked casually elegant, a façade he maintained very well to all eyes. Only Hans knew the rapacious predator which resided within the man's dark soul.

"Yes, sir." Hans never bothered to lie. He sensed Mars would know and would react poorly.

"What held you back? What held you back?" Mars tilted his head and smiled at a passing elderly couple. He looked very much the gentleman at leisure.

"I promised you I would not." Hans looked at his employer, not hiding some of the resentment he felt at this rule.

Mars nodded. "Good, good. Good, good. Keep it up and I may let you have some fun soon. Have some fun soon."

Mars walked off and Hans could hear him engaging someone in a loud conversation. But that didn't matter. Martin Mars never made rash promises. Which meant that soon Hans could accept his dark longings again and let another child feel the stroke of the razor once again. The thought was intoxicating.

With a smile, Hans began to whistle again as he sketched the weapons he sought to use against the monster known as Gouroull. The legendary creature might be mighty in battle, but all fell before the arms of modern man. And this weapon would be Hans's masterpiece. The monster of Frankenstein would soon be reduced to another exhibit in Mars's collections. And after that, Hans would hunt…

CHAPTER V

"You are just as my ancestor described. I still have his original notes right here," Elizabeth Frankenstein said. She crossed the room and lifted a large leather ledger. She placed the ancient tome on a table, facing Gouroull, and flipped open to a page. A large full page sketch in pencil appeared, a drawing of Gouroull. The source was obvious to all: the infamous Baron Victor Frankenstein had etched his creation.

And all three present knew this was in the days before the sight and comprehension of the horror of his creation had reached Victor's fevered mind. That was the time when the mad scientist was reveling in his own genius. To Frankenstein, he achieved what all of mankind sought since awareness of the universe first appeared. He, Baron Frankenstein, had thrown down God himself, grinding the creator into the dust. All of nature was subject to the whims of the brilliance within Victor.

That was Frankenstein's view at the time he had sketched this image. Soon after, he determined that his conception was far removed from the pliant creature he had imagined. Gouroull possessed a fiendish, if alien, intellect, capable of horrific acts. Instead of a lamb, Victor Frankenstein's science had given birth to a viper, a demon in a human shell.

And all three knew the test that lay at the end of this precious volume of lore. The oath sworn by Victor Frankenstein when he had tried to destroy the monster Gouroull. But the latter was hidden nearby, listening, and had remembered each word, suspecting his creator possessed some secret method of providing his end. But

42

the words were very memorable, having been read by Elizabeth and Hugh in the days as students of the work of her long-dead ancestor. The words read as follows:

"By the sacred earth on which I kneel, by the shades that wander near me, by the deep and eternal grief that I feel, I swear; and by thee, O Night, and the spirits that preside over thee, to pursue the daemon who caused this misery, until he or I shall perish in mortal conflict. For this purpose I will preserve my life; to execute this dear revenge will I again behold the sun and tread the green herbage of earth, which otherwise should vanish from my eyes forever. And I call on you, spirits of the dead, and on you, wandering ministers of vengeance, to aid and conduct me in my work. Let the cursed and hellish monster drink deep of agony; let him feel the despair that now torments me."

And the tale was well-known after that: the pursuit through the world, the death of Victor on the ice of the Arctic. Gouroull himself was trapped by the frigid ice, suspended between life and death, until a disgusting Irish trapper had freed him from his entombed existence.

Gouroull stared down at Elizabeth Frankenstein, his pale yellow eyes studying her with an inhuman intensity. Hugh felt as if they were being examined by a being completely alien to the thinking of a human. It was as if a serpent or a scorpion grew to gargantuan size with their intellect growing in equal proportion. The soul of civilization was missing, as it was in those poisonous beasts. Nothing human resided behind those ghastly malevolent orbs.

But Elizabeth was either unconcerned or disinterested in the miscreation that was Gouroull. She slapped the volume shut with a heavy bang and continued: "I am recreating my ancestor's work. We came to this place to escape the irrational conservative misguided fools that make up the modern medical world."

And that was true, to a small degree. The medical community had spurned Elizabeth Frankenstein's experiments, their disgust at her vivisectionists' attitudes towards patients being merely one in a long list of reasons to bar her from their august body of learning. And that was only the barest hint of the truth.

Born in Switzerland and raised there and in Italy, Elizabeth Frankenstein was a precocious, if disagreeable, child. She possessed no interest in toys, pretty dresses, ponies or any of the other luxuries her well-funded noble family had to offer. Learning was her obsession, the subject changing at a whim. Entomology, astronomy, botany, ornithology and chemistry were many of the all too brief passions she had indulged in with an almost religious fervor. But none satisfied her for long, the sketch books of books and the trays of beetles and butterflies being tossed aside for the next obsessional study.

Then, by pure accident, she was given her ancestor Victor's journals. It was her moth, a kind woman who loved this odd child, so different from her sensible older brother and gentle younger sister. All Mama knew was a distant relative of her husband was a scientist who had died nearly a century earlier. The books themselves were dusty tomes of science, unfit for their lovely library. Either young Elizabeth could take them, or they would be burned as rubbish.

It was there that Elizabeth had found her true aspiration, her path in the universe. The century-old diaries told of her ancestor's genius, his quest to find the method of returning life to the dead. The steps Victor took were plainly described, the mistakes and the triumphs. The fact that his name was not listed among the medical greats, such as Pasteur and Lister, was a crime against science itself!

It was then that Elizabeth Frankenstein's path had become clear. She would recreate the brilliant success of Victor Frankenstein and expand upon his genius. To do that, she needed to become a doctor, an expert in all areas of the medical profession. Building upon her studies in chemistry and biology, Elizabeth undertook the coursework required by all of the great institutions of medical science in the world. She knew the danger of attempting to recreate her exalted antecedent's perspicacity. No, she needed to be an expert in her own right, equal to Victor, when her true study commenced.

She did see one flaw in her future. Victor did possess assistance throughout his studies. This was something Elizabeth lacked, never having time for friends or her family. Socially, she was worse than awkward, she was uncomprehending as to the basic niceties that controlled societal interaction. This, Elizabeth knew she would have to remedy, but only in the most basic steps. A degree of cleanliness and basic cosmetic minutiae served for the time. She waited, knowing an answer would come to her, a remedy for this lack of human connection in her life.

That came in Edinburgh in the form of Hugh Larkin. Hugh, awkward but near genius himself, possessed few connections to the gayer members of the medical school, and spent much of his spare time staring with increasing longing at Elizabeth. Why, she was never sure. But he appeared unconsciously entranced. After a few tests, Elizabeth allowed him to observe her experimenting upon a newly-obtained limb. This was the time he would either flee in horror or swear eternal loyalty.

And the latter was Hugh's choice. Sensing he possessed a need for sexual release, a biological function Elizabeth indulged rarely and without true interest, she took him to bed one night. That, she suspected, was the final step required to make Hugh her permanent dogsbody. If necessary, she would marry him, but the need never arose. Words of their experiments emerged far sooner than she'd imagined. The elders on the various boards compared their work, Victor's magnificent legacy, to be pseudo-science, little better than alchemy! Well, she would teach them all, prove that the name Frankenstein was the only name one should remember in the world of science. Because, when they recreated and improved upon Victor's success, they would show the world that death need never be feared by mankind ever again.

They were chased away from Canada, the United States and Hispaniola before they settled in San Pedro. Lending her genius to torture a few rebels and Indians for the junta leader, Elizabeth and Hugh were granted a place of their own to work, without interruption. The only condition was they would remain on call if the new leader of the government required her genius in forcing information from unwilling subjects. This only came to pass twice. Most of the President's enemies were easily broken by the crude military methods made famous by the legendary leader known as the "Tiger of San Pedro." But a very committed priest and a true revolutionary who espoused odd Marxists beliefs were tougher subjects. But few could resist the scientific cruelty of a trained surgeon who lacked a basic moral code. These were tools she passed on to a young German boy named Szell, an intelligent lad who would make a fine scientist in his own right.

But now, all her dreams had come to fruition. Gouroull was here, standing before her in the flesh. His presence was overwhelming, causing her to feel smaller and insignificant in a physical sense. But Elizabeth's intellect, and overwhelming sense of self, rose up. She was defiant in the face of such power, her mind the equal to anything Gouroull could offer.

"I presume you are here to enlist my aid?" Elizabeth asked, looking up at the hulking form of her ancestor's terrible creation. Her small blue eyes locked with the monster's strange amber orbs.

Gouroull nodded slightly, his stillness an unsettling force unto itself. "Victor's promise." The voice emerging from the black lips was a rasp, a sound formed by organs that possessed no true human origins.

Elizabeth nodded. "He did promise to create you a mate, but destroyed his work. I believe a second scientist attempted the same on that Scottish isle, Cround. But he was thwarted by someone. Very odd reports. I had one other report from a crazed, but quite intelligent gentleman named West. Very odd little man. Intelligent, but without any conception of the true path to success."

Gouroull did not reply, but watched Elizabeth. There was no hint of his thinking, no body language. It was as if a statue suddenly appeared in the midst, alive, but not possessing the basic actions of a human being.

"I will provide your mate. But your aid is required. I require a sample of your blood. This way, I can determine the proper proportions of compounds in the reanimation reagent." She pulled a metal beaker from a nearby shelf and handed it to Gouroull. "A small sample will do. Though I will require more in the near future."

Gouroull placed the container on the table next to the diary. He then bit down upon his wrist with his razor-sharp teeth, placing the cut limb several inches above the beaker.

The fluid that issued from the wound was a thick, black ichor, a fetid flow that filled the air with a corrupt, yet slightly antiseptic, scent. The dusky discharge leaked with tantalizing slowness, but soon the beaker was filled. Gouroull tied a rag around his wrist and one word emerged from his terrible maw.

"When?"

Elizabeth looked up, having immediately moved towards with a syringe in hand. Her gaze was almost dreamy, lost to this world as she contemplated the task. "Hmm? Oh, yes! Once the proportions are determined, I will test the components on a spare limb. If the test performs successfully, assembly of the corpse will begin. I will not provide dates; to do so would be foolish. All will happen, when each step is completed. No sooner."

Gouroull stared for several seconds and then turned away, leaving the lab and vanishing from all view a moment later. Elizabeth waved towards the open door, "Close that and boil some coffee. We shan't be sleeping tonight."

Hugh shivered inside, an instinctive feeling of terror. Suddenly he sensed the direful path he and Elizabeth chose was about to become even more terrible.

As he closed the door, Elizabeth pulled up her sleeve and tapped her arm for a vein. She plunged the needle into the exposed flesh and felt the rush as the ephedrine caused her nerves to become alive. Sleep would not be required for several days now.

CHAPTER VI

"Give me that fish," said Moraika, pointing at the day's catch. Her target was a small, red creature, one that The Living would not eat. There was something foul tasting, wrong textured about these fish. Most believed they were bottom-dwellers, eaters of the foul at the bottom of the great lake. Other believed they were part of Supay, feeders upon the corpses within the water. But none ate these fish; they were either cut up and used as bait for better catch, or buried near the food groves to feed the fruit trees.

Khuno reached into the net and pulled out the fish, placing the wet, still form upon Moraika's extended claw. All knew their wise woman always had a reason for her sometimes odd actions. None questioned why she would sometimes as for a specific item, a fish, a fruit or a sharp stone. These demands only came occasionally and never to the hardship of The Living. Normally she ate her proper portion, performed her work with quiet willingness, and never requested special treatment. Therefore when these requests came, The Living agreed without inquiry, trusting their wise woman had a purpose for the item.

And so she did this time, even more so than her usual needs. The majority of her work was helping the tribe. She was tasked to appeasing Allpa and Supay and reading the signs in the sky, water, earth and animals for danger. And all signs were declaring that danger was here, and the woman in the house was the source.

This was not the first time in her life Moraika had viewed such terrible portents. The second Hortado

49

brought similar omens, his dreams of an empire in the lands of The Living was a true danger to all life. The visions Moraika received from Supay told of death, burning, slavery and horror. Ashes instead of land, destruction that spread well beyond the lakes.

This was why Moriaka, young, clean limbed and pretty to the eye, gave herself to this man for one night. He did not know she was the tribe's new wise woman, her knowledge given to her when the first Moriaka went to Supay's embrace. And as he used her for his foul desires, she fed him a little known flower from the jungle. This plant did not bring about madness, such sensations would merely be temporary. No, this flower increased the person hidden within, the beast that resides in the heart of all humanity.

And Hortado was an angry, mistrustful creature, a bestial fool who died screaming. His thigh bone became her symbol of her power, a totem to prevent any who might get new ideas and rebel against the ancient ways of The Living. Many seasons later, none of her tribe doubted her knowledge or power.

Father Pupo also fell because of Moriaka's visions, a similar dream to that of Hortado. His world would be one of slavery, metal trees and air that choked all life to death. Moriaka didn't comprehend this world, this nightmare one man could bring to all mankind. But she knew he, too, needed to die in a horrible manner. He was easily lured out, a slender slave girl on the edge of the forest, the deep dwellers grabbing the giant fat man with silent deadliness, the slow painful death at their hands.

The remaining invaders, she ignored. Allpa and Supay whispered to her that they would fall without her aid. For few were hardy enough to stand the depredations of this land. The jungle was a terrible place, full of life and death. Even those born to a life in these lands felt the overwhelming power that filled every aspect of one's life when residing here. Even members of The Living sometimes went mad and fled screaming into the night, never to be seen again. Occasionally one could find a bone or a belt to indicate the sad end of the crazed tribesman. But more often than not, they were swallowed up by the jungle forever. This was the harsh life The Living understood; outsiders were unable to comprehend this, even the realistic ones.

Moraika hobbled down a rarely used path to one of the old fruit groves. This one would not be touched by The Living for many seasons; Allpa needed to replenish the soil and bring new trees to this location. The Living planted fish and small animals in the ground to help Allpa and Supay, but only very rarely. The land didn't really require their help, only their distance.

But she was drawn here; her connection to the spirits indicated this was where she needed to find certain items. Stopping before a broken, moss-covered tree, she dug near the roots. From the tiny hole, she found a large protuberance, a brown and orange root. Cutting the vegetation free, she placed it in her hide pouch, the turtle skin carry-all that she always held at her side. Covering the hold back up, she added a circular gray stone, a large dead insect and a pair leaves to her collection.

Examining all, Moraika knew her bundle was complete. She picked a trail, hidden by thick creepers and fallen ancient trees, and headed deeper into the jungle. The scream of a jaguar filled the air and insects and other unseen creatures slithered through the bushes. But Moraika was unconcerned. The jungle would let her pass, knowing she was heading to a very special place…

CHAPTER VII

"May I ask you a question, master?" Hans reverted to his preferred form of address when they were in private. It was dinnertime on the *Princess of San Pedro* and Mars wasn't in the mood to be jolly and tell stories. He was in a black mood.

The source of his mood was the knowledge that his many attempts to bribe the crew and controllers of the liner were still proving a waste of money. Their placement on the second class accommodations deck was not to be altered.

Hans knew that, to Mars, the first class deck areas represented a passage, both actual and metaphorical. To be placed among those assumed to be the "best" of society would mean all of the killings, larcenies and toadyings would have yielded their promised prize. Martin Mars would be one of the "greats" in the world, a paragon of virtue in the eyes of all who mattered.

But this was not meant to be, nor was this likely to change. The transferring of social classes was a rarity in modern society. And for a showman like Martin Mars, this was an impossibility. To the established families of that heralded social order, he was the worst sinner of all, a climber. They knew he wanted to rub shoulders and be viewed as an equal with those whose family's fought for their positions eons ago. Interlopers like Mars were to be used, curiosities and servants, possibly even friends. But never equals. It gave those types a bloated sense of self-importance. And that just would not do.

Therefore every failure sent Martin Mars into a black mood, a depression more than a killing rage. He hid from the world, nursing his hurt with the understanding that he would make those responsible for his humiliation pay in the future. The revenge list grew with the years, but also diminished slowly and surely. From his growing heights, Mars was able to extend his influence and return his embarrassment to others over the years. A preacher who railed against his exhibits as immoral was found to be having sexual relations with three teen girls; an English lord lost all of his money in a series of card games and was forced to sell his ancestral home for a fraction of the value; a wealthy matron's granddaughter's fling with a common gangster became public knowledge... these and more were the secret hand of Martin Mars and his follower Hans.

"Ask away, ask away," Mars waved a cigarette holder in a languid manner. He thought it made him look calm and controlled, like the old money people he emulated. In fact, he resembled a tired man swiping at flies, but Hans would never say that to the man's face.

"Why hunt this Gouroull? By all the accounts you so graciously allowed me to read, this creature is a vicious, murderous and very dangerous being. Are we not taking a terrible risk?" Hans's phrasing was, as always, couched to soothe his employer's emotional responses. This was a skill that kept him at the man's side as much as his abilities as a draftsman and willingness to take the lives of any in their path.

Mars placed his cigarette in the ash tray on the table and nodded once. "The reason is simple, yet complex. Are you attending?"

Hans nodded, knowing Martin Mars was no longer using his façade. The man's style of speech, even his very vocal intonations changed in these rare moments. This chameleon-like transformation was always startling, even to someone as intimately acquainted with Mars as Hans.

"Good. Then let me start by agreeing with you. Gouroull is a true monster. The accounts we read demonstrate he is stronger than men and harder to kill than a Cape Buffalo. And he appears to possess intelligence."

"And he might not be alive, master. Your information from that island in Scotland stated that detail." Hans added this piece of information, knowing it would impress Mars, as well as flatter his researching skills.

Mars smiled slightly, hiding his crooked teeth beneath a familiar rictus smirk. "Correct. Imagine that! Gouroull walked under the North Sea from the Scottish mainland to the island. That in and of itself is a feat none ever reached. By all my information, this creature, this monster, is more lethal than anything upon the Earth. Are we agreed upon these points?"

Hans nodded again. "We are, master."

"And that is the reason, in and of itself. To allow Gouroull to live, or whatever version of life that madman Frankenstein granted upon this thing, is to weaken all of mankind. We become little more than beasts. Imagine if this demon were to reproduce and create a race, each as strong and as deadly. Our species would become prey, little more than food for these fiends! Humans must remain at the top, none above us! We prove this again and again. How many vampires have you and I reduced to dust and bones? How many shapeshifting monsters?" Mars leaned forward, almost looking over Hans in his fervor.

"Vampires? Six, if you count that one that was injured by the priest. Werewolves and the like? Eleven," Hans answered.

Mars smiled again, this time more indulgently. "The question was metaphorical. But there you have it! By all accounts, these things should be able to feast upon us with ease. Both are stronger, faster and possess natural weapons. Yet, each time we prevail!"

"But," Hans interjected, "Gouroull is far more malignant than anything we've faced to date."

"Correct. And we will use our ingenuity to overcome all of his advantages. I know you have some ideas in that area. I purchased a special weapon for this occasion as well." Mars chuckled. He was always happy to reveal he possessed a secret that his underling did not share.

"And then? If we discover Gouroull and our weapons work, what is your next step? Stuff him and place him in your traveling museum?" Part of Hans found this possible fate for Frankenstein's monster unsettling, somehow wrong.

Mars shook his head. "Not a bit. There is a museum for this creature in a small town in Ireland. You probably read of the incident in my notes. I purchased the complete stock, every stick down to the water from the melted ice tomb Gouroull slept in for decades. What I plan on doing is building a special place for the monsters we collected. Not the false Fiji mermaids and the like. No, only the true creatures of the night I own. They will be placed permanently in a special true museum. A place of learning, possibly with an attached university. Have you ever heard of the Cardiff Giant?"

The sudden shift in discussion startled Hans slightly, causing him to mumble a quick, "No, master."

"About eighty years back, a tobacco farmer hired some men to build a statue of a giant. The image was very lifelike. An excellent hoax that earned the man a fortune."

"I remember the story now. That Barnum gentleman built one of his own, I believe." Hans's knowledge of such oddities was not as wide as that of his employer. But he learned a great deal of information from the man second hand.

"Correct. But very few realize the truth. The truth was the farmer, Newell was his name, possessed a real stone giant. But he was paid to build a false one." Mars stared at Hans, a triumphant smirk across his face. He knew he possessed a special piece of secret knowledge. And he would only impart it once Hans clearly demonstrated his surprise and disbelief.

This was the showman side of Martin Mars. Though murderous, covetous, cruel and filled with loathing of mankind, he was a performer few could match. He had an instinctive grasp of the cupidity of humanity and knew the best methods to play to their curiosity. That could be accomplished simply by a pause or dressing in the khaki jacket and pants of a big game hunter.

Hans twisted his face into an appropriate mix of confusion and disbelief. He learned this was more important to Mars than shined shoes or clean hankies in his duties. "I find that hard to believe, master."

Mars chuckled. "You haven't looked as deeply as I have, my little friend. You see, I found the secret diary of William Newell. He actually found the true giant in that hole. But men came to him one night. They made it clear they were taking the true giant immediately. They then helped him plan and create the one carved from stone. Newell was quite wealthy, for the time, thanks to the fake."

"That appears…outlandish, master. It does not make much sense. Why would Newell agree to the odd terms these men insisted upon? He had, according to the diary you mentioned, the true giant. People would still call it a fake, but all of the extra work would be unnecessary." Hans chose his words carefully, believing this diary was as fraudulent as the stone figure itself.

But this was what Mars wished to hear. Disbelief without open mockery was his favorite reaction to overcome. Mockery angered him within, causing later retribution through various hidden means. Such as the anthropologist and his wife in Manhattan. Their sailboat went down in Hudson Bay and they were never seen again. The authorities found that odd since both professors were expert sailors. But in the end, no evidence of foul play was suspected and they were memorialized and forgotten. Just like the big game hunter who passed out drunk in a tiger cage and was eaten… or the wealthy man who blackballed Mars from a country club who was killed after falling beneath a streetcar… The list was long…

"I agree, my little friend. I agree! You see, I suspected I was being defrauded at first. But then I found more details on these men who visited Newell. A pair of men dressed in black suits with black hats and dark spectacles. The description intrigued me because I remember similar descriptions of such men on three other occasions. In all stories, the men were polite and would take the discovery. But they ensured the recipients would be compensated in some other way. This led me to realize that there is a secret organization in this world seeking to suppress the true history of the Earth. They wish us all to believe in a prosaic, dull planet with a simple natural order. But we both know this is far from the truth! Giants, vampires, shapeshifting monsters and other beasts strode across the land! Ancient unknown empires of inhuman monsters existed and are lost in time! And I, Martin Mars, will reveal these secrets to the world!" Mars stood with his fist held high, his shouts echoing in the tiny stateroom.

"And this Gouroull? How does he fit in your plan?" Hans heard similar speeches and was unsurprised by Mars's rants. But these added details were new.

"He is the culmination of all the lost and secret knowledge of this world! That creature, that fiend, was the product of science and alchemy. I have some notes of the ingredients used to bring that thing back to life. It reads as a list of lost and disbelieved monsters of the Earth! Did you know there are mermen in colonies who work and mate with humans? Or that there is a city of ancient vampires who enslave men and women by striking with their tongue? Or that tribes of corpse eaters exist within the militaries of the world, guaranteeing that they will have a source of fresh corpses? These are all pieces of what made the monster, Gouroull. I intend to capture this thing and rip the veil off the lies that hide the truth from mankind!" A glob of spittle formed on the edge of Mars's lips as he strode about his cabin.

"And I believe I have a method of ensuring his capture, master. I will require some time in a metal shop. But this weapon will incapacitate a creature as tremendous as an elephant. Allow me to show you my humble sketches." Hans unfolded the papers, smoothing them out on the table.

Martin Mars sat down at the table, his crazed behavior vanishing as quickly as it appeared.

"Well, well. Well, well. How very intriguing. How very intriguing."

Hans crossed the room to pour himself a large brandy. Mars was back to his old self, the pomposity filling him like air to a balloon. That was safer for this extended trip on the *Princess*. It might be difficult to explain a rash of "missing" men and women…

CHAPTER VIII

"Three parts per trillion of red blood cells, no white blood cells visible whatsoever. Intriguing." Elizabeth Frankenstein mused as she studied the ichor under the electronic microscope. This machine was a miracle of modern science, a device designed by Elizabeth with a madman named Dr. Janos Rukh. The order of magnitude of this microscope far exceeded even proposed devices. This one worked on an atomic level, and was the only one of its kind around the world. Elizabeth and Dr. Rukh could probably make a fortune by selling this apparatus to scientists around the world, but neither possessed any interest in pursuing such an endeavor. Elizabeth had her work and Rukh was now interested in outer space and new means to observe cosmic phenomena.

"That makes no sense," Hugh stepped over and examined the readings. "The white blood cells are the immune system's first line of defense. Lack of them would mean Gouroull would die from even the most common disease. The common cold would lead to pneumonia and eventual death."

Elizabeth shook her head. "You must abandon the orthodoxy of science, Hugh. My ancestor's vision was far beyond the common thought process that is modern science. Gouroull is no mere man, but a being far greater than any beings existing at this time."

"This is not merely unorthodox, Elizabeth. The volume of red blood cells alone make no sense. They provide functions all sentient life require! This Gouroull is not even slightly under the definition of life as exists in the entire taxonomy of the Earth! Fish, reptiles, apes, birds, even insects follow certain basic principles of science. This blood...no I can't even call it such, this sample of alchemical compounds, should not be any use other than cleaning stopped up drains!" Hugh was practically shouting as he waved his hands over the sample of ichor. The almost gelatinous quality of the monster's lifeblood appeared completely alien when compared to any other form of bodily fluid.

"And now you see the true secret of my ancestor's genius. To bring back the dead would serve no true purpose. Humanity is a dead end, a failed branch on the elocutionary chain. We are stagnant, no better than our cave-dwelling ancestors. Humans still battle over which mythical creator told them the true path. Battles over imaginary boundaries between people cost millions of lives. The land is destroyed for useless bits of metal or pretty stones which ultimately serve no purpose. We are still primitive, weak-willed, frightened, superstitious savages with delusions of godhood. Baron Victor Frankenstein realized this much over a century ago. Gouroull and his new race will cause humanity to either rise or fall." Elizabeth leaned forward and prodded Hugh with one finger, emphasizing her point with each poke.

"That's monstrous! We humans are imperfect, but we are the apex predators of the planet thanks to our intellectual superiority. Though the animal world possesses natural strengths greater than ours, we overcame these deficits. Humanity rose from a lesser ape form to the creators of civilization!" Hugh pushed Elizabeth's hand aside and slapped a palm hard on the table for emphasis.

"Your point being?" Elizabeth asked, a slight smile crossing her sharp features.

"The introduction of a being with greater killing capacity but a mind equal to humanity transforms the balance of nature! Mankind would no longer be the most dangerous beings on this world. This new race would eventually cause the fall of civilization!" Hugh looked terrified as he stated these words, his voice dropping to emphatic hiss by the end.

Elizabeth shook her head, "Incorrect. Humans will not lie down and die so easily. This is the very *causatum* our species need to throw off the shackles that bind us. The competition for life itself will be our greatest trial. Our race will either achieve greatness or be relegated to the dustbins of history. We can join the dinosaurs, dodo birds and the great auk. Curiosities, relics forgotten by time. This was the true vision of Victor Frankenstein, the secrets of life and death."

"Do we have that right? Through the creation of Gouroull's mate, aren't we determining the fate for all life?" Hugh stared at his hands, almost asking himself these questions now.

"Who else has the right? Victor was the first to recognize this need." Elizabeth watched Hugh and picked up a scalpel behind her back.

Hugh looked up. "But Victor attempted to destroy his creation! He chased Gouroull across the globe before dying in the polar wastes. He rejected his vision in the end! He recognized that Gouroull would be a plague upon all life and attempted to destroy his life's work!"

Elizabeth nodded and stepped closer, her hand gripping the blade tight. "He lost his nerve. He promised Gouroull a mate and then destroyed his second creation. Why? Because his nerve failed him in the end. Victor was a genius, centuries ahead of the greatest minds who ever lived before him or since. But he was not perfect. I hold him a paragon of scientific virtue. But as a man, he was weak in the end. My mind is not yet at his level of scientific mastery, but I have greater determination than

Victor. But the question is, do you, Hugh? Are you going to flee my side just when we are the verge of the culmination of all our work?"

Hugh looked away, feeling Elizabeth's eyes piercing his very soul. He knew he stood on a precipice, a metaphorical fork in his road of fate. Could he walk away from Elizabeth and the work they shared? He knew he was still a very good doctor. He could move to some small place under another name, lead a quiet life, use his skills to help people's ailments and the like... But could he spend his days talking to housewives and businessmen about gout, influenza and the common cold? Go to town meetings and fairs, church on Sundays and local sporting events? Was that possible after all he witnessed in his time with Elizabeth... the blood, the pain, stealing new bodies by night and attempting their latest elixir on the still fresh corpse...

The answer was obvious, despite part of him wishing otherwise. Hugh was too far down the path of necromantic horror to return to the life of a simple physician. He belonged at Elizabeth's side. The time of resistance ended when they stole their first body. The idealistic Hugh Larkin was dead and gone. He was a follower of the path of Frankenstein.

Hugh shook his head. "No, Elizabeth. I was merely playing devil's advocate."

Elizabeth smiled and hugged Hugh, a rare show of affection. Behind his back, she placed the scalpel on the table. Then she broke the embrace and stated: "Excellent. Now, we must continue the full analysis. Once that is complete, I will examine Gouroull's flesh as well. Based on reports, the tensile strength is far greater than human epidermis." And with that, they were back to work, their voices low as the experiments continued...

CHAPTER IX

Lowering his head to the marble floor, the servant waited. He knew the master could keep him kneeling in that position for a minute, an hour or a day. Such was the great one's patience. He was above the common herd of humanity, an exalted being with power few could comprehend. The servant had witnessed his master's power many times and knew he was capable of feats of legend.

"Rise," the voice of the great one was a mere whisper. Yet there was power in that single syllable, elemental like the wind.

The servant rose, his head lowered in obedience. Even this small contact with the master filled him with an inner terror. He felt like a rabbit before a serpent, terrified to the point of immobility. Had the great one not ordered him to rise, he would have knelt before the master's feet until he died.

"Speak," the master raised one withered claw in emphasis. The hand was like a dissected spider, mere bones and flesh without additional substance.

A wave of revulsion filled the servant, but his fear was too great to flee. The master was to be respected and even worshipped. But there was a wrongness about him, an inhumanity that caused him to be both more and less than human. To be the subject of such a being's gaze was to feel every weakness in your mind, body and soul.

Finally he mustered enough courage: "Master. The scryers sent word of the creature called Gouroull."

The master did not speak for several moments. The servant felt his heart beating against his chest. The sound was like a fast drumbeat to his ears and he didn't doubt the master heard the sound as well.

"Continue," the master replied, his obsidian eyes focusing on the servant with sudden, greater, intensity.

"Gouroull is working with a woman who claims to be a descendent of Baron Frankenstein. She is building him a mate." The servant's words fell from his mouth in a rush. It was as if he vomited the very contents of his mind out before the great one.

The master did not reply, but his unblinking gaze moved away from the servant, focusing on another area in the chamber. Time seemed to freeze as the great one pondered. The flickering fire of the braziers along the stone walls seemed to freeze in place as his terrible mind ruminated on the information. Finally, his scrutiny returned to his servant and his voice filled the air again.

"The divinators are to focus upon Gouroull. Nothing else. Report all changes. No matter how small." The master raised his withered claw again. "Depart."

The servant dropped to his knees and touched his head to the stone floor. He then rose quickly and backed away, grateful at being able to leave the presence of the master unharmed. He rushed off to obey the great one's commands. The servant was always fearful of the master's scrutiny. One did not look upon the face of those who are touched by the gods. Not if a man wished to keep his sanity. But the servant, like his father and his fathers before him, were raised in the service of such beings. There was no other life for them. No matter what terror filled each moment throughout their existence.

This was why the servant ran down the hall, heading for the scrying pools. The master's orders would be heard, understood and obeyed. They lived and died at his command. There was no other life for the great one's followers.

CHAPTER X

Moraika spotted the marker as she stepped out from under a low-hanging bough that hung over the path. The vines which weighed down the tree limb were crawling with life, yet all of the creatures ignored the wise woman. To almost anyone else, the insects would have swarmed, protecting their homes and feeding upon the flesh and blood of any intruder. But Moraika possessed no fear of such threats. She was a part of the land, part of Allpa and Supay and their spirits guided her each step of the way.

The marker was a small pile of stones, tightly stacked and uncovered by the creepers, mosses and creatures of the jungle. A small circle of gray earth surrounded the small stone monolith. It was as if the land itself rejected the creation of this monument, viewing it as an invader upon its realm. Moraika, as always, felt a slight chill in the air as she approached the marker. There was a something about this marker, a wrongness, a transgression upon the natural order that repelled her. And this repugnance was within her memory. All of the wise women before her had experienced the same distaste for this location.

Leaning upon her thighbone cane, Moriaka waited. Time passed with agonizing slowness, but still she stood before the marker. Waiting. Staring at the jagged expanse before her and waiting.

It was nearly night when the hidden trail to her right appeared to open and disgorge a man. He was tall and straight, proud and powerfully-built. He carried an ancient spear of black wood in one hand and a small bow was across his back. His face and body were painted in a riot of colors, red, blue and yellow. The lip plate that caused his lower lip to jut out many inches beyond his face was of a dark wood, one given to his people by the Living many generations ago. This was the wise man of the deep tribes, a being nearly as old Moraika and possessing just a deep a memory.

The shaman bowed his head to Moraika, a token of respect. Never a word passed between them, none was needed. They were more than simply ancient founts of wisdom. They were two halves of the lives of all beings of the jungle and beyond. Male, female, warrior, wise woman. They were equals, partners and servants of the greater beings who created and protected these lands.

And both were summoned by the appearance of the living dead man. It did not matter that he was inhabiting the lands where Moraika's tribe dwelled. They both knew this being was a canker, an alien danger who could destroy all life. Both warrior priest and wise woman were called to this location. The ancient powers, normally sleeping and dormant, called to them and demanded their attendance. And both complied without question. This was their way, their path in their extended lives. They would follow the forms and discover the commands of their masters.

Moraika was first, stepping up to the marker, she pulled the dead fish out of a pouch. She placed it reverently on the left side of the flat stone cap, positioning the head and tail exactly north and south. Next to the fish she added a small bulbous root, a flat yellow stone and a few sprigs of a reddish green vegetation. Bowing to the offering, the wise woman stepped back and leaned on her cane.

Her male counterpart stepped up to the marker, the bangles on his ankles jangling lightly as he moved. He pulled a petrified lizard from a pouch and placed the ancient creature's head and tail facing east and west on the marker's stone cap. Next to the lizard he added a red flower with broad leafy petals. The petals were of an odd consistency, almost flesh-like in texture, and exuding a bizarre noxious scent. The shaman then placed a forked stick below the flower, bowed and stepped back next to Moraika.

Together they pulled out a matching set of metal daggers. The blades were made from an odd metal, dark and non-reflecting. There were deep swirls across the surface of the knives, the patterns seeming to change before one's eyes. These weapons were ancient, created by their masters eons ago. Back then, the lands were shaped far differently and possessed different names, different people. There were land masses with vast horrific empires of inhuman beings, their names lost or thought to be myths or legends. The Living and their inner jungle counterparts, led by this shaman, were once servants to those creatures, a cold-blooded race who were closer kin to the fish or the lizard than humanity.

Those demonic fiends were long gone, possibly extinct back in the times when the giant lizards ruled the land. But their gods, ancient and terrible, still existed. The Living called these deities Allpa and Supay, but they possessed thousands of other names. They were spirits of life and death, the true powers of the universe. These two, wise woman and shaman, knew this better than any. There were other gods, other spirits of the world which men worshiped. In ancient days, it was fire, the sky, the seas and the earth. Later, as humans grew more mindful, their gods became more theoretical...war, wisdom, craftsmanship, medicine and the family. But these were mere pretenders, lesser creatures before the true powers of the Earth. Life and death, the circle of existence that all living beings were enslaved to for all time.

Wise woman and shaman each lifted a hand, his right, her left, and cut their palms with their ancient blades. The edges were so keen, neither felt pain, merely an instant numbness to the area. Red blood welled up on their skins, the coppery scent filling the air.

Raising their hands, their palms touched, their blood intermingled. After a few heartbeats, they separated and placed their bloody flesh upon the face of the marker. The red fluid fell liberally on the surface and then vanished from sight. The offers also disappeared from view and the wise woman and shaman removed their hands. Binding their wounds, they stepped forward, entering the ruins of their holy site.

The land was subtly different, a clearing hidden by unusual plants. These plants resembled ferns, but grown to monstrous side, possessing boughs as thick as the most ancient trees of the dense jungles. The ground was thick with a greenish brown vegetation, resembling a mixture between moss and grass. The air was also far thinner, as if they were suddenly standing on the top of a small mountain. A light chilly wind blew, rustling the odd trees and grasses. But no other forms of life could be heard. No birds, no insects of small lizards. This clearing was devoid of any living creature beyond Moraika and her male counterpart from the deep jungles.

Their eyes took in these sights, or lack thereof, which were startling to both, no matter how many times they had visited it in their lives. Following a carefully cut path that appeared to be made from on extended piece of yellow stone, each step seemed to cause the temperature to drop noticeably.

Turning a corner around a copse of trees, they spotted the temple. Their ancient memories remembered this location as once huge, busy and teeming with acolytes, beasts of burden and visitors of the alien masters from over the great waters. Many thousands of years passed since those antediluvian days and all that remained were silent ruins.

A pair of stone plinths rose above the path. Both once possessed statues of the founders of the ancient lost empire who ruled these lands in archaic eras. Those monuments were shattered back when the land known as Atlantis fell beneath the waves, their evil naught but a memory.

Random piles of gray stones lay scattered across the grasses, their carefully carved edges and rounded faces the only hints these were more than boulders left behind when ice covered the lands. These were once houses, administrative buildings and storehouses that were important to the running of such an important site. Now all lost and forgotten.

But it was the monolithic sculpture carved out of the hillock that held their attentions. The structure rose above them, a massive stone elevation, rounded by time. Carved in the north and south facings of the mound were two faces, massive imposing with only slight difference to distinguish their representation of the spirits of Supay and Allpa. Allpa possessed a softer countenance, subtly female yet androgynous enough to be male. The lines of Supay's face were harsher, colder and yet there was a gentleness the sculptor brought out in the eyes. Both spirits were carved by hands long lost in time. Both wise woman and shaman knew the creators of these ruins, of these images, were not human. No, they were ancient creatures who ruled a form of humanity that was closer to the beasts. Until these beings used their sorcery and odd metal devices increased the minds and skills of their servants. The path of Allpa and Supay were a lesser form of worship these beings taught, a barbaric following meant more for control than actual faith. But when the masters fell into dust, their few remaining members hiding deep within the Earth, Allpa and Supay endured, their power respected by the two tribes that resided in this terrible land.

Nestled in the center of the hillock was a cave. The cave possessed no visible light, but the gentle downward slope was inviting. This was their path, their destination. Each time wise woman and shaman came to these ruins, their only interest was the deep recesses of the cave. This was not a temple, oracle or locale for veneration. But was a direct connection to the spirits both tribes honored through their daily actions. The hermaphroditic entities were nature in the rawest form. Adulation was alien and unnecessary. Respect and obedience to the proper treatment of the land, air, water and life were the only important factors. Other behavior was man seeking to impose their will on a high order of being. To attempt to codify and venerate a form of the universe was to lessen the greater, making it familiar and easier to comprehend. This was insulting and foolish, ultimately leading to a bad end to the people in the end.

Side by side, wise woman and shaman headed into the cave. They would learn the method of correcting the imbalance to Allpa and Supay, caused by the Frankenstein woman, her follower and the walking dead man.

CHAPTER XI

"Radio is gonna die soon, my friend. You just watch," the film producer attempted to sound wise and venerable. This affect was spoiled by his thick New York accent and calculating eyes. The producer, Jack something...Wolf? Walt? Walters? Waltz? was a vulgar man, a newly wealthy first generation American who took over a small ailing film production company and turned a profit in a short time. He was a power in the imaginary world of movies, a producer and owner who was capable of making or breaking the careers of anyone he focused his gimlet eyed gaze upon.

"That seems doubtful, sir," Martin Mars knew the extra bit of civility was required for this coarse man. He expected a certain degree of reverence. In a small way Jack the film man reminded Mars of himself; the need to be seen as greater than other men. The difference was Martin Mars wished to be embraced by the leading lights across the globe. Jack the film man wished to bend them to his will, while never altering from the boorish *nouveau riche* he was to this day. Admirable, in a way, but also unwise. In the end, when Jack would be in trouble, his so-called friends would be the first to desert his side. Because followers who stayed with you because they needed your aid were the least loyal creatures.

Jack smiled, his face creasing and some hint of wrinkles were developing. He would fight aging for as long as he could, but in the end, nothing could fight what nature granted him from birth. He looked older than his age and only his power kept people from sneering about that flaw to his face.

"You're a smart man, Mr. Mars. So let me tell you something. Radio will be around for a long time. But motion pictures, they're on the rise. Soon picture palaces will cover the globe. And whose movies do you think will they be watching?" Jack's grin was both mocking and predatory. A lion teaching the proper feeding techniques to a lesser member of the pride.

"Your studio's," Mars replied, knowing that answer was expected of him now. He could have named one of the other players in California or New York, Hal Roach, Louis B. Mayer, Alfie Alperin…there were so many churls in that business. But it never served to anger any of them, they might be useful in the future.

"Right you are, my friend!" Jack beamed upon Martin Mars in a paternal manner. He continued to talk, his words fast and filled with promises.

Mars stopped listening, having already decided to agree to the offer. He would be better paid and could use the funds to finance even larger expeditions. There were certain locations in his files, inhabited by creatures known to only a few men around the world. Taking credit for their work would be easier, but the treks would be riskier. Still, the rewards would be greater. And possessing a foothold in a rising business, such as films, would be a good means of increasing the Mars fortune.

"I will have my attorney speak to your studio's once the contracts are available. But it appears we are in business, sir." Mars rose, not wishing to stay in the man's company any longer. There was something loathsome about the film producer, his vast, obvious ego and need to demonstrate his wealth and power at all times. But there was something worse there; Mars's instinct said as much and he was rarely wrong.

The answer came mere moments later as he exited Jack's office. Seated in the waiting area was a girl, no older than twelve. She possessed shoulder length golden blonde hair that fell in large sausage curls and was dressed in a short blue dress. Her eyes were fixed on the ground and she appeared stiff and emotionless. Something was dead within this child, a piece of her psyche seemingly removed or lost. An older woman, the child's mother, or minder, sat ramrod straight, her thin lips tight, her chin determined.

And now Martin Mars knew why he found Jack the film producer so pestiferous. His tastes were less than that of Hans, whose despoiling of the innocents was based in an in-born need. Jack chose to despoil the innocent as an expression of personal power. If this child did end up in a film, a doubtful factor at best from the start, Jack would revel in his wickedness. He would look up on the screen and think of the girl's tears, of her blood and pain. And he would feel satisfaction that he was powerful enough a man to desecrate the innocence of that child, and none would dare to suggest such a terrible deed had occurred. Mars knew that this girl, if she did become an actress, would be of sweet, happy, angelic adolescence. But all the while Jack would laugh inside, would stare at the girl and silently dare her to refute the image he created. And the child would falter, knowing the truth of the lie, and would forever possess horror and contempt for herself as this man's victim.

Martin Mars noted this truth and placed it within his list of future weapons to use against Jack. Should the film boss attempt to control Mars, these facts might one day cause the man's untimely end. But for now, they would do business. Because in the end, Martin Mars didn't care how mankind treated each other behind closed doors. Only that they looked upon him as a great man.

Hans held the door of the car open and jumped into the front seat. They pulled into the light traffic of Park Avenue, heading back to their hotel. "Did the meeting go well, master?"

"Very well, very well. A great deal of money may come our way. A great deal." Mars settled back in his seat, the offer already receding from his mind. He needed to complete all his business before the *Princess of San Pedro* left Manhattan and headed its slow journey back home. But the trip was already better than expected. A good omen? Possibly. If Gouroull was as easy to kill as these well-fed fools were to manipulate, Martin Mars would own the creature's corpse very soon...

CHAPTER XII

Elizabeth Frankenstein didn't speak for another week. She worked from morning until late at night, her attention totally and completely focused on her test tubes. Eating and drinking only happened because Hugh cooked and left food for her next to her microscope. He knew this behavior all too well, having seen her enter this state several times since medical school.

This was a form of mania on Elizabeth's part, a total and complete inability to seen any other facet of life as higher than her calling. Back in medical school, he'd been forced to drag her into a shower, fearful one of the elderly hidebound professors would declare her pungent body odor to be a symptom of a mental imbalance. Hugh knew they would be right, Elizabeth Frankenstein was insane. But that insanity was caused by her brilliance, possessing a mind capable of universe transforming science. The universe created such beings rarely. And their very presence revolutionized life itself for all mankind.

And this was the ultimate reason for Hugh's presence in this jungle. Besides the unspoken love he felt for Elizabeth, he believed in his heart of hearts that her work was essential for humanity's future. He learned this much from his very religious nanny as a child. According to her teaching, great people were touched by God. Their place in the world was often short, but important, essential for all life. Her philosophy was an odd mix of half-understood Christian theocracy and parochial school taught history. In her mind Jesus, Moses, Richard the Lionhearted, the Duke of Wellington, Queen Victoria, Louis Pasteur, John L. Sullivan and Sherlock Holmes were all the Lord's messengers on Earth.

Though Hugh abandoned much of the old woman's philosophies as he grew more educated, a version of this belief remained. He did believe that the universe provided, probably through chance, created genius. Men and woman beyond the norm, capable of enacting forced metamorphosis upon mankind. But unlike his old nanny, Hugh believed these people operated by science, not religion or war. Did not the great Imhotep create the first pyramid and birth medicine upon mankind? Did not Aristotle teach the Greeks and Alexander the philosophy that lead to all science? Or Alfred Nobel and his discovery of dynamite? The list of greatness was long, but always with one individual forcing humanity to take a new and radical path.

And in Hugh's mind, Elizabeth and her long-dead ancestor were such people. Victor Frankenstein had created an entirely new species of life, a being far more than human. Gouroull was not the same species as *homo sapiens*. That much was established when they began examining the ichor within him that passed for blood. Though shaped like a man, the similarities were merely superficial. The same could be said for man and gorilla, but the differences were all too stark.

This was why Hugh knew that Elizabeth would recreate Victor's genius. She was the only scientist alive who could comprehend his genius and improve upon his accomplishments. It was his duty to the world to help her achieve her vision. If that dream was somewhat terrifying, it was something he had learned to sublimate. Possibly a new race, such as that created by Gouroull and his proposed mate, would improve life on Earth. The new race was more dangerous than anything on the planet. Possibly they would end all wars and bring about a world of peace. Hugh could only hope this would be Elizabeth's effect upon the future.

Placing a tray of meat and vegetables and a pitcher of cold tea by her microscope, Hugh began to clean the lab. Elizabeth ignored his presence, her back hunched over a beaker which she was heating with a gas flame. Hugh didn't ask what she was doing, an attempted interruption was nearly impossible when she was in this state. And to do so would cause her to rant and rave for hours.

Hugh was just placing a bottle labeled *lupus lycanthrope cerebral spinal fluid* back on the shelf when he nearly shrieked in surprise. Gorouull stood just outside the window near the cabinet, his phosphorescent yellow eyes staring unblinkingly into the laboratory. Hugh knew he had looked out those windows mere minutes ago and the creature was not there. For such a massive being, Gorouull had an unnerving ability to move silently. This time, it was as if Victor Frankenstein's creation had just materialized into this location. But Hugh knew the truth. As a predator, Gorouull used stealth as a weapon, a means of defeating his prey, in addition to his other deadly inborn assets.

Hugh stared at Gorouull and watched as the tremendous creature's black lips slowly peeled back. Serrated canines glinted in the strong sunlight and Hugh shuddered involuntarily at the sight. There was something so terrible about Gorouull, so frightening. Staring into those horrific yellow orbs was like looking into death in the purest form. Hugh knew that he only lived now because he was serving Elizabeth. Otherwise Gorouull would have destroyed him without compunction.

As if reading his mind, Gouroull appeared to smile a little wider. His chalky gray skin reflected the light, giving his already inhuman appearance an even more terrible aspect. The only time Hugh ever viewed light in that manner was when he had viewed an odd statue in that town in the United States, Innsmouth. There was a statue in a hall near their dwelling, a large sculpture of a marine creature they called Dagon. Hugh had never learned more, but he remembered the peculiar way the light danced across the surface of the stone. The fact that Gouroull's skin reacted the same way was terrifying to say the least.

Shuddering again, Hugh continued to clean the lab. He felt Gouroull's gaze on his back and he hunched his shoulders and tried to pretend the cold sensation down his spine didn't exist...

CHAPTER XIII

Martin Romero was a happy man, but not a content one. The newly-appointed head of the Santa Clara docks, he knew this was just the first step in his career as a member of the San Pedro elite. But he needed to prove himself indispensable at his current job first.

The son of a city police chief, Martin's father was known to be willing to look aside from crimes by the wealthy for the right price. More than a few sons and daughters of the upper class indulged themselves a little too freely at times. Rather than destroy the lives of these future leaders of their country, Alberto Romero was willing to place the blame on the poorer members of their flourishing society. And if that led to his receiving gifts from the grateful family's, then all the better. Because this money allowed him to set his children's future on the path towards greatness.

Martin's older brother, Jorge, a massive brute with a surprisingly clever mind, earned a place in the elite San Pedro Military Academy. Now he was a Captain in the Federal Army, a rising power in the military. His recent marriage to the youngest daughter of General Ruiz ensured he would rise even faster in the ranks.

Martin's sister, Ana, was quickly married off to an older, but very wealthy, banker whose family were one of the twelve greats that controlled the county. Their children were the future diplomats, presidents and elites of San Pedro.

As for Martin, he was determined and possessed a quick, active mind and almost no conscience. The best private school followed by university placement had resulted in his earning a degree in law and a place in the lower levels of the Federal government. His big step had come when he had discovered the elderly head of the docking commission was pocketing 90% of his bribes. At least 40% of those funds were supposed to be sent to the minister of customs, who would provide the Coast Guard leaders with a piece of the action. This discovery led to a big show trial and a public execution of the traitor to the people of San Pedro. And, of course, Martin Romero's quiet placement as head of the Santa Clara docks.

This was the first step, just a rung on his ladder. Martin knew he would never be president or even a cabinet level politician. That was for the twelve families or military men like his brother Jorge. But the functionaries who actually ran the government, who possessed the real power, that was his future. With the increase in bribe money, he was already viewed as a possibly important cog in the Federal machine. If he continued on this path, one of his new patrons would ensure his marriage to a daughter or cousin of the twelve families. Then it was a short time before he was made a deputy commissioner or minister in some agency.

But this path was not nearly quick enough for Martin Romero. Oh, he was already making more money than his brother or father. One of the best parts of being the head of the Santa Clara docks was the second income he earned as a naval reservist. A no-show position meant to supplement his pay and prevent him from getting too greedy with the many bribes which passed through his hands.

But he was not yet one of the great men in Santa Clara, let alone the rest of the nation. Martin Romero was still not invited to the balls and shooting parties the twelve families held regularly. To them, he was a potential ally, but nothing more. Until he rose to a greater position, they would not assist his career. His predecessor was an example of one who never rose further in the world. The man had been too dazzled by the impressive sums of money passing through his hands. Instead of working on a way of taking the next step in government, he had held onto the docks post with an almost religious fervor. The man—Velez had been his name—had reminded Martin Romero of a bloated, elderly spider squatting in its web. But like a spider, he had forgotten that his tiny universe was merely a miniscule part of a greater cosmos.

Now, Martin Romero sat in his office, happy but not content with his place in the world. He didn't wish to be a spider, or even the bird who snapped up the insect. No, Martin Romero wished to be the hawk who fed on the birds and soared above the world, a power unto himself, answerable to none.

And the method to ensure this future was through two areas: money and patronage. The money continued to flow at an impressive rate. His first act, upon taking control of the docks, was to fire Velez's toadies and surround himself with a core of young men. They were loyal to him and knew he could make or break their futures. Then he increased their pays and rewarded loyalty on their parts. Disloyalty, like pocketing too much of the bribes, resulted in a quick, often violent, response. This increased the amount of money Martin Romero passed on to his leaders, a demonstration of his skills and leadership.

But it wasn't enough, at least not yet. The increases were good but not unexpected. He needed to give the government something more, a scandal they could exploit to attack their enemies. Because there were always those looking to attack the San Pedro government. Ever since the Tiger had been toppled from power, the infighting had become fierce. With the late, legendary leader's family back in control, they often required ammunition which could be turned towards attacking their enemies. If Martin Romero provided such information, the rewards would be as fast as his appointment to the head of the docks…

This was why each day he poured over every single movement on the Santa Clara docks. These docks were very busy, the river traffic connected to the coast and ocean-bound custom. And it led to the interior; all of the small cities and towns on the great interior lake were connected to the Santa Clara docks. But the paperwork was all in order. Nobody was shipping guns to the Indios, or stolen gold from the mines to the Church, or enemies of the twelve families. All was in order.

But one regular shipment caught his attention. Nothing remarkable, but one of the notes by the new inspection agent was different. Instead of the simple word "*chemicals*" in the contents section, the recently appointed inspector wrote, "*chemicals, medical*." Frowning, Martin Romero checked previous paperwork and found most shipments were chemicals. But a few were large boxes, some listed as fragile.

"Flora," he called out, knowing his secretary was always listening, "please send someone to get me Roberto Rubio. As soon as possible."

"Yes, sir." Flora's voice was high-pitched, the squeak of a mouse rather than reply of a woman. The wife of a drunken fool, she supported her immediate family by her job. She was completely efficient and almost disinterested in anything other than keeping her position at all cost. A tall, insect-like, thin, pinch-faced woman, she kept her graying hair in a tight bun and often worked late into the evening to ensure all knew she was indispensable to the office.

Placing the paperwork in a file, Martin Romero continued his work. But he would soon understand the details of these odd shipments to a woman named Frankenstein. If she was one of those foreign women who believed the Indios were humans, she might be a perfect victim of San Pedro justice. If not, he could increase her shipping taxes. The increased funds would help; the government was hinting at war with distant Hidalgo to the north...

CHAPTER XIV

Moraika and her male counterpart stumbled out of the cave. Their bodies were soaked with sweat and they both stank of blood, shit and fear. Contact with Allpa and Supay was painful, harmful for humans. Both wise woman and shaman were changed each time they ventured into these caves, subtly altered by the powerful beings from beyond.

To Moraika, the experience left her feeling like clay. Supay and Allpa molded her, twisted her body and innards completely out-of-shape and dumped her back in the sun to bake and be used. Because in a very real sense, she was merely their vessel, their pot to be used to pour out their wisdom. She did not know how her shaman ally felt about these moments. As always, he stunk as badly as herself, but remained silent.

Leaving the ruins, they stepped past the monolith. The silence of the rain forest hit them like a force, an absence of all sound and life. Moraika knew this sensation would end when they parted ways, each proceeding to their own realms to prepare. There was so much that needed to be done.

Raising their hands, they touched fingers and palms again, a silent acceptance of their duties. Standing in the clearing for several seconds, they slowly stepped apart and turned away. Without a word, the shaman vanished into the hidden trail he always used. And Moraika stepped onto her path, her cane tapping away as she slowly trudged towards the lake.

But she did not head back to the shores of the like and her tribe. She had so much to do, so many steps to take to save her lands. The vision she still held within her made that very clear. All life, from the smallest insect to the largest jaguar, from the fish not visible to the eye to the members of The Living, all would perish in flame and terror, with naught but ashes and dust left in their world. This was a harsher, more terrible prophecy than any she had viewed in the past, more horrific than the horrors the outsiders had planned for these lands. For this time, creatures of darkness, rather than the greed of mankind, would bring about the terrible end for all.

Moraika trudged a smaller trail, a forgotten path made by animals, but long since abandoned. She walked each step with sure feet, knowing every root and fallen branch, every loose rock and small hole to avoid. Though she was usually able to navigate the paths of the lands with such skill, after her time with Allpa and Supay, her instinct was heightened. It was as if she was somehow merged with life and death, a piece of Allpa and Supay in human form. But this period as an avatar of the great powers would not last, could not last. It would dissipate as soon as her duties were complete.

Her destination appeared into her view a short time later. A long, flat white stone with an imbedded circle of red crystals within the rock. Next to the stone was a small brook, a waterway which started deep within the distant mountains and ended within an ocean she never viewed with her eyes. Animals regularly drank from the clear waters, though they never crossed the rock with the crystals.

Moraika understood why the creatures avoided this odd natural formation. This comprehension was within her, was part of her inheritance as the Moraika of The Living. Whether the first of her kind had learned the truth or was granted the knowledge by her patrons was unknown to her, but still the answer lay within her deepest mind. The creatures of the land knew with all their innate spirits that this circle was connected on a deeper level to the spirits of the Earth. This was the place where Allpa and Supay met, a nexus point in the world. This was not a place of contact for those ethereal beings like the cave. No, this was a point of convergence where their power lay, usually dormant.

And this was where Moraika could center herself, prepare for the last battle. One of the details she had learned in the cave was that this was the end of her time. Soon, she was to join with Allpa and Supay, and another would take her place as Moraika. She was surprised that she felt no fear at the news of her forthcoming death. Perhaps it was because her trail through life was far longer than any human was meant to travel. Or maybe, because she had viewed so many horrors in her time, had prevented so many tragedies as a servant of the lands, that she embraced her final days, and would do her best to succeed in her final task.

Seating herself in the circle, she closed her eyes and immediately felt contact with all beings near her location. From the smallest insect to the jaguars creeping through the trees a short walk away, they were all part of the same spirit. The Living possessed a tiny comprehension of this simple fact, but even they could not comprehend the magnitude of this small piece of the Earth. But that was not the reason she was in this place.

Slowly her mind focused, ignoring the unimportant details and discovering that which was necessary. Moraika's mind drifted far beyond her body, seeking the required items.

She felt the presence of her male counterpart, his essence working his own direction. His path was different, yet connected to Moraika's. They would work together at the time of battle. Their unspoken connection was such that each would do as they were required, accepting their mutual demise. But they would meet it together.

CHAPTER XV

The man that lay at their feet wasn't a man. Oh, he was similar in shape and dimensions. There was a single oblong-shaped head, two arms and two legs. But the differences were distinct enough to cause them to realize this was no man, just like the old drunk informed them that morning.

Martin Mars squatted next to the corpse, the coppery smell of blood rising as he approached. Even in the twilight, the taxonomy of this creature began appearing in his head. Had this not been so, he would merely have Hans toss the body into the gulley and they would have returned to the boat. No loss to them in the end.

"Hans, your pad. Then we must make plans," Martin Mars stood up and smiled.

They were in the American South, stuck at a port for a week because of a series of storms further down the coast. The city, if you could call it such, lacked any true diversions. But Martin Mars was nothing if not ingenious Contacting a local museum and the most read newspaper, he scheduled two lectures of his travels to entertain and earn a little money. Plus the appearance allowed him to keep his name on the minds of potential sources of fame and fortune. That was, as always, his first priority. Fame was a form of worship, which was the point of all he attempted to do in this world.

Then the old drunk had approached him, just after the lecture. The man was taller than Mars, beefier, with a tangled reddish gray beard and wild, unkempt hair. He smelled of sweat, dirt and very cheap whisky and he held a battered straw hat in his shaking hands. The man's eyes were large and watery and reminded Mars of a pair of fried eggs left too long on a plate.

"Mister Mars," the man attempted to speak in a humble whisper. But his frame was not made for soft words and each sound came out with a hushed explosion of noise. "My name is Oscar Jakes. And I have a proposition for you."

"Do you now, Mister Jakes?" Mars spoke in a calm, soothing voice. He often discovered treasures by simply being polite and treating even the most disgusting, twisted dregs of society with a degree of dignity.

Oscar Jake's beefy hands began turning the hat slowly in his hands as his massive head nodded quickly up and down. "Yes, Mister Mars that is so. There's a man who I know is not really a man. My folks used to call them the Pine People. They is shaped like you and me, but when you look close, you can tell they're not made by God."

Martin Mars had heard many such stories in his travels, though not about this region. In Germany, the Black Forest was said to contain the last tribe of Neanderthals. In the American South West, there were the Raven Mockers. The long line of near human races hidden in the world was staggering. And as always, Martin Mars was on the hunt. There was always room for another addition to the collection.

"Please tell me more," Mars kept his distance but knew Hans was moving into place.

Oscar Jake's huge Adam's apple jumped up and down as he swallowed and shook. Anyone could see the man was in need of his drug. In this case, based on the scent, Oscar preferred the cheapest but strongest possible liquor. Similar behavior crossed Mars's past in the past, a morphine addict in Florence, a gambler in the south of

France, and others throughout the globe. Each were addicts in their own way, barely functional without their chemical or emotional refuge. They sought numbness or heightened pleasure each day. Without this sensation, they were reduced to pitiable wrecks, shells of living men and women. Wretched wastes, in Mars's opinion, but easily used and forgotten.

"Well, Mister Mars, it's like this. My daddy told me there were people like the Pine People about, but I didn't believe him. Until some of them took over the Roarke Farm when Mrs. Roarke died from a lung disease. They bought two other pieces of land nearby and were looking to take my Daddy's place, but I wouldn't sell. But I watched them and learned they were the Pine People. Only one is still there, calls himself Paul Pulver and keeps to himself most days. But he and his type aren't human." Oscar Jakes shifted from foot to foot as he spoke a little dance more reminiscent of a child trying to hold off the need for urination.

"What do you suggest I do?" Mars always asked this question, looking for malice on the part of the addict. Often rage was proof this was merely an attempt by the user to obtain revenge on one they felt wronged them in the past.

But Oscar Jakes looked frightened, his huge frame almost shrinking as he moved back and forth before Martin Mars's eyes. "I don't know, sir. But you track down creatures I heard you once killed a man wolf. My granny told me they can only be killed by a pure-hearted man. If this Paul Pulver is one of the devil's children, maybe you can chase him and his kind back into the hills."

"Tell me more." Mars wanted to laugh, but held himself from reacting in any way. The old wives' tales were very amusing to him, an easy method of manipulating the gullible. Try killing a werewolf with just a pure heart and the creature will end up eating said organ before your dimming eyes.

Oscar Jakes reached into his sagging pants and pulled out a folded map. He unfolded the soiled, damp paper and stepped closer to Martin Mars. "This is the way to get to my farm. The Roarke spread is a short walk east. Paul Pulver lives in a three room cabin made by Mrs. Roark's husband's grandfather. They got the land after marrying one of the Johnstone family, who claim they were given the place by the Ancients."

Martin Mars didn't listen to the details of the backwoods real estate history. All he needed to know was that this man was in earnest. And that a near human creature lived in the hills outside the city. This could be a good addition to his collections.

"Hans, pay the man." Mars turned away as Hans handed Jakes a small collection of bills. At the same time, Martin Mars reached into his valise and pulled out a large pistol with a very narrow barrel. Pulling the trigger, the weapon snapped and a tiny projectile struck the large old drunk in the neck.

Oscar Jakes gasped and grabbed his neck, a tiny drop of blood appearing between his fingers. He toppled over and Hans deftly yanked the money from his now nerveless fingers. This was one of Hans's inventions, a dart gun which fired an exotic poison-covered wooden spike. This was the best method of preventing anyone from taking credit for his work. And all that was left behind a body usually believed to be a victim of a heart attack.

The trip to the farm was uneventful and the cabin on the Roarke land was easy enough to spot. Mars and

Hans just strode up to the porch and sliced his throat before he could ask who they were and why they were on his land. Paul Pulver fell off the porch and died, choking on his blood.

"The hands are human-shaped," Mars dictated as he prodded and moved the body, "yet the index fingers are elongated past the middle finger. Nails are black and sharp. The eyes are narrower than human and the eyes possess pupils reminiscent of felines. The same narrowing and widening irises. No doubt they see well in the darkness. Skin is an odd tan color, closer to maple than human shading. The hair is thick and does not appear human in texture. Teeth are sharp. These Pine People appear to be an aboriginal race that developed along a different route than mankind."

"What shall we do with the corpse, Master?" Hans asked as Mars stood up after wiping his blade on the corpse's brown shirt. "We cannot bring it aboard the ship."

"Correct. But we will be passing this way again on our return voyage. On our return voyage. There was an old cemetery a short distance from that fat drunk's home. A short distance. We will bury the body and come back. Bury the body and come back," Mars explained, rubbing his hands together and stepping into the cabin.

"And by the time we return, the insects will make cleaning the body to the bones simplicity. Very clever, master," Hans completed the thought, smiling.

"Yes, yes. Very correct. Very correct," Mars confirmed and searched through the late Paul Pulver's possessions. He liked to take something as a memento of a hunt, something connected to the victim. Pulver must possess something worth taking.

Hans hoisted the dead body across his shoulders and headed towards the graveyard. He knew it was his job to carry the body and dig the hole. Happily, he packed a shovel before they headed out on the hunt. You never knew when Martin Mars wanted a body buried.

CHAPTER XVI

The coast guard cutter was named the *St. Helena* and it smelled fresh and clean. They were a new class of ship, a gift from a foreign Colonel named Bozo or something. The man had established himself with the twelve families as well as the most important men in government through a series of impressive gifts, bribes and blackmail. The new ships for the coast guard were one of his gifts. This way, the officers could seize cargoes of people the Colonel didn't like.

This also allowed some ships to move items without customs or searches. Nobody was sure what the Colonel's business was, but it was obviously profitable. The few who attempted to find out the contents of the Colonel's shipments vanished. No violence, no blood, no word. They simply left their home or office and never appeared again. The cold simplicity of attack was terrifying to the leadership of San Pedro. Some hotheads suggested breaking the agreement with the Colonel and attacking his interests. They, too, vanished, but the bribes and gifts did increase. The survivors accepted the greater payments and gave up questioning the foreigners. After all, they kept to themselves and didn't seem to be doing anything dangerous.

This, Martin Romero knew and was grateful for as he crossed the long lake. The previous ships were castoff merchant vessels, barely functional rickety boats with a stench that could be smelled for miles. But the coast guard wasn't considered particularly important until recently. But these days, San Pedro's growth meant an increase in imports and exports. This led to a need for more customs inspectors, coast guard officers and better boats to catch smugglers. The Colonel's gift solved the problem of finding the money as well as where to purchase the ships. These vessels were built in Boston by a firm called Lyte & Tremain, and they were envied, even by San Pedro's small navy.

Martin Romero straightened his naval reservist uniform, an unnecessary movement since his outfit was perfect. It was easy to stay clean when you spend the majority of the journey reading a book in the captain's cabin followed by several walks around the deck. The coast guard crew, for the most part, ignored him and went about their business. They only knew he was the head of the docks and could make their lives difficult if they made him angry. Best to call him sir and ignore that he looked ridiculous in his fancy uniform.

"Captain," Martin Romero stepped onto the bridge and gave a crisp salute.

The Captain, a thin, gray-bearded man named Campos, merely nodded. He was an experienced river pilot and sailor and a high-ranking member of the coast guard. He chose the safe life of the coast guard over risking his life against pirates and bandits as a merchant seaman. Occasionally, a smuggler might try and run or fight, but they were rare. Pirates and bandits were more common and dangerous along the river. They were a genuine danger to small ships and seemed impossible to stop.

"I will need at least three of your men to accompany my men when I speak to the people ashore. Armed. Do you possess large guns?" Martin Romero pictured himself stepping ashore, an honor guard preceding him as he strode with the calm assurance of a warrior.

"We have rifles for each man and revolvers," Campos said, sounding bored, but he waved over his first mate.

The first mate, who was introduced as Raul Soto, was as tall as his captain, but wider and possessing a moon-shaped head and face. He didn't speak, but his slanted dark eyes seemed to always be moving and examining his surroundings.

"Tell Bravo, Salinas and Contreras to draw revolvers and rifles from the arms chest. Then send them to me," Captain Campos ordered and glanced over at Martin Romero, "It will be done. You had best get ready, the dock is in sight."

Martin Romero saluted again, turned on his heel and headed below. He wanted to check his uniform and put on his peaked hat that completed his uniform. This foreign doctor named Frankenstein would be overwhelmed when he realized his contact wasn't some elderly dock inspector.

On the deck, Captain Campos checked to make sure Romero was gone. A moment later, Bravo, Salinas and Contreras stepped onto the bridge. They were the three largest and youngest members of the crew, each distantly related to each other. Why they all signed up for the coast guard was a mystery, but they did their jobs as sailors well-enough.

"The little prick is going on shore to demand more money. Go with him and salute him like he's Admiral Munoz inspecting a parade. Make sure he doesn't get himself into trouble." Captain Campos was well aware that the head of the coast guard was planning on retiring in the next few years. Romero might be responsible for suggesting who would take that position. Best to keep him happy.

"Sounds more like we're guarding Admiral Munoz's son." Salinas was a handsome man, tall, muscular with classical good looks and thick curly hair. He always looked as if he was posing for a statue, such as one of those Greek athlete figures in the Santa Lucia art museum.

"More like his daughter," Contreras tossed in. Taller than Salinas, he was the opposite of the man in many ways. Huge, fleshy and covered in coarse black hair, he resembled a bull which had happened to evolve into a human.

"Or his wife," Bravo had to put his view in, disliking both beat him to the funnier comments. He was as tall as Contreras, but thinner. This made him appear slight, but Campos knew Bravo was the most dangerous of the three men. A heavy drinker and brawler, Bravo was scarred across his face and arms and always looked like he was itching for a fight.

"Yes, yes. Just do as I said and there will be an extra rum ration for you each tonight." Campos gave all three men a smile and watched as they filed out. The nightly rum was a tradition back since San Pedro was helped to freedom by an English sea captain. There were a few blond-haired, blue-eyed families in San Pedro who claimed lineage from the legendary Captain Jack of the English Navy.

Both sailors smiled slightly and nodded their agreement. They knew the manual of arms, having been forced to learn it as a punishment from a previous captain. That man had an unfortunate "accident" that cost him a leg. He was another pensioner, hoping the government's money came as scheduled in the right amount. A sad life, one Campos vowed to avoid at all cost. He'd prefer a death on the river or lake than years sitting ashore, drinking himself into a stupor every night.

The rest of the ship's small company made preparation for pulling into the distant dock. They were an efficient crew, proud of the new ship and hopeful their work could lead to greater things. None of them wanted to merely be stuck chasing smugglers or rescuing ships in trouble from the river's powerful and sometimes treacherous currents.

Their dreams went two distinct directions, both known to Campos. A few wished to make the coast guard their career. They wanted to lead ships of their own, wear a captain's cap and receive the respect of such a position. This was a good dream, if somewhat futile. Few men were leaders, most were followers. Campos knew this since he was a child and watched his uncle's dog lead a group of sheep from their fields to the barn. The sheep clearly preferred to stay outside eating grass. But his uncle needed to shear them for wool. The dog, a little black and white mutt named Dog, barked a nipped the larger animals until they fell behind him and walked into the spacious barn. That was the day learned an important lesson. For every dog, there were many sheep which followed.

Most of the men wishing to stay in the coast guard were sheep. Young Baez had potential, but he was the only one Campos viewed as a possible captain. The others were more like Duarte and Franco. Strong, capable sailors, but followers. Sheep.

The other set of sailor's dreams was equally simple to comprehend. They wished to go into the merchant trade and earn wealth. Also very unlikely. These sailors failed to comprehend that the merchant shipping trade was as dangerous as navigating piranha-filled waters.

Everyone was out to cheat you and enrich themselves in the process. Knowing how to navigate a rip tide or ride a ship through a bad storm when your mainmast is close to snapping were impressive skills. More difficult than almost anything on the planet. But it didn't make one an expert in commerce. More than a few dreamers of wealth found themselves both broke and returning to the coast guard. Or, worse, they became smugglers and were hunted down by their former comrades. Either way, the thought was quite depressing to Captain Campos. Because either a shell of a proud sailor would return to his ship, or he would be forced to arrest someone he once trusted.

The rare few that would succeed in either dream would hopefully lead happy lives. But Campos knew those would be a rare breed. This was somewhat depressing to Campos, though he never discouraged his men. The Good Lord gave all men the gift of free will. How they chose exercise that heavenly treasure was between them and God. To intervene would, in Campos's mind, be a contravention of the will of the Lord. He prayed each night against such, knowing this would be the sin of pride.

Martin Romero returned as Campos mused on the pitfalls of pride. Here was one who clearly lived with an excess of such a sin. This much was obvious based on the way he preened in his military uniform. Campos knew the navy reserve was merely a means of giving a pretty uniform to government officials. Then they were allowed to come to parties dressed up in a costume that made them look like proud warriors. Most carried swords and wore their decorations and medals, both the government's way of keeping the ambitious happy, with extraordinary pride. It was a pathetic sight, though one you could not comment or laugh about, even secretly. Because these powerful peacocks would feel slighted and strike with all their power to destroy the one who told the truth or their true status.

But Campos also reflected that this Martin Romero was a creature who would violate many of the other deadly sins. Pride was proven and he was willing to bet Romero had an excess of envy. No doubt Martin Romero coveted the positions of those above him in the government. That was how he had earned his place as head of the docks. He was probably considering similar actions to others in the future, wishing to take what they possessed, no matter the cost. Sad, because he would never be satisfied. If Martin Romero rose to be the President for Life of San Pedro, he would then wish to attack their neighboring countries. Then he could be an Emperor or a King. But it would never be enough.

Midway through these thoughts, Romero started to speak, forcing Captain Campos out of his reverie. He turned his head slightly and saw the young man was waiting for an answer.

"Forgive me, sir. I was paying attention to the barometer. What did you say?" Campos knew that invoking one of his instruments would satisfy the man. Like all non-sailors, he was amazed by any trinket of the trade.

"What I asked is, if you would please blast your horn. I wish to alert the inhabitants that we are to arrive shortly." Romero nodded at the now visible house in the hills beyond the dock.

Campos restrained himself from explaining that this was a waste of time. He knew anyone, even the least observant, would have noticed a ship approaching for the docks for the last four hours. But Campos knew that

Romero wished the horn as a method of control. He wanted the people he was coming to threaten to know that they were about to meet an important man.

"Of course, sir." Campos pulled the line and released two long blasts of the horn. This was normally reserved for fog safety, preventing possible collisions. But if it soothed this ambitious little man, so be it. There was no helping a sinner like Martin Romero, they had to determine their own path in the world.

A pair of figures could be seen, walking from the house to the dock. Both wore gleaming white jackets which appeared to shine in the bright light. Otherwise they were indistinct, the distance being too great. Captain Campos had no interest in examining them with his telescope. This was Romero's mission; Campos knew he was merely the man's driver.

Romero, for his part, vanished below and returned with a well-polished set of brass binoculars. He handled them with exaggerated care and it was obvious he'd bought them specifically for this journey. After playing with the dials for a few minutes, he finally focused on the two figures in white.

"A man and a woman. She must be the doctor's wife or nurse. The man is speaking a lot. Typical of doctors. She looks angry. Too skinny, too. He should slap her across the mouth. Women need to learn their place," Martin Romero narrated before closing up the binoculars in their case and returning below.

Captain Campos was grateful he held his tongue. Though he knew his career began and ended with the bridge of ships, such as this one, he wasn't unaware of the political situation in his country. For Martin Romero to rise up in politics, he would be forced to either marry the daughter of a military strongman or one of the wealthy families on San Pedro. In either case, the woman he would marry would be well-bred, born to wealth and related by blood or marriage to important people. If he were to lay a violent finger, or even to speak a nasty word, that woman's relatives would destroy Martin Romero. The destruction could be of his career or his life. That happened all the time. Romero's swaggering was a front, a ploy by a frightened little man to hide his terror.

They pulled up to the dock, Campos's men tying the cutter up and lowering a gangplank. With exaggerated solemnity, Bravo, Salinas and Contreras marched down the walkways and formed a tight corridor for Martin Romero to pass. They knew it would be several minutes before he appeared, but they were getting extra rum for behaving like this was an important occasion. They would act in an appropriately military manner, holding in their laughter and eye rolls.

The doctor and the woman were waiting on the docks as well. The man looked confused and a little frightened. The woman looked, as Romero stated, angry and impatient. The man was wringing his hands and sweating rather profusely as the female strode back and forth. Her pacing appeared to be making the man even more nervous.

Eventually Martin Romero appeared, his white uniform gleaming even brighter than the white lab coats on the two he was coming to meet. He saluted with slow, deliberate movements and marched down the gangplank. Campos knew he was attempting to look a proud and expert commander whose very walk showed his precision and warrior intensity. Instead, he looked like a child in a costume, a mummer attempting to act like an adult. Campos viewed such behavior in the past, the son of an admiral or a general in a miniature version of their parent's uniform. But in a full grown adult, the behavior was ridiculous.

Stopping several feet and standing at attention, Martin Romero stared at the man for a moment. "Doctor Frankenstein, I am Ensign of the San Pedro Naval Reserves and head of the Santa Lucia Docks, Martin Romero. Your regular shipments of medical supplies must be examined and understood by my government. You will cooperate."

The woman stepped in front of the man, her blue eyes flashing with open contempt and menace. "I am Doctor Elizabeth Frankenstein," she said. "This man is my assistant. Follow me, I will answer your questions. We must be fast. I am at a critical juncture in my research."

Bravo, Salinas and Contreras all choked back laughs at Romero's shocked expression that this skinny woman was the doctor. For her part, Elizabeth Frankenstein turned on her heels and began stalking back towards her home in the distance. She didn't ask them to follow. In fact, she didn't give any of them a choice but to do so as her quick pace lead them up the hill towards her lab.

CHAPTER XVII

Life with Martin Mars could be difficult, but Hans was happy enough. He had money, a form of respectability and all the work he would hope for in one life. It kept his mind and body engaged, prevented his... urges... from returning. Hans didn't want to do what he needed to do to the children. But that was in him; it was who he was all the time.

But work was better than doing what he knew was wrong. Mars was constantly demanding something. It could be as simple as getting his tuxedo ready or as complex as poisoning the food at a party so the host was humiliated. And, of course, there was the killing of monsters, enemies, annoying people and reporters. Oh, and hiding bodies or planting them in places so it didn't affect Martin Mars's life. Yes, Hans was a busy man.

But the best part of this work was the designing and building of weapons. Trained as a clockmaker, Hans enjoyed the intricacies of devices. He'd tried in the past to bury himself in the creation of clocks and toys, but the gadgets always somehow reminded him of children. Their soft skin and unsullied... it was not a distraction, or at least not enough.

But weapons, they were so much more vital than a cuckoo clock or a dancing clockwork clown. The potential for destruction kept him engaged each time he sat down and set pencil to paper to design something for another hunt with Martin Mars. There was something intoxicating about designing, building and testing a weapon. Every small detail was critical, could mean the difference between life and death when faced with something monstrous.

This part of their working relationship appeared during an early hunt. Mars wanted to kill, stuff and mount a near-human creature which was faster and stronger than human and could smell gunpowder from miles away. This Canadian forest-dweller was capable of hiding from any who carried guns or explosives in their chosen location. And all attempts at close combat resulted in bodies so torn, the woods were believed to be inhabited by ghosts according to the locals.

"No guns, no knives, no dynamite! How can I catch this monster? How? How? No guns, no knives, no dynamite! How can I catch this monster? How?" Martin Mars was raving, walking back and forth, kicking over furniture and making a huge mess of the cabin he rented.

"Why not use a crossbow, master?" Hans heard the recitation ten of twelve times by that point and had to break in with his thoughts.

"Did you just say a crossbow? Did you just say a crossbow? Did you?!" Martin Mars froze in his tracks, his hands balling into fists as he stared down at his diminutive assistant.

"Yes, master. A crossbow." Hans knew Mars wasn't listening right now, but this would allow him to rant in a different direction and eventually pause and listen.

Martin Mars stalk across the room and lifted a huge rifle in his hands. "This, you little, stupid fucking fool, is an elephant gun. It fires a .577 Nitro Express round. That is a bullet that is so heavy and powerful it is capable of knocking over a full grown elephant. At 750 grains, the projectile travels at roughly two thousand feet per second. But I should leave that behind in favor of a dark ages' weapon that couldn't penetrate the side of a small barn?! Hans, are you simply a complete idiot or were you kicked in the head by a cow as a child? Because clearly, you're the stupidest being walking the Earth!"

"Master," Hans ignored the insults, now seeing his chance to be more than just a servant to this man. He could be a vital part of Martin Mars's growing empire. "A crossbow need not be a hand-held weapon. In ancient times, some were so large they required animals to move them to the battle. If I had the equipment, I could design and build one large enough to kill a charging beast or monster. A clockwork mechanism could pull back a metal string and reload seconds later. But I will need to design the device and test the results…"

Martin Mars returned the gun to the walnut rack against the wall. He clapped Hans on the shoulder and smiled. "If you can build such a device, my friend, I will know we are meant to work together for all times. Build it for me! Build it for me!"

And so he had, and many more weapons and devices since that day. And he learned the art of gunsmithry, explosives, poisons and oh so many other lethal skills. All were used to serve Martin Mars and hold back the urges. Always to hold back the desire to take the children once again.

This was why Hans was deep in the hold of the *Princess of San Pedro*. As expected, a metal shop was deep within the bowels of the boat. All large ships possessed somewhere the sailors could repair important equipment. After a few well-placed bribes, Hans was granted full access. He'd brought aboard several crates of metals and other items he required in the creation of his latest hunting weapon. Because this hunt was the most dangerous they'd even undertaken.

"Gouroull," Hans whispered as he lifted a metal rod. "You are about to meet your end."

CHAPTER XVIII

If there was anything Elizabeth Frankenstein despised more than stupidity, it was interruptions. Even back to her childhood, she was renowned for her fury when even her parents attempted to tear her attention away from her work. Even her teachers in medical school walked carefully, resenting her brilliance and furious responses to their inquiries. She didn't care. Elizabeth knew her work was more important than any foolish query.

Therefore she was less than amused when Hugh informed her that a ship was sighted and was approaching. Her disinterested grunt was not unexpected by Hugh. He was used to Elizabeth's moods. But when it was clear this was not a cargo ship, but was in fact some type of government vessel, he risked her anger. After verifying with their telescope, he went back to the lab, wishing he'd had a drink before taking this step.

"Elizabeth," Hugh knew his voice was a little high-pitched and weak now. But he was exhausted and knew her rage would be terrible. "That ship, it is coming our way."

"Mmmf," Elizabeth grunted as she poured some saline into the vat she was studying.

"I believe, based on the boat, that it is a government vessel. They will want to speak to us." Hugh's each word emerged from his mouth in hesitant gasps. He knew he sounded like a foolish coward, but this was his least favorite activity in his rather unusual life.

"What of it?" Elizabeth didn't look up, but she was gripping the edge of the table with tense, white knuckled hands.

"They will want to speak to you and will ask questions. We need to speak to them... greet them when they arrive. If we don't, they may become angry." Hugh took a step back, knowing this would ignite the tantrum.

Elizabeth slapped the tabletop with a palm as she snatched up an empty beaker with her other hand. She hurled the glass beaker at Hugh's head, missing by inches. She followed that with two test tubes, a metal ring and a heavy leather-bound book.

"How dare you interrupt me! How dare you! I am in the middle of a critical juncture in my work and you bother with... with... boat? BOATS?" Elizabeth screamed and stepped forward, her eyes searching for more items to throw or hit Hugh with now.

Straightening, Hugh stood his ground, "Elizabeth! This is not Europe! We are in San Pedro and the government is different!" Hugh knew his voice was squeaking as he yelled back at Elizabeth, but part of his duty to her was to deal with the reality they faced in each location they chose to reside.

"What do I care of governments and differences? Science, Hugh! Science is all! My work will change the world! I care not about little men and their games!" Elizabeth stopped searching for something to grab for the moment. Her hands were on her hips and she stared at Hugh with a challenging look in her eye.

Hugh noted Elizabeth's lack of tribute to her ancestor's work in her statements now and as of late. She appeared to have forgotten, or chose to ignore that all of her work was his concepts from centuries earlier. This oversight on her part was worrying to Hugh. But there was little he could do at this time. The current problem was far more important.

"Elizabeth," Hugh lowered his voice to a calmer level, hoping he could reach her now. "You may despise officials and bureaucrats, but they can make our lives difficult. And in a backward hellhole such as this part of the world, they have even more power. We need to deal with them when they arrive and make sure they do not return. Otherwise our work will not proceed!"

Elizabeth frowned, her body still taut as a steel spring. Yet a measure of doubt entered her still hostile demeanor. "Just like in Boston and Toronto. Little men who cannot conceive of anything beyond filling their bellies and filling their pockets with gold. Pathetic little fools!"

Hugh nodded, grateful for an opening. "Yes, yes! And we are so close in your breakthrough! We need to keep these men from stopping your work. A brief delay, but nothing more than a postponement of your production."

Elizabeth sighed, her hands dropping to her side, "So be it. Take the extra limbs in the cabinet and throw them into the brush on the north side of the hill. The animals will consume the remains. They're useless in any event. We'll need fresh specimens soon enough. Save me two arms and a leg. And sweep up the glass on the lab floor. I am going to prepare myself."

Not willing to say anything, lest he ruin this rare acceptance on her part, Hugh rushed over to the cold cabinet. Removing the tray, he carried three arms and four legs out of the lab, heading for the thicket in the rear of the building. There were often wild animals nearby and this would serve them a rather huge meal. Tossing the body parts over the small cliff, he ran back inside and began to clean the lab.

That was the situation a short time ago. But now the circumstances were once again in danger. When the round-faced, pudgy man in the white uniform failed to address her as Doctor Frankenstein, Elizabeth's fury rose once again. She was in a foul mood just walking to the dock. Now her temper was in danger of erupting once again.

The man who introduced himself as Romero spoke up again: "My apologies, Madam Doctor. But you are the first lady doctor I have ever met. This is very odd in my country. I am not sure many of our people would find a lady doctor acceptable. But since you are a foreign female, they will understand somewhat."

Elizabeth's fists clenched and unclenched as they headed up the hill. "I do not practice the sort of medicine you would need to consider. My work is exclusively re-search."

Hugh could tell she bit back an epithet or two at the end of that statement, but he was grateful to see her control so far. They couldn't afford to move to another country and start over. Physically it would be difficult. And there was the question of Gouroull...

"What type of research?" Romero asked, lengthening his stride so he was at Elizabeth's side.

"Organ transplantation. I am determining the best method of ensuring this will work properly without tissue rejection." The lie was a familiar one, used many times in the past. But Elizabeth always knew her true work was never greeted with social or even scientific acceptance.

"Please explain more," Romero stated, straightening his uniform as he struggled to keep up with Elizabeth's fast pace.

"The organs of the human body," Hugh jumped in, knowing Elizabeth's responses would be biting at best. "…periodically fail. Whether it be from birth defect or disease. If a matching organ from either a living or recently deceased donor was transplanted into a person, a life might be saved. It is an important advancement we are working to perfect."

"That sounds like witchcraft." Romero's voice sounded both skeptical and repulsed by the explanation.

Elizabeth whirled on her heels, facing her. Her face was a taut mask of rage and she looked ready to attack him with her fists. "Witchcraft? If you are attempting to be ignorantly insulting, you are succeeding, Admiral!"

Romero looked surprised, but Hugh noticed he didn't correct Elizabeth's mistake about his rank. "I am a good Catholic, Doctor Frankenstein. What you are doing sounds like something the Church would find quite objectionable."

"The Church were the first people to engage in such experiments." Elizabeth's lie came easily. Hugh knew she loved to state such false truths and could supply a complete set of false and hard-to-follow facts that would overwhelm the listener.

Why did she lie so easily? Hugh once thought it was a means of protection against those who found her work objectionable. He knew her determination to complete her ancestor's work was a mania, a form of illness that could change the world. A form of defense against doubters was understandable.

But later, he realized this belief was quite incorrect. Elizabeth didn't provide these false statements as a form of protection against doubters. Quite the opposite, in fact. Her real reason was based in her contempt for most people upon this planet. She viewed anyone who was not a scientist with her depth of knowledge to be an ignorant simpleton. Therefore, flooding them with a seemingly endless stream of nonsense facts was merely her demonstration of contempt for their imbecility.

Romero looked stunned by the information Elizabeth was tossing his direction. The three large armed men who followed him alternated between looking amused by the leader's discomfort and stunned by the statements made by Elizabeth Frankenstein.

Arriving at the house, Elizabeth led them through several corridors and down into her laboratory. The room itself was far cleaner than before and smelled faintly of alcohol. The more unusual ingredients were placed on high shelves or in drawers in other rooms. The lab resembled a hospital operating room rather than the site of the resurrection of the dead.

"Here you will find my latest experiment." Elizabeth led Romero and his guards over to a table. On the table was a large clear glass vat filled with saline. Within the liquid, attached to two thick copper wires was a heart. The crimson organ pulsed with an irregular movement, vibrating the vat slightly. The wires lead to a large black metal device which lit up with each beat.

"A human heart? What kind of a monster are you?" Romero recoiled in disgust, his face pale. He made a loud sound and looked as if he was beginning to retch.

"Sir," Bravo said, stepping closer to Romero, "that's not a human heart?"

"What? What? Of course, it's a human heart you stupid fool!"

Romero was obviously attempting to bluster. Hugh believed Romero knew he was making himself look like a sad, pitiable sight. This meant he needed to hide himself beneath a veneer of anger and attitude.

"My uncle was a butcher in our town. I worked with him mornings. That's a cow's heart. Too big for a man," Bravo explained and gesticulated broadly to demonstrate the size differences.

And Bravo was right. They'd substituted a cow's heart for the human one Elizabeth had been using earlier. The reasoning was that, if the ship had a doctor aboard, he or she would tell them they were looking at a bovine organ.

"Ah, well, I see..." Romero straightened and looked at Elizabeth, confused.

"You wonder why I work with animal organs." Elizabeth smiled, though there was a predatory, amused quality to her grin. "Only a monster would work with human organs."

Hugh could have laughed at this bald face lie, but he held his tongue. The thought that either he or Elizabeth possessed the slightest degree of interest in the ethics of human experimentation was ludicrous at best. But she was playing the part very well.

"That aside, why are you in this distant jungle in my country, Miss... er... Doctor." Romero regained his bluster and stepped closer to the cow's heart. He examined it quickly and looked away after a moment.

"My work is very advanced. I cannot risk theft by other scientists. San Pedro was distant enough to prevent discovery." Elizabeth waved at several advanced-looking devices in the laboratory.

Romero nodded once. "Understood. However your taxes were improperly assessed. They are hereby doubled."

Elizabeth nodded to Hugh, who removed a small pouch. He handed it to Romero, hearing the clinking as the man nearly dropped it in surprised. "Will gold coins be acceptable? That should cover the next two shipments. And I will write my factor in Santa Lucia to make the adjustment."

Romero nodded, still surprised and barely under control. "Acceptable, yes. Thank you."

Elizabeth waved her hand, "My assistant will see you out. Thank you for your help, Señor."

Romero almost fell over himself as he left the elderly house. He remained silent all the way back to the boat and merely nodded to Hugh as he stepped back aboard the cutter. Within a few minutes, they were gone.

Hugh rushed back up to the lab. He hoped this was the last they would hear of that repugnant little man.

CHAPTER XIX

It was an hour before Romero returned to bridge. He'd taken the time to change out of his uniform and was straightening his tie as he appeared. The linen suit was slightly more appropriate, but would doubtless be sweat-stained in very little time. But to a man like Martin Romero, dressing like an old-fashioned land baron was a part of his act. To him, it was essential that at all times, he looked and acted like a man of great importance. This was why he would suffer in a lightweight suit rather than wearing a light shirt and short pants.

"This trip was better than I hoped," Romero sat down in the Captain's chair, ignoring the dark looks from some of the crew. Captain Campos was holding onto the wheel and appeared disinterested in the lack of propriety.

"How so, sir?" Campos wasn't actually interested, but he knew asking would keep this little man happy.

"The Frankenstein woman is conducting evil, terrible experiments upon human beings!" Romero wasn't hiding his glee at this discovery.

"Bravo told me the heart she was using belonged to a cow, sir." Campos wished this little monster of a man would go below and sleep. He disliked Martin Romero and knew he would be a plague upon the people, should he rise to a position of great power. But there was little that he, a simple ship's captain, could do without destroying the lives of his family. Because killing Romero would be easy, a quick slash of a knife and dump the body overboard. But this act would come to light and those connected to Romero would see to Campos's de-

116

struction. Then they would go after his family. That was the way of the men in power. No, the risk was not acceptable,

"Bravo and the rest of the men missed the large collection of vultures circling the rear of the house. This bitch Frankenstein thought she could fool me with platitudes and some pieces of silver. But I am not so easily led by the nose. A woman doctor is a bad enough thought, but this one must have been chased all the way from Europe to our fair land. She is a witch, hiding behind science!" Romero rubbed his hands together, delighted by his statements.

"Then it is good you came here, sir." Campos didn't want to encourage more contact with Martin Romero.

"Yes, it is, Captain. In my report, I will state how well you did assisting me. You and your men demonstrate the best of our country's coast guard service." Romero stood and straightened his jacket. "When dinner is served, please have the food sent to my room. I will be writing the rough draft of my report to the minister and others."

Campos signaled to the men nearby to keep their mouths shut. There was an undercurrent of amusement filling the air. They all heard how Martin Romero almost vomited at the look of a cow's heart. And now this so-called navy reserve officer proved he did not know the most basic nautical terms. A room? Did Romero believe this ship was a hotel? They'd given Romero the first mate's stateroom, knowing he would demand nothing less. But his ignorance was a source of glee for the crew. Campos needed all derision to occur after the little man left.

Receiving the crisp salutes of the Captain and the others in the wheelhouse, Martin Romero headed down below and into his assigned room. It was small, slightly larger than a closet. But the only one larger belonged to the Captain, and, wishing to appear somewhat humble, he hadn't protested when assigned this small chamber. Apparently the crew slept on hammocks slung below. This was good, the separation between officers and men was important to maintain social distance in the caste system of society.

Inking his pen and pulling out his least expensive paper, Martin Romero began to write. He listed his concerns regarding the Frankenstein woman's shipments and, with suitable drama, his investigation. He wished to look humble, as well as important and intelligent. This was not easy, but he endeavored at the task, scratching out unacceptable words or sentences. He was just starting a paragraph on the excellent qualities of Captain Campos and his crew, when a sound caught his attention.

The sound was a harsh grinding noise, a rumble that rose to a high-pitched screech. It was a horrific noise, the wails of the damned in the mind of Martin Romero. Suddenly the ship lurched violently, tossing him about and almost spilling his ink pot. The steady hum of the ship's engines cut off and the screeching sound ceased. The sounds of the crew moving about, with harshly toned shouts drifted down to Martin Romero's ears.

Putting away his writing material and hiding his notes in his suitcase, Romero headed up the companionway and onto the deck. The whole crew was up in force and he could hear the metallic rattle of the anchor chain being run out. Two men were going over the side and Captain Campos was out of the wheelhouse and standing near the railing. His usually placid face was tight with anger and concern.

"What is happening?" Romero pushed up next to Captain Campos, ignoring the man's tense anger.

"Something caught in the screws. Please step back. I need to work now." Campos's eyes never left the location of his two divers.

Respecting the Captain's professionalism, Martin Romero stepped back several paces and moved closer to Salinas. "I didn't catch what the Captain said is wrong. What happened?"

Salinas was no fool. He'd clearly heard what Campos stated to Romero from this distance. It was clear that this little man didn't understand the answer. "The screw, the propeller of the ship. Something snagged it and damaged the machines. The Captain needs to know how badly."

Martin Romero, realizing this was important and very beyond his knowledge, nodded with what he hoped was a solemn look. "What would cause such a calamity?"

Salinas shrugged. "Could be an outcropping of a rock, a tree. Many things can snag the screws. We look, we find out. Then we fix or we raise sail and go back slow. It happens to all ships."

Romero nodded again, grateful this wasn't a danger. In fact, it probably gave him more time to work on his investigation report. The only future problem was that his supper would be late in arriving. But that could not be helped. The safe running of the ship was more important. If this meant a missed meal, Martin Romero was willing to make the sacrifice. This way he could get back and do his very important work.

"If the Captain requires my assistant, tell him to let me know. I will be in my room." Romero gave Salinas a waving salute and headed below. He missed the rolled eyes and look of amused derision on the face of the larger sailor.

Locking his door once again, Martin Romero returned to his work. His plans were very simple in this situation. He would compose a perfect investigation report and send copies to his minister, the minister of the navy and the archbishop of Santa Lucia. The government's ties to the Church were currently weak. The President and his family possessed very little interest in religion. This led them to acts of impiety that were often used as weapons by enemies of the government as well as the Church itself. This was his chance to forge closer ties with it, at least temporarily. With the Church on the side of the government, even the rebels would be forced to silence for a short time. Politically this was a good move on his part. All three men would share in the credit and they would all be grateful to him for presenting this excellent opportunity. This would lead to better positions and the friendship of powerful men, exactly what he required to advance. The fact that all three men were members of the twelve families of San Pedro didn't hurt his chances either.

The only downside was that he was not able to involve the army. That branch of the government was inordinately powerful. The legendary "Tiger of San Pedro" was a former general, as were many of his successors. But Martin Romero had no true contacts in that body. His connections, thanks to the docks, were with the navy. They were less important, but not weak like the department of Indian Affairs. Once he was promoted to a better job, Romero knew he would need to make some friends and contacts in the army. It wouldn't be healthy to have them seeing him as an enemy. Men who placed themselves against the generals had a habit of dying accidentally or suddenly simply disappearing forever.

Romero worked steadily for half an hour, hearing the movement on the deck in a distant manner. He was lost in his work until the first gunshot rang out. The movement upon the deck became more frantic and a high pitch shriek of agony seemed to fill the air. Romero stood, tossing the inkpot onto the floor and soaking his shoes. The scream abruptly cut off followed by a loud crashing sound. A howl of fear, deeper than the first yell, suddenly emerged and was cut off a moment later. Another gunshot followed and the sounds of a man cursing floated down to Martin Romero's ears. The man's voice stopped with a gasping cry and another loud clatter and a wet, meaty thud. The sounds of running feet heading towards the stern sounded over his head. Shrieks of panic were audible from several voices, each cutting off as abruptly as the earlier screeches.

One voice called out, a strong, stern sounding inflection. The words were indistinct, but the tone of the speaker was unquestioning and harsh. There was a silence that followed, one that seemed to stretch endlessly. Then the speaker, who Martin Romero believed to be Captain Campos, barked out what sounded like a command. There was a yell of triumph by several voices, followed by the thud of rushing feet. Then the screams began again. Multiple voices crying out in torment, their wails like the howls of the damned. Martin Romero covered his ears and sunk to the floor, trying to drown of the lamentations from the deck. Nothing, nothing in his whole life sounded so horrible and he prayed the sounds would go away.

And then the screams and crashing sounds ended. The only sound was the gentle movement of the water against the hull of the ship. Slowly, Martin Romero moved his hands from his ears. He didn't know if he wanted the silence to continue or not. In truth Romero wished to hear the calls of the low-class sailors, their crude, rough voices and oaths. But no, not a sound emerged from the deck.

Barely able to breathe, he reached for his suitcase and reached inside. For a moment, he felt around and finally touched cold metal. Quickly he pulled the object out, his revolver. The blue steel of the weapon was a comfort, death to anyone who crossed his path. Standing up and extending the gun ahead of him, Martin Romero exited his stateroom.

The silence lengthened, but a new sensation entered his world. A wave of scents filled the air, so many it was hard to discern. Martin Romero stopped and tried to figure each out, hoping this would give him a clue as to what happened earlier. The first scent was odd, a coppery smell, like a group of pennies left in the hot sun. It was a sensation he recognized, but the source eluded him at the moment.

The next scent was easier to comprehend. The smell was noxious and caused him to gag and place a hand over his mouth. This was the scent of shit and piss, the two substances the body released during a violent death. Martin Romero learned this after watching the execution of General Huerta, the former leader of San Pedro. His execution was public and the whole Romero family was present. The formerly proud military man soiled himself in the end, an important lesson.

Martin Romero was about to try and figure out the coppery smell again, when an object was hurled down the stairs. It fell at his feet, stopping just against his shoes. Looking down, Romero shrieked, his wail a high-pitched screech of terror. He backed away, his cries echoing in the ship.

The object was the head of Captain Campos. The face was twisted in a rictus of agony, the skin a sallow white. Lifting his pistol, Martin Romero pointed the weapon up the stairs, his hands shaking. Then a shadow filled the doorway, moving downward towards the quaking bureaucrat.

Martin Romero took one look at the twisted face and elongated, predator's teeth and pulled the trigger. The hammer rose and fell with a metallic click. He pulled again and again, the hollow sound of the gun even louder than the footsteps of the giant being approaching. It was then that Martin Romero remembered: he never loaded the gun. It was easier to carry without bullets.

Screaming and weeping, he fell to his knees and tried to crawl away. A large hand grabbed his ankle in a grip of steel. Martin Romero squeaked like a mouse before the sound was cut off a second later...

Later that night there was a flare of flame, a bright inferno that could be seen for miles along the lake. None ever knew the source. But the coast guard cutter, the *St. Helena* was never seen again.

CHAPTER XX

The work continued. A momentary interruption by government officials merely spurred Elizabeth to work with greater intensity. It was a full four hours before she looked up at Hugh.

"Get me the remaining limbs. I wish to conduct a phase one test upon each. Hurry!" Elizabeth crossed the lab and produced several large syringes. She filled each with a yellow fluid. In each syringe Elizabeth added a reddish black fluid that mixed with the yellow fluid. The compound bubbled ominously for a moment and slowly transformed into a glutinous, viscous solution that appeared more solid than liquid. Even Elizabeth Frankenstein recoiled slightly at the sight of this compound. There was a wrongness to this liquid, an unidentifiable quality that was alien to any who observed the solution. The chemical did not resemble any solid or liquid seen on the Earth, but possessed an otherworldly quality that was hard to observe for long.

Hugh returned a moment later, the remaining two arms and one leg in hand. He'd hidden them in the cellar in a cold chest earlier. They were close to putrefaction, but still possibly of some use to Elizabeth. He placed each body part on the steel table and stepped back, waiting. Elizabeth would reveal her plans soon enough.

I am injecting each of these limbs with a compound similar to that which runs through Gouroull." Elizabeth tapped the glass of each syringe, releasing any air bubbles before injection.

"For what purpose?" Hugh was confused. The ichor which provided Gouroull with his unique form of life was highly toxic. It was merely one component in the larger work of Victor Frankenstein.

"I wish to see the reaction this ichor has upon a dead body part. The results will be quite exciting. This fetid fluid is unique, possessing qualities of solid, liquid and gas. It should have a unique reaction." Elizabeth carefully injected both arms and the leg and stepped back to watch.

Hugh watched both the body parts as well as Elizabeth. Her face was slightly flushed and she was breathing a little deeper. There was a feral quality in her eye, a predatory lust that he'd only observed on rare occasions. Those were always when Elizabeth made a small breakthrough in her work. On those rare moments, the normally cold scientist became crazed, indulging herself in any area she desired. Would this be one of those moments?

Elizabeth reached behind her and pulled out three meat thermometers. With cool precision, she thrust the metal tips deep into the exposed flesh and watched with rapt attention.

While musing about the last time this occurred, Hugh's attention was caught by the three limbs. All three began to twitch. At first, it was a slight movement, almost impossible to discern. But the extremities, the fingers and toes began to move. The movements were jerky and spaced out in random intervals. But slowly, inextricably, the fingers and toes began to flex and move. The movements were at first slow and increasing in speed and length of time. Then the spasms began to emerge in other areas. Larger muscles began to jerk and tremble, their motions growing more visible with each passing minute. A full hour passed and still they stood rooted to their locations, staring at these limbs as their motility slowly grew more apparent.

Then a hand moved. At first, the extremity merely flopped about, a light weak shudder resembling that of a beached fish dying on land. The other hand soon moved in the same unnatural fashion, a quivering that slowly grew in intensity. Meanwhile the foot began to slowly move, up and down. This limb resembled a person attempting to get the feeling back in their leg after sitting in an uncomfortable position.

"The average temperature of all three limbs has doubled in the last hour." Elizabeth's eyes never left the body parts. He breathing grew deeper as the vibrations of the limbs appeared to increase.

As if on cue, both arms and the leg began to move with greater speed and intensity. The hands balled into fists and the arms flexed causing the muscles to bunch and tense. The leg also quaked, a rhythmic movement that was rapidly increasing. It was like watching a St. Vitus Dance conceived of by a madman, a terrible, bizarre, horrific sight.

"The endothermic reaction is increasing exponentially," said Elizabeth, stepping back, feeling a wave of heat rising from the limbs. The body parts thrashed with increasing violence, hammering the metal table.

"Internal temperature still climbing!" Elizabeth didn't mention the cracks which were appearing in the exposed flesh. Or the scent of putrid cooked meat which filled the air. No, she leaned in closer, keeping just far enough away from the body parts to insure she wasn't punched or kicked.

"Elizabeth," Hugh checked the numbers on the thermometers, shocked as the needles rose with increasing speed. "We're approaching a dangerous level. The endothermic reaction can't rise much further without consuming the remains."

Elizabeth nodded and smiled. "Watch, Hugh. Watch. If my theory is correct, the heat will drop off momentarily and there will be an internal attempt to stabilize."

Hugh was about to stated that her theory made no sense. Unless she meant that the flesh and bones would be consumed. That would cause the temperature to drop dramatically since there would be no fuel left to supply heat.

But before he could state these very basic scientific principles, the needles of the thermometers dropped. The fall was sudden and dramatic, as if all three limbs were suddenly dropped in a pool of ice. Their thrashing grew less frantic and the heat around the table grew more bearable by the second.

"That… that's not possible…" Hugh leaned in his head almost touching Elizabeth's as he watched the numbers drop as quickly as they rose. "Scientifically that is…"

Elizabeth released a bark of laughter. "We are confronting sciences far beyond the knowledge of mankind, Hugh. Abandon your preconceptions. The universe is ours to manipulate as we require!"

"Core temperature approaching 98 degrees Fahrenheit." Hugh looked at Elizabeth and smiled.

She smiled back and was about to open her mouth, when the three limbs suddenly began to spasm and shake with increased violence. And then the two arms and one leg exploded. A small tidal wave of fluid and meat struck Elizabeth and Hugh, covering them with red, black and yellow juices and pieces of flesh. The stench filling the laboratory was a nauseating combination of rotted meat, putrefied fluids and other identifiable odors.

They looked at each other, covered with the juices that once made up the three body parts. And without a word, lunged forward. Their mouths met in a hard, violent embrace, their tongues dueling. The bodily fluids which covered their faces mingled with their saliva, but neither appeared to notice. Hugh reached under Elizabeth's skirt and tore away her panties as Elizabeth's deft hand unbuttoned his pants.

And then, he was thrusting in her, his low grunts mixing with her loud snarls. She pushed him down to the floor of the lab and mounted him again, riding Hugh as he hands scratched him deeply across the chest. Elizabeth leaned down and licked the blood, now mingled with the fluids from the exploded limbs. Hugh ripped her blouse open, twisting her small breasts with increasing violence.

There was no sensuality to their coupling. Every time they were together, it was closer to an animalistic rutting. There was a sadomasochistic thrill each received at these moments, one which they never discussed.

But this time their abuse of each other was increased to new heights. Elizabeth's teeth bit down on his arms and she tore away small bits of his flesh. She swallowed the bloody skin and moaned as Hugh's hands began strangling her, his fingers slowly cutting off the precious oxygen she needed to live.

And then, they both screamed, their cries intermingled as the orgasmic bliss struck them simultaneously. Elizabeth collapsed on his chest as Hugh's hands dropped to the hard lab floor. They lay together panting for several minutes, neither moving nor saying a word.

Then Elizabeth stood up and began straightening her torn clothing. Hugh joined her a moment later, a little more unsteady on his feet. She tossed him a towel and began wiping some of the body fluids off her face with another cloth.

Hugh broke the silence. "Bones. There were no bones left in the arms or legs. Had there been, we might have been injured rather badly."

Elizabeth nodded and smiled again. "True. But I also theorized that the calcium in the bones would be consumed by the elixir. It would take too long to explain, but I realized this would occur. And do not say again how this is not possible Hugh. The laws of the universe are suspended by my science."

"I wasn't about to say that; I witnessed as much. But exploding body parts are not about to bring about a mate for Gouroull. I doubt he will look upon this experiment as a success." Hugh was frightened of the monstrous being. There was an inhuman lethality about Victor Frankenstein's creation that caused him to shiver like a rabbit before a serpent.

"He should," Elizabeth tossed her cloth to the ground and reached for a second one. "This reaction proves I am on the correct path. Gouroull's form of life is quite different from that of a mere human. For the next step, I require a dead body. A recent corpse, no more than 24 hours expired. Contact our factor in the capital. He can pack the corpse in ice to maintain freshness. But stress I must have the body within 24 hours. Male or female, it matters not."

Hugh knew their representative in Santa Lucia well and frowned. Jennings was a huge fat man who was easy to underestimate. But he was also a former Austrian cavalry officer who was very dangerous, despite his effeminate airs and passion for very young boys.

"I'll contact him in the morning. By now, he will be drunk and abed with someone. I'll also send word to the police chief at that mining town, Valparaiso." Hugh knew both would demand payment in advance. This was an odd request, even for these two less than scrupulous men.

"The mining town? What use will they be to us?" Elizabeth knew the location. It was reputed to be either a gold or an emerald mine. Well-guarded and about six hours away by boat because of its location up a dangerous channel connected to the lake.

"They have three taverns and a brothel there to keep the workers content. There's bound to be violence rather often." Hugh heard rumors from the sailors from the sailors of the dangerous nature of Valparaiso. If true, they might be a one-time source for their needs. Any additional requests would probably be noted and become a source of blackmail for the police chief. Never a good idea, such men were often impossible to satisfy. Elizabeth and Hugh had killed a few blackmailers over the years, their body parts used for experiments. But the disappearances led to questions, causing them to flee once again.

Elizabeth nodded once and turned away. "Very good. That as well. But stress what I said about the age."

"Understood," Hugh answered her retreating back. She would head for the bath and a few hours of sleep. Hugh knew he would follow, after the lab was cleared of the contaminants. That was always his duty, cleaning up after his beloved Elizabeth.

CHAPTER XXI

Gouroull watched the sexual congress of Victor's ancestor and her assistant. The visual exhibition was amusing and the various mingled odors an olfactory memory of the past. The place was France during the last war. The humans were slaughtering each other with impressive skill. Science took their species from the time where skill was required to murder your fellow to the modern age where death could happen merely by breathing. In days past, a trained archer could kill another from a distance through the skill of his arm or by chance. Now such men were rarities. Gas, bombs and guns dominated the trenches of battle and the skills required were far less than the comprehension of how to swing a sword without cutting off your own or your comrade's arm.

It was there Gouroull had haunted the battlefield like a ghost. He watched as each side attempted to defeat the other by charging men directly into the guns. The slaughter was massive; death swept over the fields of battle like a spectral wind. Bodies of both sides littered the landscape, some merely pieces of what was once humanity.

It was there that Gouroull had learned this stench, this intoxicating aroma that permeated the very landscape. Scorched flesh, rotted corpses, fear, lust and so many other scents mingled into one fragrance that he could never forget. It was the scent of horror, of destruction of all life. And to Gouroull, this was as delightful and the perfumed scent of wildflowers on a spring day would be to most humans. Though he did not need to breathe, Victor Frankenstein's terrible creation intentionally inhaled the spoor with greedy gulps.

All too soon the two humans were done with their sex play and were speaking of the experiment. Apparently, the explosion was exactly what the female wished. Odd, but she did seem to comprehend Victor's science better than those who attempted to help him the past. Dr. Pilljoy possessed only the barest knowledge, and that strange little man, West, had other, odder ideas. The female Frankenstein was mad, that was unquestioned, but she did possess the same insane spark of genius he'd once viewed in Victor Frankenstein. Could this lead to his mate after all this time? Possibly.

Hearing the need for a human, a newly dead one, interested Frankenstein's most lethal creation. The male stated something about a mining settlement nearby. Gouroull knew the location, had sensed it when he had first sought this woman out. Finding it would be easy. He also remembered her earlier admonition of leaving the tribe of natives alone. They were, according to the Frankenstein female, unsuitable for her work. If they had been suitable, Gouroull would have slaughtered them without pause. He would leave those which were still in one piece stacked in the house and the piles of limbs, heads and torsos nearby. But if they were of no use, they would be ignored. For now, at least.

Heading into the deep forest, Gouroull moved through the rough terrain with a speed that belied his massive size. He had no worries about the inhabitants of this jungle hindering his passage. Animals were creatures of instinct, born with the comprehension of danger in its myriad forms. To the animal kingdom, Gouroull represented a clear sign of danger, death on two legs. No matter how starved they were, no matter whose territory he crossed, they would stand aside and wait for him to pass. To do otherwise was to court instant death, and their inbred drive to survive would overwhelm any other inner urges.

As to the terrain, that was even less of a limitation. Gouroull walked on the bottom of the sea, though boiling desserts and freezing wastes that would destroy even the heartiest man or beast. All without pause. Even a crevice in the Arctic had merely paused his journey for a few years. In the end, he had revived and continued his quest.

Climbing over a fallen tree, he turned west. The settlement was mere miles away; he would be there in the early hours before the dawn. Then he would retrieve the next subject for Elizabeth Frankenstein's mad experiments. Gouroull was unwilling to wait for some businessman in distant Santa Lucia to help their plans.

Antonella Santos sighed as the mining foreman fondled her large breasts with one hand while his other hand shoveled rice and pork in his mouth. The mouth was the one part of Oscar the Foreman she tried to never look at when he paid for her "friendship." Oscar the Foreman's mouth was huge, with vast rubbery lips that resembled bloated red worms. When he spoke or ate, it looked as if the worms were trying to escape his face, an understandable sentiment.

Most in Valparaiso called Oscar the Foreman, behind his vast back, names such as pig, ox… basically any animal that was bloated and looked unattractive. But Antonella disagreed with those sentiments. Oscar the Foreman didn't have the intelligence of a pig, or the calm of an ox. No, he was a human. The worst thing one could be in her opinion. His job was to bully, berate and beat the miners, as well as inform about the troublemakers. The lowest position one could occupy in terms of honor.

But in occupying the post of chief informer for his shift, Oscar received benefits. The first was his little apartment in the manager's wing of the Valparaiso dwellings. He was in the basement, which was befitting given his low station. Even the managers, a collection of money-hungry second sons of the wealthy and the likes, viewed him as a repugnant creature. But by giving him a place of his own, his loyalty was assured. Also they gifted Oscar the Foreman with more money, use of the company hospital without charge, and two free trips per month to the nicest brothel in town.

And that was where Antonella came in. For some reason, despite her total lack of interest in him, Oscar developed a fondness for the youngest whore in town. Antonella, whose drunken mother was a prostitute herself, had sold her children by the time they'd hit age 10. She knew her brother had died in the boy's brothel after a customer caught him attempting to steal his watch. Her sister toiled away as a maid for a wealthy family in Santa Lucia. But Antonella had been bought by Madame Fargo, the owner of a string of brothels in Santa Lucia. Her girls were better treated than most, taught to read, speak with accents that didn't make them sound like *barrio* trash, dance and serve drinks. Many girls, the ones not poxed or killed by customers, often continued to work of Madame Fargo as maids and helpers. It was a better life than many received in this world.

But there were rules in Madame Fargo's world. And these rules must be followed to the letter. First and foremost was to never refuse a paying customer. If the customer was too rough or disgusting, leave it to the bouncers to ensure they were dealt with properly. Madame Fargo's bouncers were well trained in diplomacy as well as horrifically effective violence. A damaged whore was bad for business, fewer customers wanted to use them and that led to less sales of wine and other spirits. Because in the end, the girls were there to sell all the other services. Madame Fargo's food was far more expensive, her drinks outrageously priced. But the men and women who used her establishments were induced to pay prior to, and often after, one of the girls had been chosen. Sales, that was the true duty of all of Madame Fargo's whores.

Antonella knew this was a better life than many in her profession received. Most women who sold their bodies for money ended up used up, disgusting hags by the time they reached their twenties. Antonella's own mother, dead these five years, was forty when a sailor rammed a knife in her gut. And she looked a wasted, emaciated sixty years-old when Antonella had been forced to identify the body. No, Antonella knew better than to violate Madame Fargo's rules. To do so meant either being turned out to the streets and dying like her mother, or worse, being sold to a brothel known as a slaughterhouse in the Santa Lucia *barrio*. There, the girls slept in bare cots with tattered curtains between them for the customer's privacy. There, a customer would pay a San Pedro dollar and get five minutes to mount and use a girl, longer times extra. It was said the girls could entertain fifty men a night. The whores were kept drunk or drugged on cheap wine or drugs until they were used up or died.

That was Antonella's recurring nightmare. It kept her willing to take Oscar the Foreman, smile at his poor jokes, and try and ignore his revolting mouth. She was new in Valparaiso. Madame Fargo liked to move her girls around to her different locations. It kept customers from getting too fond of any of her employees. Also it brought in fresh faces, renewing interest in customers who might drift over to the competition's brothels.

"You're mine for the night," Oscar shoveled another forkful of pork into his mouth. He liked to announce this to her, as if it was a surprise. She was already informed as much by Luis, the bouncer on duty. To get a girl for the night cost extra and happened rarely.

"Oh, good," Antonella gave him a wide smile, knowing this would be an easy one for her. She usually managed to get a few bottles of wine in him on a regular evening. A full night meant she could get Oscar the Foreman to spend more and pass out after a few pokes. Antonella would get a good night's sleep in his oversized bed and would ply him with lies about his prowess as a lover. "Let's drink to that."

Oscar smiled, his gruesome lips convulsing and causing Antonella to fight back the desire to throw up. But he raised a hand and signaled for another bottle of wine. He never realized that all of Madame Fargo's girls were experts at pretending to drink. They would taste the cheap wine, pour full glasses for the customers and send back half-empty bottles. These bottles were then remixed in the back and returned to the customer, who was charged again. On a good evening, a customer who paid for four bottles, rarely completed more than two. Antonella already got Oscar the Foreman to buy six, drink two, and eat two plates of food. Her bonus for this night alone would be better than her week's wages. All of which she would save. Antonella vowed to never live and die in the pathetic fashion of her mother or brother.

It was another hour and three more bottles of wine, before Oscar the Foreman decided it was time to leave. Wrapping a meaty hand around Antonella's slim wrist, he led her out of the brothel and into the cool night air. His step was unsteady, his gait a weaving stumble. She knew his normally pathetic stamina in bed would be even less tonight. In truth, she hoped she could induce him to pass out before mounting her. Usually when Oscar the Foreman was in this state, he would thrust in and out of her a few times, missing more often than not and would fall asleep. It wasn't easy to slide out from under his substantial bulk. Oscar the Foreman possessed a huge paunch and immense, flabby, hairy men's breasts that were almost as large as Antonella's own. Maneuvering herself out from under his bloated body was far from easy. But, occasionally, she could get him to pass out just after undressing. Then he would gratefully accept her tales of his sexual prowess. Antonella spun stories of Oscar the Foreman in which he resembled a randy, rampaging bull. Not the squeaking, moaning mouse he actually appeared to imitate when he did his business on her body.

"Eggs," Oscar the Foreman was speaking, having difficulty forming words.

"Hmm?" Antonella asked as they left the porch of Madam Fargo's and entered Valparaiso.

"Bought eggs for you. Will cook them for breakfast," Oscar the Foreman managed to say, spraying spittle with each sound.

"Oh, thank you!" Antonella pretended to sound grateful. But she would induce him to return to Madame Fargo's for food, increasing her bonus. She didn't need him viewing her as his property.

Valparaiso was a new town, an artificial one. When the emerald mine was rediscovered by an engineer employed by the Murillo family, they realized they had found their way for returning to power. Rather than trying to secretly exploit the mine, they created a business concern with the twelve families as lesser partners. The town of Valparaiso, formerly a tiny village of half-Indios, was taken over and real buildings were built. Madame Fargo was consulted and she supplied the brothels and the taverns. A percentage of her profits went to the corporation as well. And the miners received decent wages. This compensated for the daily full body searches they underwent daily to prevent the theft of the uncut gems. Yes, Valparaiso was a town where everything cost and the Murillo family and their partners received vast profits.

The town itself, oddly enough, resembled one from the past Wild West of United States history. The roads were unpaved and the low buildings were built from wood and possessed large gaily painted signs. Day and night didn't really matter in Valparaiso. The two shifts of miners were either working or in town spending their wages. A busy location, teeming with life.

Antonella worked in the better of the two brothels in town. Oscar the Foreman and Javier, the other Foreman, were the lowest class allowed inside. Their place was used by the managers, engineers and other skilled classes. The girls within were prettier, better trained and very skilled and making their customers part with their money happily. The other whorehouse was for the miners. It was more raucous, the girls less pretty but more skilled at please a greater number of customers each day. Less money was made there on food and drink and more on fast, pleasurable sexual acts in the small back rooms. Very profitable for Madame Fargo but far less refined.

Oscar the Foremen led Antonella through the streets to the manager's apartments. The impressive front doors were visible for a great distance, but they didn't head in that direction. Despite having one of the basement dwellings, Oscar the Foreman and his fellows were not allowed to walk in the front door. No, they were relegated to entering through the tradesmen's entrance in the back. This was where maids, cooks, mistresses and other lesser beings were admitted. As with all things in Valparaiso, this was a form of enforcing the clearly delineated social caste system within the town.

Oscar the Foreman was of a higher position on the social order than the miners. But the managers and others who ruled the town did not allow him to believe his station in life was of the higher order. If they had the time, the managers and their unspoken caste would have had foreman, police officers and their ilk reside in a complex all their own. But the corporation had denied that request. Therefore, the basement was used to denote the person in question was higher caste than a miner. But they were still lesser people in the end. Servants that were of some use, easily replaceable.

Circling around the back, Antonella spotted the smaller wooden door which was the servant's entrance. It was unadorned, not even possessing a door knocker. But there were three locks visible, as well as a guard who sat inside. His job was to ensure that only the proper people were admitted within. Early attempts to steal from the managers had taught them to never trust the people of Valparaiso too much.

As Oscar the Foreman fumbled with the keys attached to his belt, Antonella rubbed her wrist. Oscar's grip was always too tight and she hoped he hadn't bruised her arm. An unsightly blemish like that was a mark against her in the customer's minds. This time, it didn't appear so, but you never knew. The wrist was as bad a location as the face in many cases. Customers like to touch arms and faces of the whores they purchased for the night. Seeing a blemish spoiled the illusion that this was not a transaction of services.

Oscar the Foreman finally opened the door lock and turned to smile at Antonella. His mammoth maw flapped open as he gave her what he thought was a lascivious grin. In truth, he resembled a large fish whose hook was removed and was slowly gasping as the air suffocated his bloated body. He was about to speak, when he froze. His fat face was still, his head tilting, as he studied something over Antonella's shoulder.

Antonella turned and stared into the lower chest of a man. The body was clothed in tattered, torn, blackened rags. The visible skin beneath the cloth scraps was pale. But the light color was odd, closer to that of flour than that of a pallid person. Antonella lifted her eyes and was surprised by the uncanny height of this stranger. He was taller than the giant bodyguard of Madame Fargo, a monstrous, silent man named Felix. Felix was reputed to have once torn off the head of one of Madame Fargo's clients with only the power of his hands.

All Antonella saw of the man's face was a heavy mass of dark hair. His head was a mere shadow, a huge black object without form. The darkness seemed to cling to this titanic figure, wrapping around his body and giving him an otherworldly image. But it was the stillness that frightened Antonella. This darkness-covered pale man seemed as motionless as a block of stone. There seemed to be no signs of life visible around him, yet she instinctively knew he was not a statue.

"Hey!" Oscar the Foreman pushed past Antonella and stepped closer to the stranger. He raised his elephantine fists and waved them before the taller man's face. "Miners and tramps ain't allowed around here! Go on! Get away!"

The massive man merely stood there, looking down at Oscar. He didn't advance or retreat, no sounds emerging from his hidden face. This was a surprise. Even the largest and most dangerous men in Valparaiso walked carefully around a gigantic bully like Oscar the Foreman.

"Speak or I'm going to break your face, friend!" Oscar the Foreman was breathing heavily as he cracked his knuckles. The resulting sound was like that of pistol shots. It was one of his classic intimidation tactics. The sound often made strong men wince, knowing violence was coming soon. To be a foreman in Valparaiso meant you enjoyed bullying and beating your fellow man. Squeamishness was not allowed; they were paid to ensure the company's will was followed to the letter.

Yet, this unknown man still failed to react. This simple fact filled Antonella with a greater terror than if he'd been barking threats while waving about a bloody blade. Something was very wrong here, something horrible and evil, and she really wanted to flee. But her training from Madame Fargo rebelled at such an act. Fleeing from a customer was a violation of the rules. And that was one which brought about punishment. Antonella warred with herself, her fear fighting her desire to continue her life with Madame Fargo.

"You asked for it, friend!" Oscar the Foreman lifted his ample arm and threw a hard punch towards the unknown man's face. Antonella viewed that blow in the past. The results were often catastrophic, teeth shattered, noses flatted and gushing blood in vast pools. Oscar's enemies rarely last longer than that one punch to the face.

But the stranger appeared to be made of stronger stuff. The fist struck him on the chin and he did not so much as flinch. Oscar shook his hand, feeling some pain and threw a heavy fist into the unknown man's stomach. Most people hit with that punch fell over and would violently vomit the contents of their belly. But again the stranger appeared unmoved, disinterested in the attack.

This caused Antonella to shiver involuntarily. She was knowledgeable about the human body, for obvious reasons. And in her profession, since childhood, she'd witnessed more violence than most professional soldiers. And in all her time, Antonella had never witnessed a man able to ignore powerful blows such as the ones delivered by Oscar the Foreman. Some men, strong ones, could fight on with such pain. In fact, some seemed to be able to ignore attacks. But they, even in the smallest way, acknowledged they'd been struck. But not this shadowy man. There were no hints he even knew he was being attacked.

Oscar the Foreman, shocked and enraged by the lack of fear or pain by his opponent, reacted in the only way he knew how. With greater violence. Reaching into his belt, he pulled out an immense silver bladed knife. Everyone in Valparaiso knew this weapon. Oscar the Foreman made it a point of honing the knife with an oiled whetstone around members of the work force he believed to be troublemakers. A powerful intimidation tool. But he had used it on an occasion, stabbing a sailor who was threatening an engineer who had cheated him at cards. And also in a fight with Gonzalez and his friends when they had tried to organize a union.

With a snarl of rage, Oscar the Foreman lunged forward. His blade flashed in the moonlight and was aimed straight for the stranger's chest. Antonella watched, disgusted and fascinated, but unable to look away. She knew that, once that wicked blade pierced the silent stranger's body, the end would come quickly.

But the stranger appeared to have other ideas. His arm moved, so fast it was a mere blur to Antonella's eyes. An enormous hand seized Oscar the Foreman's arm, freezing the huge man's attack in place. A moment later, the knife dropped to the ground, released by Oscar's hand as the grip on his wrist slowly tightened. The hand holding him was hard and cold, feeling more like it was made of stone than flesh. Just as Oscar the Foreman was about to scream in pain, he was lifted off the ground by another powerful fist. He dangled in the air, a pitiable, ridiculous figure. Antonella realized Oscar resembled a marionette used in a particularly silly story about foolish peasants. Then, the stranger slammed Oscar to the hard earth, where he lay without moving.

Stepping over Oscar, the stranger loomed over Antonella. A terrible, spectral figure whose luminous yellow eyes were suddenly visible in the spare light. She stepped back in fear and saw the man's face. It was terrible, twisted and inhuman, the stuff of nightmares. She opened her mouth to scream, but a huge palm was slapped over her mouth and she was lifted from her feet.

Seconds later Antonella passed out, her last sight of Valparaiso being the fallen form of Oscar the Foreman.

Oscar the Foreman was discovered early the next morning, asleep and snoring on the ground outside of the apartment complex. It wasn't the security guards that discovered his bloody form, but the bouncers from Madame Fargo who had come to collect Antonella. Once they confirmed that the young whore never arrived inside the complex, they hustled Oscar the Foreman off to the police station and deposited him in the nearest jail cell.

Though Oscar, no longer a foreman, claimed a massive stranger bore off the young, lovely Antonella, nobody believed his tale. A search was performed for the poor whore, but it was believed that her torn corpse had been carried away by the animals of the thick jungle. Three days later, the company hanged Oscar in the town square and left him there to rot. It was a good way to teach the people not to get above themselves. And it kept Madame Fargo happy, which was very important too.

Hernando was appointed foreman, now that there was an opening. He was wiser than fat, bullying Oscar, but also could be crueler when pushed. But life in Valparaiso continued, and poor little Antonella was soon forgotten. After all, a new shaft was being dug and the workers had, oh so much to do, now. Who cared about one murdered whore more or less?

CHAPTER XXII

The woman was unconscious and would stay so for an hour or more. Gouroull could tell that he damaged her slightly, though not a great deal. With rest, she would recover if he let her free. But he would not; she was to be the subject of Elizabeth Frankenstein's next experiment. What she wished to do, Gouroull did not know. And in truth, he didn't care. He could tell she and her servant were committed to the completion of Victor's work. They would provide him with a mate.

But what to do with this woman, his gift to Frankenstein? She would die, but the method was interesting to Gouroull. He could bring about swift ends to lives. That Irish fool, Vrollo, had died swiftly. In a way, it was a gift to the man. Vrollo had thought to use Gouroull as a servant or slave, a poor choice. The people of Kanderly hated the tramp for good reason, knowing he was disgusting and lusted after a villager named Helen. Gouroull had been tempted to kill Vrollo slowly, but he had chosen a quick death. The man had freed him from the ice after all; a fast end was a gift.

And he could grant someone a slow, terrible end, one of terror and misery. That old man in Antwerp for example. Gouroull remembered locking him in a cellar infested with hungry, diseased rats. That end was monstrous all the more so because the old man's son had found his torn, bloated corpse. Delightful, almost poetic.

But this time, there were other choices. He could free from her suffering and kill this woman before Elizabeth Frankenstein and her sexual slave, Hugh, got their hands on her. Gouroull decided against that path of action. After what he had witnessed between Elizabeth and Hugh, one death more or less would not affect them at all. Possibly they would enjoy the killing, which he didn't need. They needed to remain focused on the duty at hand, the creation of his mate. Their lusts would merely slow the process.

Raping the girl would cause massive suffering. He knew this all too well, having indulged himself once or twice in that fashion. That was less forty years ago in Gottwohl, that insane Pastor... Schleger was his name. He'd believed that mating with a human woman was possible. The false holy man's plan was to create a new race, a race of supermen as written by his favorite philosopher. Gouroull had found the idea intriguing and waited as kidnapped women were supplied. But these women were far from compliant. One look at Gouroull and they panicked. In the end, their terror-filled shrieks had angered him and he'd killed each female. Enraged by this failure, Gouroull had raped Schleger's wife, Ingrid, and killed the Pastor.

That should have been the end of the tale. Ingrid was meant to die in the frigid Swiss Alps. She'd been driven mad by his depraved treatment and was suffering from the snow, ice and cold. But Ingrid had survived. He'd found her six or seven years ago, still insane and in an asylum. He learned she'd been pregnant and that had rendered her permanently lost to the world. Sadly, the child wasn't his, but the Pastor's son. Gouroull had learned then he could not mate with human women, but needed one of his own kind.

But rape was still a weapon, though one he did not use often. Male or female, rape was a violent assault that destroyed the souls of humans. Gouroull appreciated that, there was a symbolic verisimilitude to that idea.

The concept that an act that brought about love or joy could be transformed into the lowest, most horrific form of violence was proof that humanity was not fit to survive. Actions such as these made them lower than the basest animals. And he would use their weapons against them; they deserved nothing less.

But in this situation, Gouroull had no need for the torment of this human female. She was his victim, yes. But her suffering wouldn't grant him any gain. He wasn't a vampire, an undead leech feeding upon the life energies, blood or emotions of the living. Victor Frankenstein's vision was that of a new race, not a new revenant existing and sustaining itself like a parasite upon all life. To stoop to that lowly station would betray Gouroull's very existence. And that was also why he happily destroyed any vampire who chose to oppose his will. They were corpses with megalomaniac ambitions. He was Gouroull, something altogether different and more vital.

Which was why, a short time later, Gouroull killed the girl with a simple twist of his hand. Her neck and spine twisted and seconds later, she expired as he continued to walk through the forest. That was as gentle an end as he could offer. Gouroull could have suffocated the girl. But that would have taken time and was occasionally less than perfect. He attempted that once in the past, while traveling back from China after battling that vampire with many bodies... what was his name...? Dracula! Yes, Dracula! Calling himself the "King of the Vampires," he'd appeared multiple times in Gouroull's wanderings. And each time, he appeared to inhabit new bodies of varying strength. Gouroull destroyed at least two; yet, the undead fiend always seemed to return. Was he an immortal bloodsucker with powers beyond the realm of imagination? A series of vampiric pretenders using the same name? Or a creature with the ability to possess other members of his kind? Gouroull didn't know, and, frankly, didn't care. The creature was a nuisance, but one he hadn't dealt with in decades. That was merely a side-note, a distraction

But the suffocation killing was one Gouroull remembered, even more than the immortal leech. He was returning from China, when he witnessed a young man murdering animals with a gun. Gouroull was disinterested, the killings were silly, a child's cruelty upon lesser creatures. No doubt this young boy, a teenager whose name Frankenstein's most terrible creation never bothered to learn. But the young man appeared bored by his pathetic cruelty and appeared to have a notion to take the next step in his path of blood and death. Viewing Gouroull's ragged clothing and ignoring the chalk gray skin and enormous height, the young German man decided to murder what he took to be a tramp. Pulling out a hunting knife, he rushed at Gouroull, intending to stab him multiple times. Apparently, this would be his first step in a festival of blood, death and destruction. That was a path Gouroull could appreciate. In fact, he would have allowed it to happen since the murder of humans was of no interest. But Gouroull had no desire to participate in any way, having his own plans. And he possessed no desire to be this little man's first true victim.

Which was why, that day in Germany, he'd slapped the knife aside, and decided to kill his attacker slowly. It didn't matter to Victor Frankenstein's creation that the knife would not, could not, truly injure his unique body. Gouroull wished to visit suffering upon the human who did not possess the basic survival instincts necessary to all predators. For that alone, a terrible end was necessary. One filled with torment.

Never having killed by suffocation, Gouroull decided to test this experience. He held the teen down, covering the mouth and nose with his hand. The end was slow and twice, when bored, he let go and decided to check if the young human was alive. In both cases, near death, the young man would gasp and begin to breathe again. Finally, bored and wishing to move on, Gouroull held the young man under water until his heart stopped. Death came, but the slowness in this situation wasn't enjoyable. It was merely tedious. And it appeared gentle at times, like falling into slumber. Then and there, Gouroull abandoned suffocation as a means of killing. Possibly he would use this method again, abandoning someone in a room filling with water. But the likelihood of such an event seemed small.

But there was something else he needed to do this day. Gouroull knew Elizabeth Frankenstein and her sexual slave would build his mate. They were committed to this end, an objective they'd sought for years. Gouroull knew this form of madness well. He'd viewed it before, in the eyes of Victor. But also in those who had undertaken to repeat his creator's work. Dr. Pilljoy on Cround Isle possessed the same brand of insanity. As did Herbert West in the battlefields of France. Though West's aberration was slightly different. To him, the recreation of Victor Frankenstein's work was a scientific exercise to help his own odd research.

Elizabeth Frankenstein possessed characteristics of all three men. She was as megalomaniacal as Victor, as deranged as Pilljoy, and as arrogantly scientific as West. This was very useful for Gouroull's needs. No, the creation of his mate would happen. But there was another issue that needed to be addressed.

Such mad geniuses also held the belief that their creations were their property, their slave. Victor's fears of Gouroull began when he determined that his creature possessed a mind of his own. A fiendish one capable of terrible acts of cruelty. This lead to Victor's shouted declaration, words burned into Gouroull's memory for all time.

"The hour of my irresolution is past, and the period of your power is arrived. Your threats cannot move me to do an act of wickedness; but they confirm me in a determination of not creating you a companion in vice. Shall I, in cool blood, set loose upon the earth a daemon, whose delight is in death and wretchedness? Begone! I am firm, and your words will only exasperate my rage."

Victor snarled while destroying Gouroull's mate before its final creation.

Why did his creator gain such a conscience at that late hour, a few short years after his successful creation of Gouroull? There were many possible reasons, but one seemed most apparent. His creation, terrible, lethal and malevolent, was not a grateful, lovely slave, worshipping its creator's genius. This was in opposite to the madman's dreams, a direction he didn't imagine possible. Such was his insanity.

Elizabeth Frankenstein, like her ancestor Victor, could fall victim to the same foolish notion. Gouroull knew he needed to establish the division between them, teach both scientists that he was the master of their shared destiny. Their genius would bring his mate into the world. But neither of them would be their tools in the future. This was an arrangement, nothing further.

Slowing his pace slightly, Gouroull arrived back at Elizabeth's dwelling just after dawn broke. As expected, she and Hugh were already in the lab, toiling away. An odd odor filled the air, the ingredients of their chemicals being otherworldly and vaguely disturbing. Perfect. The disquieting effect of the compounds would only add to the image he wished to project upon their minds.

Opening the door with a loud crash, Gouroull strode into the room. The dead girl was in his arms, lifeless, her head lolling at an odd, disjointed angle. Though the corpse's weight was insignificant enough that he could carry her in one arm, Gouroull knew this visual would make a greater impression. And that was his aim here, in addition to assisting their research.

Dropping the body on a long table, Gouroull stared at both scientists. His yellow, unblinking alien eyes appeared to bore into both for a moment, before he turned and left the building. Their work would proceed, but without any illusions that he would be their slave or friend. This was business. They would accomplish their goal; he would gain a female of his species. What Elizabeth and Hugh did with their knowledge after he and his mate left was of no interest to Gouroull.

Heading into the rain forest, Gouroull smiled slightly, his predator's teeth glinting in the sunlight. The shouts of surprise of both humans were very amusing. He would check on them later and see if his beliefs as to their character were correct.

CHAPTER XXIII

"Dear God, almighty! What? What? What did he do?" Hugh stared at the twisted corpse Gouroull deposited on the table moments ago. The body was that of a girl. He revised his mental statement based on the jutting round breasts of the dead body. This was a woman, though probably in her early twenties at best. And she was, based on the odd angle of her neck, quite definitely dead.

Elizabeth stepped forward, grabbing a subcutaneous thermometer. She thrust the sharp end into the abdomen as she answered Hugh: "Obviously Gouroull heard us earlier. I told you I required a dead body to continue the next phase of my work. I surmise he went to that mining town and obtained a specimen for us. She is a female, approximate 18 to 24 years of age, dead no more than two hours based on her temperature. Perfect!"

"Elizabeth! She will be missed! That town is not like Santa Lucia or Casablanca. There a missing person or six is expected. That is just a mining town!" Hugh stared at the dead woman. She was pretty, in that earthy, fleshy way peasant girls managed to be for a few years. Once in a while, when Elizabeth was away for a week or more to procure equipment and the like, he would find such girls. Usually, they were available at local taverns or bordellos. Then he would overpay them, out of guilt, and indulge himself. That would sate his burdening lusts for a time. Once in a while, he couldn't find anyone to fit his needs. Then a little chloral hydrate or chloroform would be applied and he would make use of the first female that stirred his loins. He felt some guilt afterwards, but only for a short time.

Elizabeth looked up as she pulled out the thermometer. "You believe so? I doubt it. But we can take steps to ensure otherwise. Prepare the body the normal manner. Then use the extra measures we used in London. I believe we shall have little evidence for authorities to discover in a few days. This portion of the experiment will be as intriguing as last night's endeavor."

Hugh didn't respond, but immediately went to work. Cutting away the garish, yet cheaply made clothing, he was unsurprised the woman possessed no under garments. No doubt she was a whore, like so many females in this world. Taking the tattered remains in hand, Hugh crossed the lab and dropped all in the sulfuric acid. Very little time was required to destroy the fabric, with no traces visible. A far better method of destruction than fire, fewer traces remained.

Returning to the corpse, Hugh checked her ears and fingers for any jewelry. These two were often easy to identify and therefore needed to be destroyed. But this woman appeared to have none. This was good. He disliked spending too much time near the acid. The fumes were noxious on the best days.

Next he began a minute search for tell-tale birthmarks, scars or other physical blemishes. In this case the dead woman's skin was imperfection-free. Her complexion was turning sallow in death. But Hugh was willing to believe her skin possessed a golden sheen in life. Perhaps it would again under Elizabeth's guidance.

Checking to see that Elizabeth was still out of sight, Hugh paused to grab both of the large, round mammaries upon the corpse's chest. He massaged them, fondled them gently. He didn't want to leave any marks. But he wanted to know how they felt, even as the skin cooled in death. They were silken soft, yet possessed an inner firmness. Perfection. Exactly what those women always seemed to feel like before the tribulations of peasant life took a toll upon their bodies. Then those delectable bosoms became softer, mushier to the touch. They would hang like the teats of a cow and disgust Hugh to his very core.

One time, he had been fooled by a woman with such prominent mammilla. It had occurred in Madrid. Elizabeth was away in Toledo, purchasing several odd chemicals she wished to test from a friend of some book sellers named Ceniza. A woman, Marta by her name, enticed him back to her house with the promise of ecstasy for a small price.

But when Marta unclothed, Hugh was dumbstruck by her fleshy body… her stretch marks from childbirth. She was old, at least thirty, and he was disgusted by her coarse corpulence. With a small scream, he threw Marta down and took her violently from behind. Grabbing his tie, Hugh strangled her and continued to thrust into Marta's ample rear as her flesh began to cool. Then, he fled into the night, determined to only use women that he knew were young and still possessing the bloom of youth in their body. His seed deserved nothing less.

With a guilty look in Elizabeth's direction, and uncommon haste, Hugh removed his hands from the corpse's breasts. The cheap titillation he received was now lost in a wave of shame-filled remorse. He knew he was a weak creature. But Hugh worked to prevent Elizabeth from knowing of his pitiable indiscretions. Though capable of astonishing sexual compulsions, she prized self-control above all. Giving into her base desires was a function of existence in Elizabeth's mind. But to indulge it was to lower one's self to the level of the animal.

The thought that Elizabeth would think he was not worthy of her was the reason Hugh ensured none of his sexual conquests spoke of him again. To the prostitutes he had two approaches. Street-walkers were considered the lowest of the low in society. Like in the land of India, where all men and women knew their place, their caste in the whole of the social structure. Street whores were the untouchables, lesser beings below that of an animal. These he murdered once his lusts were sated. Easily forgotten in the sea of humanity that made up most cities.

The prostitutes who worked in houses could not be killed. Large men guarded those women and they would harm anyone who damaged their product, because the women of a brothel were as much goods as anything one could purchase in a store. Therefore killing them was not possible. But he could cover his face with masks, false beards and dark spectacles. The amusement these items raised did not bother him in the least. It was just important that Hugh was never recognized.

Cutting away the dead woman's scalp, nose and ears, Hugh deposited each into the acid. Once they were properly dissolved, he removed the remainder of the face as well as the fingers. Each dissolved slowly in the sulfuric acid, even the finger bones. After medical school, Elizabeth and Hugh experimented with acids and the disposal of human remains. They were working at a private madhouse and using some of the prisoners for their experiments. There were enough ill and abused men and women available. A quick injection of a large air bubble in a vein and soon a corpse would be found. They would then claim the body under a false name and went to work.

But hiding the bodies became a difficulty. Depositing a few in the Thames was easy enough, but a dangerous risk. They were just beginning to consider the use of acid, when Thomas Bascomb came into their lives. That was when everything changed.

Bascomb was an orderly at the asylum. He was a large, slovenly drunkard who was brutal to the patients as well as much of the staff. Bascomb stole from the hospital and was believed to use the maddest females as a bizarre form of a harem. He was obsequious to the doctors, knowing they could fire him with a word. But he was no fool. There was a cleverness within Thomas Bascomb, despite his oafish demeanor.

"Isn't it interesting that the last three patients who died were claimed by a man with handwriting just like yours, Mister Larkin, sir?" Bascomb was seated in Hugh's office, the door closed. He was smiling, his yellow and brown teeth barely visible in the spare electric light.

"What are you implying, Bascomb?" Hugh sat ramrod stiff and looked at Bascomb with the cold expression Elizabeth used when speaking to fools.

But the nasty look was lost on Thomas Bascomb. He merely shifted his bulk in the uncomfortable chair and chuckled. "Oh nothing, nothing at all Mister Larkin, But I think matron and the director might be interested in such fascinating information..."

"What do you want, Bascomb?" Hugh knew better than to fence with the man. Intimidation would not work. Bascomb was larger and willing to use violence to accomplish his goals. And it was apparent that to threaten his job would endanger Elizabeth and Hugh's experiments in reviving the dead.

"Ah, good. I was afraid you'd try and talk at me for a long time. I like you, Mister Larkin. You're a decent sort. Now when I saw that you was claiming bodies, I said to myself, Tommy, this isn't regular. I reckon Mister Larkin must have a good thing going and is trading dead people for a bag or three of chink. Now that makes old Tommy Bascomb happy. But I'm sad you isn't sharing the wealth. That's what our good Lord would want." Bascomb pulled out a small cigar and lit it with a tarnished silver lighter. He puffed away happily and leaned back in the wooden chair, causing a large creak to emerge from the backing.

"Continue, Bascomb." Hugh also knew better than to deny or agree to anything this lout stated. Just keep him talking and see which direction this discussion proceeded.

Bascomb leaned forward and blew a stream of smoke in Hugh's face. He chuckled as the latter coughed and tapped some ash on the office floor. "Half. Tommy Bascomb is your new partner, Mister Larkin. And I'll help you get new bodies. With your brother Tommy at your side, Mister Larkin, we'll both do very well."

Hugh smiled back, though secretly he was terrified. If Bascomb revealed their work, all the whispered tales of their activities in Scotland would be proven true. Their reputations would be lost and they could even be jailed for their activities. This was even more terrible considering they were attempting to defeat death. This service to mankind was the reason they stole the dead and killed people who didn't deserve to live. And all could be lost if this lummox was given a chance to spread the truth to those incapable of understanding the purity of Elizabeth's vision.

"Come to my house tomorrow night, Bascomb. I'll provide you with your...chink, and we will determine who we will take next." Hugh wasn't sure this was the best step. But he scribbled down the address of their laboratory in hand he knew did not resemble his normal handwriting.

Hugh rushed home that night and found Elizabeth pouring over the papers of a Victorian scientist she revered named Moreau. Hugh had to admit that man had a certain impressive mad vision. But his work went a less interesting direction involving animals. Elizabeth had a greater knowledge of the man, but refused to say how or why.

"Elizabeth! Our work is endangered!" Hugh spilled out his tale, speaking quickly and not sparing any details. But Elizabeth was unmoved.

"You did correctly, Hugh. I assumed this would happen sooner or later." Elizabeth put down her papers and appeared almost disinterested in the discussion.

"But Elizabeth..." Hugh wasn't sure Elizabeth understood the gravity of this situation. Though brilliant, she occasionally lacked comprehension of the basic social niceties of society. Hugh understood that she chose to ignore anything unrelated to her work, but recognized that appearances could affect their lives. "If Bascomb tells others we could be removed from the medical rolls and even arrested. This is a true danger to our lives."

Elizabeth rolled her eyes and shook her head. "Demonstrate more self-control, Hugh. This Thomas Bascomb is nothing more than a nuisance. But he is also an opportunity. He is fairly young. Or at least younger than the last two specimens we obtained from the hospital. And we can test our disposal techniques upon his body. Living tissue as well as expired."

"But Elizabeth..." Hugh was more desperate now. She didn't realize the danger Bascomb represented. "This man is experienced in the use of violence. We cannot simply stab him with a needle and watch as he dies. He'll be ready and will fight back!"

Elizabeth shook her head. "I think not. There are several methods we can employ for recalcitrant individuals. The first is a specially prepared room. A deranged individual named Holmes in the United States employed this method for procuring victims."

"That sounds like an excellent notion!" Hugh rubbed his hands together, smiling at the thought of Bascomb falling victim to special traps.

However Elizabeth shook her head. "No. We are not attached to a gas line in this laboratory. That is the essential element. But it is a future consideration. Next we can drug his drink. He strikes me as one who enjoys his spirits of some type."

This time Hugh shook his head. "I believe he does not trust me. He would either refuse to drink or wish me to imbibe first."

Elizabeth frowned, but nodded. "Well reasoned. Therefore there is a device I shall build. It shan't take me long, but I will require a few items."

She crossed to the table and pulled out the Moreau papers. Shuffling through the pages for a moment, she stopped suddenly and nodded. Grabbing a piece of paper, she scribbled a small list for Hugh and sent him into the night.

The next evening, Thomas Bascomb arrived precisely at seven. He appeared happy and convivial. But this was clearly an act. Bascomb was tense and his eyes darted about the room, seeking anything suspicious. Seeing nothing out-of-the-ordinary, he took a seat with his back to a wall. With greedy eyes Bascomb watched as Hugh counted out eight pounds and four pence on the table.

"A pleasure doing business with you, Mister Larkin. I think Miss Cabot in the west wing, second floor, should be our next... how shall I put it...? Sad victim of circumstances?" Thomas Bascomb pocketed the money and headed for the door, keeping Hugh in front of him at all times.

Hugh nodded and watched as Bascomb opened the door and was about to step out. There he was stopped by a shadowy figure on the porch. Bascomb was about to open his mouth to protest, when the other raised a hand and a slight coughing sound was heard. Thomas Bascomb gasped and stumbled backwards, falling back into the house, dropping to his knees. A dart was visible in his neck and, a moment later, he fell sideways onto the living room rug.

Elizabeth stepped out of the shadows, a small metal tube in one hand, a watch in her other. "Twenty-three seconds. I believe I underestimated his weight slightly. But not enough to be a danger."

All Hugh could do was nod, amazed by the speed of the tranquilizer dart. The gun itself was an adaptation of an air gun designed by a blind German engineer several decades past. The dart itself was, according to Elizabeth, a creation of the late scientist Moreau.

After dragging Bascomb into the laboratory and strapping him to the table, Hugh performed a simple operation to remove the man's larynx. Then the experiments began. Sulfuric acid versus hydrochlorate acid for dissolving skin, bones, organs, hair and clothes. And other work performed upon the body of Thomas Bascomb. He took several days to die, but they learned a great deal. And after Bascomb died, they learned how to best hide all evidence of his identity in case someone happened upon the lab. In a way, Thomas Bascomb helped keep out of prison. Because his body taught them the best means to clean up after themselves.

"Is she prepared?" Elizabeth asked, returning to view. She had four large hypodermic needles on a tray before her as well as a clean mortar and pestle.

Hugh checked the acid vat and nodded. He crossed to the unrecognizable corpse and began covering the head and face with a heavy linen bandage. Though he and Elizabeth could function fine with the stripped corpse, others were not so sanguine. If, on the very outside chance, an outsider came into the laboratory, they would react poorly at a faceless, fingerless nude woman. Once, in Rome, a servant happened upon a similarly stripped corpse. First, they were violently ill, destroying the sterility required for that experiment. Then they ran to the authorities and reported Elizabeth and Hugh as murderers. Happily, they were able to dispose of the evidence and place a waxen dummy on the slab before the Carabinieri arrived. The servant looked ludicrous, but the police were now suspicious. Hence another location was lost, forcing them to move to Istanbul for a time.

"Then we shall now begin the next phase. Wheel the corpse over to the tank and place her on the table. We shall soon see another facet in the creation of this new form of life." Elizabeth filled the hypodermic needles but her voice was filled with anticipation and triumph.

CHAPTER XXIV

Elizabeth Frankenstein knew her destiny was about to be met. That it was happening in a small laboratory in a backward country of savage was not important. The great moment would happen, no matter the location. And then she would change the world. The name Elizabeth Frankenstein would be listed among the greats in science, an achievement her ancestor never managed.

She checked the solutions in each hypodermic needle, recognizing the precision of these compounds was essential. Elizabeth was always careful, but a second look was never a bad idea. Additionally it gave Hugh a chance to collect himself and regain control. The man's lustful actions always caused him to be both slow and secretive for a period. That would waste Elizabeth's precision time. An unacceptable course of action.

Hugh's groping the corpse didn't bother her. In fact that was preferable to their early days. Then, during the occasions she craved sexual congress, Hugh was a willing and useful participant. He liked to receive and deliver pain, which was part of what she craved at those moments. They fit well sexually, fulfilling the others needs with enthusiasm.

But Elizabeth only required those moments on rare occasion. To her, sex was something that was only needed on rare moments, when her body craved release. Otherwise the need never arose. Elizabeth knew, based on research done by alienists and the like, that this behavior was considered by many to be abnormal. Possibly true, possibly not true. Elizabeth Frankenstein was unconcerned. She embraced her unique qualities. The world would not be changed by the normal men and women of the world. The mad were the true visionaries; they realized paths the average fool would never comprehend.

As to Hugh, he craved sexual release regularly. This was something Elizabeth would not, could not, accommodate. Why should she waste time in bed rutting when the secrets of life and death were still a mystery? But Hugh watched her with lustful eyes, perpetually licking his lips and attempting to move closer to her while working. This was a distraction. He needed to be redirected.

Finding the location of a brothel, she sent him on an errand that would pass him by the building. The errand was unimportant. She could have just as easily obtained the items on her list from a chemist a few blocks away. But if Elizabeth could find a means of keeping Hugh's sexual impulses under control, the deception was worth her effort. She needed Hugh, focused on her goals, not behaving like a satyr in search of a nymph.

Because Hugh was the partner she sought in her work. While studying in her youth, Elizabeth recognized her work required aid. To do so alone would slow her down. That was unacceptable. But her experiments were too unusual for most men or women. Oh, there were a few she met over the years who possessed similar, strong minds. A woman in Japan for one, another female who claimed to be Moreau's daughter... there were first-class minds in the world. But they possessed their own agendas. Elizabeth didn't possess the inclination to debate the efficacy of her research as compared to their ideas. No, she needed a follower. Not a partner.

But what type of assistant? She read of a twisted man named Fritz who had assisted another of her ancestors who had attempted to recreate Victor's research. This Fritz was said to be a hunchback who was willing to dig up dead bodies or cut down the bodies of hanged men. Useful, but apparently the failures that followed lay at the door of this twisted little man. According to her ancestor, Fritz tormented their creation with fire. This led to the hunchback's death and the madness of that revenant. That creature was useless, a childish brute. Elizabeth abandoned the majority of that research along with the idea of using a simple-minded murderous servant. She didn't have time to waste on fools or shambling corpses like the one that idiot ancestor designed.

No, she wanted a doctor. A man or woman of science. One with brilliance, but no fixed direction. And without any true scruples. Not an easy combination to discover. There were always men and women with few interests beyond their own needs. But they all too often placed their personal safety as paramount. And usually the first person they chose to betray was their employer. The lessons of the past were not lost on Elizabeth.

Then she spotted Hugh Larkin. To all outward appearances, he was the model of a future medical man. His bloodline was considered acceptable and his manners impeccable. He possessed an impressive mind and was believed to be a doctor who would rise high in the establishment. Hugh Larkin was the correct combination of intelligence and dull deportment that was the hallmark of hospital supervisors and medical school principals who populated that world.

And it took a very short time for Elizabeth Frankenstein to recognize this was all a facade. Her first clues were the guilty glances at the breasts and bottoms at any females who were present in the university and hospital. These looks were not the pathetic peeks of a deprived schoolboy who was inexperienced with the female sex. No, there was a cannibalistic hunger, a violent desire to possess and rend within Hugh Larkin's gaze. He was a definite possibility.

Elizabeth decided to watch him further and additional information caused her to believe she'd found her follower. Hugh was unconcerned by the worst accidents in the hospital, wading through blood and bodily fluids with remarkable aplomb. But he did always volunteer to assist the worst injuries and surgeries. Then Hugh watched the blood with the greedy eyes of a predator, reveling in the sensations.

Deciding to take a chance, Elizabeth allowed Hugh to "discover" her experimenting on a limb she took from a recent victim. His feigned outrage didn't fool her. His eyes almost glowed as she hinted at her larger research. There was a lust to break the rules and cross new grounds in this man and Elizabeth Frankenstein knew he would serve her faithfully forever.

Her only difficulty was ensuring he was kept sexually satisfied. Their occasional bouts of rutting kept her slaked for long periods of time. But not so Hugh. He needed regular sessions of intercourse, as well as the occasional murder of his sexual partner. This forced Elizabeth to utilize her distraction techniques by discovering the locations of fallen women, preferably young ones. This way, Hugh remained continually focused on the work. Happily, they were both satisfied for now. But in a month or so, Elizabeth would send him to Santa Lucia or that mining town and would allow him to slake his hungers.

In the present, Elizabeth waited until Hugh began to wheel the corpse over to the tank. She joined him in moving the woman's body onto the platform above the structure and stepped away. Grabbing a test tube, Elizabeth dipped the glass into the liquid-filled tank and took a sample. Stepping over to the chemical bench, she quickly performed several tests and nodded.

"Ph level is exactly correct. Place the wheel above the corpse and prepare the generator. We will run the current through the body four times. Three second bursts. Understood?" Elizabeth checked the hypodermic needles a third time. They were still correct, to the last milliliter. That much of her personality was a clear inheritance of the Frankenstein family. Her father, the current baron, always counted the amount of steps it took to get to every location in their home. If the numbers were different than previous trips, he was bothered for hours, possibly days. Her Uncle Ernst recorded in a diary exactly how much food he ate. He then weighed himself three times daily to ensure the body mass fluctuation was minimal. Every member of the Frankenstein genetic line, as far as Elizabeth knew, possessed a mania for precision. But only a few members, such as herself and Victor, used this inner derangement for scientific purposes capable of transforming life on Earth. The others were merely odd people whose wealth had them labeled "eccentric" rather than insane.

Hugh moved a circular metal frame which hung on a heavy chain along the ceiling. He stopped the device several inches above the corpse. Hugh then stepped back and watched as Elizabeth fitted the hypodermic needles into the metal frame. He then returned to her side and thrust sharp metal rods into the barely exposed flesh. Each rod was attached to large heavy rubber-wrapped copper wire.

"We begin." Elizabeth donned a pair of heavy gloves and dark goggles. She grabbed a large metal lever built into the wall.

CHAPTER XXV

Hidalgo was an unusual country. It was clean, well-run and the people appeared both prosperous and hard-working. There were no dangerous *barrios* in the port city according to the guides and police. The passengers of the *Princess of San Pedro* were encouraged to visit the many neighborhoods, the beautiful church and a hospital that was said to be even better than the one in Mexico City.

The city itself was very picturesque, with older Spanish style buildings as well as ancient structures on the outskirts of the metropolis. Upon disembarking, several men were visibly shouting at the tourists. These men were guides, promising to show the many antediluvian ruins and mounds. Their stories about the builders of these fallen stone structures were often wild and bordered on the mythological. But most agreed the Mayans resided in this area hundreds of years ago.

As to the lives of the Mayans, those tales ranged from the prosaic to the penny dreadful. Some of the guides spun tales of ancient rites of a lost terrible religion. Warriors with blood tipped ruled villages with murder in the heart and evil in the intentions. And sorcery slew their enemies with as much impunity as blades cut from obsidian. Nonsense, of course. But the tourists loved the stories and drifted to these men in droves.

To Hans, this three-day layover was well-timed. He needed to test his hunting device for taking on Gouroull. To present it less than perfect to Martin Mars would result in much recrimination and punishment. Hans knew better.

There was a difficulty in testing his equipment. Hans's devices were all devoted to the wholesale murder of humans or monsters. You could not test such weapons on wooden targets, but on living, breathing humans. A human would react with fear or fury. Either way, they could discover faults in the machines. That was why Hans always carried a pistol and a knife when he tested his inventions of people. If something went wrong, he could still exterminate the intended victim.

But Hidalgo was different. There were no poor areas where beggars could be killed and their fellows would ignore your actions. Nor were there any small slums near the rubbish pits. Those scavengers could be killed en masse and no police officer would care. In fact many would be grateful for the removal of a segment of society they pretended did not exist.

That was a simple fact of life. People preferred to believe that the poor were merely something you viewed from a distance. To kill peasants or poor people was only a tragedy, in many rich people's minds, if they were forced to acknowledge such an issue existed. In many countries, you could shoot three beggars a day and get away with your crimes. Perhaps the poor people would organize to protect each other. That could stop the tide of violence for a time. But society viewed such actions as illegal vigilantism. Therefore such behavior was viewed as an act as criminal as the original murderer. This was Hans's protection in his work for Martin Mars.

But he still needed to test his new weapon. With no human subjects, the trials would not be as exact as he would like. At first, Hans considered hunting down some animals, but that was troublesome too. The land about the port city was agrarian, with cows, chickens, dogs and cats being the only visible living creatures beyond the farmers. To kill a cow was easy enough, not even sport. A chicken might be harder, they ran fairly quickly. And Hans liked dogs and cats, killing them might be upsetting. But the point was moot. If he murdered some poor, dumb animal, he wouldn't learn much of his device's capabilities and deficits in the field. But more importantly, killing farm animals attracted notice.

This was an area Hans knew about all too well. Before he embraced his darker side and was rescued by Martin Mars, Hans knew he possessed the urge to kill. The despoiling of the innocence, the taste of the blood. The need called to him every day. He didn't want to be a monster, but his blood seemed to sing at the thought of grabbing a child and releasing all his urges. The corruption of the innocent soul before the embrace of the blade. He could smell the coppery scent in his nose every time he passed a young one. It was driving him slowly mad. The need, the desire to sate himself, it never seemed to grow away. In fact the more he attempted to avoid the sensations, the greater the compulsion propagated within his very soul.

There were times, in those dark days of denial, when Hans was positive the impulses within him were an actual living being. The longing for the rape, for the screams, for the blood gnawed his innards like a rat feeding on a carcass. He tried prayer, alcohol, self-abuse, and strong narcotics. The result was the need was never satiated, merely briefly delayed.

In desperation, he drove outside of town, seeking an alternative. The answer came in the form of a cow, placidly munching away upon grass in a lonely field. Waiting until dark, Hans crept up to the gentle creature and released the beast with him in a rush. He feasted upon the blood and pain, somewhat satisfied for the first time in his life. Hans slept well that night, a dreamless sleep for the first time in many years.

But the next morning was a different story. News of the butchered beast filled the newspapers and in the gossip of the villagers. Though there were no witnesses, the local police vowed to track down the monster responsible such an act of barbarism. Fear and anger filled the hearts of the townspeople and Hans's joy was snuffed out as quickly as it appeared.

Burning his bloody clothes and cleaning his auto of the blood, Hans thought long and hard upon the results of his actions. The fury over the cow was almost as great as that of a murdered child. The reason was many prized animals for their utility, their wealth. To kill such a creature was to assault the lives of the owners. To murder a child was to assault the soul of the parent. All with children would feel the pain equally. In Hans's mind, the equation was simple. He must perform these acts, embrace the beast within his soul. This was the only way Hans felt at peace. But if he must risk his life, his freedom, to perform such killings, he must do so for a good reason. Loss of his whole life over a cow or some other piece of barnyard filth? Ridiculous! If Hans was truly a monster, he would embrace that facet of his soul. The children. He would take the children. Hans knew the big cities were the place he would truly be at home. There he could be a wolf, hidden among the sheep.

And Hans remained so until rescued by Martin Mars. He was still a fiend, but his master helped him placate his inner demon through the hunting of monsters. And the killing of any possible enemies or inconveniences in Martin Mars's path. But the lessons of the past were not forgotten. Killing the lesser beings created more problems than he wished to confront.

This was why Hans stood in a lonely copse of trees, several hundred yards away from a quarry of some type. He knew such locations were often the site of explosions and very loud noises. The perfect place for early testing of weapons. Though this time, this would be the only tests he performed. Hopefully the device would not require too many corrections. There were always problems in every weapon, some more than others. This one was an ambitious advancement. Anything less would not allow them to take on the infamous Gouroull. Because this monster would truly become the prize in Martin Mars's collections.

Readying the weapon, Hans smiled to himself. Hopefully this Gouroull would bleed and scream in agony. The ones who died without a squeak were unsatisfying. And a quick hunt failed to calm the fiend within Hans. That was what he lived for in the end. That and serving the great Martin Mars of course.

CHAPTER XXVI

"Lower the wheel," Elizabeth's voice was loud, but very calm. She was excited, yet would not behave like a schoolgirl about to try a special sweet for the first time. Still, this was a very momentous moment. The second stage of the creation of Gouroull's mate. Of proving that her ancestor was a genius, and that Elizabeth Frankenstein was his equal, or greater, in all areas.

Hugh acknowledged Elizabeth's order with a quick wave of his hand. The whine of the electrical generators was rising and soon any sounds would be impossible to hear. Normally, to produce the sheer volume of energy to power such experiments, they would need either a bolt of lightning, or a machine capable of powering a small city. But thanks to another of Elizabeth's contacts in the scientific community, a crazed self-purported genius with the bizarre name of Fen-Chu, that was not an issue. In return for some favor, unknown to Hugh, he gave her a pair of simple, small machines capable of producing enough electricity to satisfy their every need. Why this Fen-Chu wasn't using his incredible invention to change the face of mankind was a question that occasionally haunted Hugh. But not today. Today Elizabeth's work occupied his fullest attention.

His hands were covered in heavy rubber gloves and his eyes by dark-lensed goggles, Hugh pulled a heavy metal switch down. The metal wheel slowly descended from the ceiling, the chains barely audible over the screech of the generators. Upon the wheel were placed four large, thick hypodermic needles, their glass cylinders filled with an opaque yellow and purple liquid.

The needles punctured the corpse's chest and legs without any visible resistance from the cold, dead, flesh. And as the wheel continued to drop, the fluid was dispersed within the flesh evenly. A simple method of performing multiple injections at the same time in different parts of the body. That was one of Hugh's few additions to the creation of this new brand of science. He realized Elizabeth required a simple, efficient method of performing such a small task. A wheel that allowed her to inject living or dead bodies in multiple locations saved time. And this wheel granted her access to twenty possible zones of the human body, no matter how large or small.

"Withdraw the wheel." Elizabeth command somehow rose above the high-pitch sounds. But she watched as Hugh pulled up his level and locked the wheel in place away from the tank. He then stepped behind the lead shield and watched, rocking back and forth on the balls of his feet with nervous anticipation.

Elizabeth watched as the pointers on the dials before her eyes rose at a steady rate. Within a moment both climbed and were about to point at the red painted zone denoting the generators were in danger of overload. Just as the needle touched the edge of the red, Elizabeth pushed up two knife switches, completing the circuit. The corpse in the tank vibrated, almost leaping out of the heavy liquid. The lights in the lab, as well as the whole house, flickered on and off and an arc of electricity flashed through the air above the tank.

After counting aloud to five, Elizabeth released the switches. She watched the generator needles climb again and pushed up the knife switches. The scent of ozone and boiled meat filled the air and the arcs once again flew above the corpse. Both Elizabeth and Hugh were unaffected by the flashes, their dark goggles designed to protect their vision from such harsh flares of light.

And again, after five seconds, Elizabeth pulled back the knife switches. The tank of fluid was still boiling and steam emerged from the edges. Then, when the generator was ready, she pushed up the levers again and watched as the body performed a bizarre St. Vitus Dance within the fluid. The image was made odder by the flashing lights as the house's current was funneled into the dead body that was once a living woman from a nearby town.

After the final transmission of power, Elizabeth placed the knife switches in the safety position. "Drop the power down to optimum levels on both generators. I shall raise the platform."

Hugh disappeared from sight, scurrying off to carefully perform his task. The controls on the generators were astonishingly simple, yet he treated their use as if he was performing some form of delicate surgery. This was an endearing quality to Elizabeth. Replacing those machines would be next to impossible. She doubted Fen-Chu would agree to help her a second time. And there were few others in the world capable of building such an incredible device. The ones that could were geniuses like Elizabeth and Fen-Chu. They would be reluctant at best to share their ideas with a mind as impressive as hers. Hugh's gentle, almost reverent, care for the machines was an additional example of his unwavering devotion.

Elizabeth pulled up the lever that raised the platform, stepping back as viscous liquid poured off the body and along the floor. A carefully cut channel in the stone floor prevented the fluid from spilling across the lab. The heavy nearly gelatinous chemicals vanished into a small metal grate. Elizabeth planned this accordingly, having forced workmen to build a small sewer line which led to the lake. Her fears of contamination were such that she pulled heavy Wellington boots on as the chemicals vanished from view.

Stepping gingerly over to the corpse, Elizabeth waved to Hugh. He stepped to the opposite side of the table and sliced away the bandages. The face was still a ruin, but there were differences. A thin layer of tissue covered part of the empty holes that were once ears. And before their eyes the nose was slowly emerging. The new skin was dark gray in color and the growth across the face and head appeared to be spreading.

"Exponential cellular growth. Hugh, cut off a sample and place it in a sterile dish. A new one." Elizabeth watched as the gray epidermis appeared to be absorbing the dead flesh at an explosive rate of speed.

Hugh pulled a very sharp scalpel out and sliced off the tip of the newly forming nose. The tissue was pliant, like human skin. But it felt different, thicker and rougher. The sample felt more like a thin slice of a thick bone rather than a layer of skin. Despite himself, Hugh shuddered. There was a wrongness to this flesh, an inhumanity that caused him to feel a sense of revulsion. Hugh felt as if he was touching, even through heavy gloves, something otherworldly. He recoiled from the image with the instinctual terror an animal feels of a predator.

Elizabeth took the sample and fed the dish into the electronic microscope. The machine shuddered and belched and whirred to life. The green screen turned white and then a close up of the cells appeared before their eyes. The microorganisms were perfectly octagonal in shape and connected to each other with unseen bonds. They were all uniformly gray in color and appeared far thicker than typical epidermal tissue.

"Look, Hugh. They're multiplying at an exponential rate. This is unprecedented!" Elizabeth tapped the screen as new cells continued to appear before their eyes. Each new cell grew out of the mass of tissue forming a tight gray honeycomb.

Before Hugh could respond, Elizabeth dashed past him and returned to the body. He followed and gasped. The cellular growth was spreading everywhere, turning the corpse of the woman into a dark gray mass. The body resembled a statue more than a human now, a gray, vaguely human mass. The only way to tell this creature was female were the jutting breasts. But even these mammaries were covered by the dark gray membrane.

"Is she...the body...she's...longer?" Hugh realized the corpse was altered in and unexpected manner. Formerly about the height of Elizabeth, the dead woman was now approximately Hugh's size and appeared to be slowly growing larger.

"Yes," said Elizabeth, taking a bone saw and cutting deep into the flesh. The saw appeared caught as she attempted to examine beneath the skin's surface. But eventually an incision appeared and she shined a lantern within the corpse. Elizabeth was silent for a full minute, barely breathing as she examined the corpse.

"Cellular growth is subcutaneous. The new tissue is inhabiting the skeletal structure and strengthening outer shell. The incision is vanishing at an uncanny rate." Elizabeth's voice was clinical and cold. But Hugh detected the excitement beneath her scientific detachment. All of her dreams were coming to fruition in an instant. The creation of life from the dead, the work of the legendary Victor Frankenstein. Recreated, possibly improved, by his descendent Elizabeth Frankenstein.

"That...that is not how organisms operate, Elizabeth! This cannot be, it is impossible!" Hugh watched as the body shuddered visibly, growing several inches before his eyes.

"Stop behaving like a childish moron, Hugh. We are operating in realms of science undreamed of, even by the most advanced minds. Only a Frankenstein possesses the genius required to even begin to understand the concepts created here. Like my ancestor, I realize that we are creating new life. Not merely reviving the dead. We are improving upon the design the universe foisted upon our species. The result is a new race of humanity. Better, stronger and capable of bending nature to their will. This new race will subjugate the universe and create a new future." Elizabeth spoke with an intensity that Hugh never witnessed before this day.

It was frightening, like seeing a facet of her personality he never knew existed. But secretly, Hugh always suspected there was a bit of megalomania within her. To be willing to devote your life to her work required a degree of obsessional psychosis. After all, she was willing to move all around the world to continue her research. But not to the degree Hugh was viewing on this day. This was new and terrifying.

But Hugh also knew that would make no difference in the end. Even if she stood on the table and declared herself to be the new messiah, he would stay at her side. There was nothing else for him in the world. Hugh Larkin made his choice all those years ago. He devoted his life to the dreams of Elizabeth Frankenstein, no matter where her mad genius took him in the world.

For want of anything else to say, Hugh looked at the face of the remade creature. The face was recreated, but the results were different from the attractive young woman that Gouroull had murdered the other day. The face was, for want of a better word, disturbing. The bone structure was transformed. Formerly, the dead whore possessed a round, pretty face, a peasant girl. She was the dreams of many a writer, waxing poetic of the beauty of the earthy young lass of the soil. Now the face was longer, narrower and possessing no traces of that loveliness. There was a twisted, demonic quality about this reconstructed countenance. The face was lovely in an inhuman way, the visage of a succubus capable of stealing your very soul. But the very alien nature of this remade female was chilling.

Elizabeth stepped up the face and appeared disinterested in changes. Her curiosity was entirely clinical, "Facial structure is also strengthened. Cheekbones are higher, chin in sharper and more pointed. Ears, once rounded, are now longer and possessing sharper edges."

She pulled out a pair of forceps and forced open the wider mouth. The teeth within it were larger and slightly sharper. They were not the ivory razor fangs of Gouroull, but closer to that of a wolf or a large dog. They were big and terrifying-looking, but appeared less dangerous than that of Victor Frankenstein's creation.

"Interesting jaw and teeth changes. Teeth are lengthened and jawbone is strengthened." Elizabeth released the mouth and stepped back.

"Gouroull's teeth are different. His are larger and sharper." Hugh knew he was stating the obvious, but what else could he say at this juncture?

"Male and female battle forms are rarely alike, Hugh. This new race follows those few natural laws." Elizabeth moved up and lifted the eyelids, examining the orbs and shining a light in each.

"Elizabeth, look!" Hugh noticed something odd near the injection sites upon the corpse. Dark spots appeared in all four locations. They were a tiny series of tiny brown stains which slowly darkened to a deep black. The blemishes slowly grew larger, spreading in a circular pattern from the point of injection.

Elizabeth watched the slowly spreading stain for a moment and then dashed to the electronic microscope. She increased the resolution and stared at the vast collection of honeycombed cells. She stood ramrod stiff as she stared at the screen and then slowly nodded as a discoloration began to appear within the nuclei. The stain grew darker and spread to the other tissue, with the originators of the change transforming from brown to black in moments.

"What is happening?" Hugh's question was rhetorical. The answer was obvious, the new cells were dying. Their death rate was as explosive as their growth had been.

"Come and see. It is as I expected." Elizabeth turned off the electronic microscope and returned to the table. She stripped off her gloves and stared down at the corpse with her hands clasped behind her back.

The black discoloration spread across the chest, legs and arms as they watched. Hugh reached for a pair of forceps to examine the mouth, but Elizabeth waved him back from the table.

"There is no need, Hugh. This is as I expected. The new tissues are dying and collapsing. They are losing all tensile strength. Step away and you will see an astonishing sight. This will not take long." Elizabeth's voice was light, almost happy as she watched the destruction of her latest experiment. The reaction was incongruent with what was occurring. Why was she delighted by this apparent failure?

The body was soon a uniform obsidian in tone, with every inch transformed. A moment later, the face fell inward, crumbling upon itself. The head and neck soon followed, as did the breasts and arms. In less than an hour all that remained was a large pile of fine black powder.

"Excellent! This is just wonderful!" Elizabeth almost bounced in place in her glee. This reaction was unusual for her, possessing a dour, focused personality. To demonstrate such happiness wasn't in her character. In truth, she often became amorous during moments of scientific success.

Hugh was about to ask why she was so delighted, when the outer door opened with a loud crash. Gouroull stood framed in the doorway, an enormous figure covered in shadows. But his luminous amber eyes were visible in the gloom. Their alien aspect focused briefly on Elizabeth and Hugh before coming to rest on the dusty remains of the corpse he procured. Stepping in the room, he tossed aside a table in his way and began to move in their direction. His immense gray hands lifted and the fingers slowly flexed as he approached.

"Why?" Gouroull's voice was a harsh rasp upon the ears. The sound was oddly formed, as if the mechanism within his chest and throat were formed from organs different from those possessed by humans. "Why?"

Hugh immediately realized Gouroull believed they had destroyed his potential mate on purpose. According to Victor Frankenstein's notes, he had destroyed a potential mate for his creature while working on the Scottish isle of Cround. In this monster's eyes, Elizabeth was betraying him in the same manner.

"No! We didn't...that is to say..." Hugh shrank away from the advancing antagonist. There was nothing he could do if Gouroull attacked him. The creature was legendarily lethal, a monster capable of destroying any human in his path. An unarmed medical man was no threat. Hugh Larkin would be destroyed as easily as a child stamping on a bug.

"Gouroull." Elizabeth appeared almost disinterested in the enraged fiend, "Calm yourself. You forgot what I said to Hugh. This was an experiment. The next phase in the creation process."

Gouroull stopped and looked down at her, his un-blinking yellow eyes boring into both humans. He did not speak, but merely watched them, his massive body as still as a stone statue.

"This was a test. Your body is a very unique organ-ism. Without the knowledge of how the compounds work, we would fail." Elizabeth looked up at the mon-strous figure. But he gave no sign of reacting in any manner. His stillness was unnerving, inhuman, and cre-ated an unpleasant silence about the lab.

Seeing that Gouroull was not going to react at the present, Elizabeth continued with even greater confi-dence: "The internal and external elixirs operate in con-cert. The energy created by your lifeblood is... it is un-precedented and does not follow any physical law. And your epidermal layer is able to contain said energy. Your system is a marvel in and of itself. I will not fail in the creation of your mate now that I comprehend how you function."

Yet still Gouroull stood there, waiting and watching them both. His unyielding figure was frightening, a monstrous entity that appeared to grow larger and more imposing in the silent darkness.

"We will proceed to Santa Lucia and find the body or bones of a worthy female. My ancestor's notes mentioned something about a being of strength of mind and purpose necessary for the proper creation of yourself and your mate. Superstitious nonsense, no doubt. But at this juncture, I shall not risk our success by rejecting details. Within two days, three at the most, we shall begin. All of my work will be proven correct! Oh, and your mate will live. Or the closest equivalent your species has to life as we comprehend the meaning." Elizabeth was gesticulating by the end of her speech, proof she was excited by her statements.

Gouroull stared at her full minute. Then he turned and walked back into the night. Within a few seconds, he was out-of-sight, no trace of his presence.

Hugh closed the door and sighed. "I was positive he was about to murder us both."

Elizabeth smiled, though no trace of humor was present in her face. "Yes, he was about to destroy us both. Happily, I was able to tell him truthfully my next plans. Otherwise, you would have been torn to pieces. No doubt, my own fate would have been far less savory."

Hugh shuddered, unable to imagine what that monster would do to Elizabeth's body. Betraying Gouroull in the same manner as his creator Victor would no doubt cause the fiend to react with terrible retribution.

But Elizabeth was already thinking of the future. "After you clean the laboratory, contact the shippers. I want a boat here by afternoon. Find us accommodations in Santa Lucia and have our factor prepare what we will need to unearth our subject. I wish to return as fast as possible. Once all is ready, come to my room. And bring the ropes."

Elizabeth caught the lustful look in Hugh's eyes, nodded, and left the lab. She had no real desire for Hugh this night. But her assistant used trips to Santa Lucia to sate his lustful needs. By being present, he might become sullen and withdrawn. And at this point of her work, she needed him concentrating only on the coming creation. If that meant Elizabeth needed to use him sexually, so be it.

Heading to her room, she checked the strength of the rings on her bed. Finding them still strong and in place, she opened her closet and began to search. Cat-of-nine tails tonight? Or the riding crop?

CHAPTER XXVII

The Living went about their lives with Moraika
gone. Their wise woman was given to vanishing for a
time without word. That was part of her ancient mys-
tique. To the tribe, she was an eternal symbol, a being
above and yet below them all. Her wisdom made her
their leader in all matters. She rarely invoked this privi-
lege, making her assertions into tribal matters all the
more important. There was a healthy fear of Moraika;
her age and wisdom possessed an almost sinister quality.
No matter what issue arose within The Living, she
would view the situation with the amused condescension
of an ancient observing the actions of children.

But The Living also regarded the ancient crone as a
lesser being among their ranks. She was an anomaly
among them, an oddity. Moraika birthed no children,
caught no fish and tended to no plants. The Living
wouldn't even ask her to help mend the nets, a job even
the youngest children performed. To The Living,
Moraika was a barely human object. Her only duty, self-
imposed, was to watch the children. And when she vanished for a time, that obligation easily fell to the other
members of the tribe. No true loss, unless one of the
hunters fell ill. The wise woman was a being they venerated and respected, even obeyed, but not truly of their
number.

This time, her stay away was particularly long. But
none questioned that fact. Nor did they believe she was
gone. There was always a Moraika among The Living.
That was as much of a fact as the rising sun or the crawling dark of the night. If the question of where she went

came up, usually from a child, the answer was always the same: "Moraika walks with Allpa and Supay. She will return when she returns," was the response. All repeated those exact words. No variations. Even chatty members of the tribe, like Killa the Gatherer, stated this mantra with no additions or explanations. If the child asked again, or in a different manner, the answer was always the same words. "Moraika walks with Allpa and Supay. She will return when she returns."

And the child would soon join the others, repeating the words. None questioned the exactness of their reply. Nor that there was an almost lost, inhuman quality to the manner in which they spoke on these occasions. This was just the way you answered anyone questioning the location of the missing Moraika.

But then she returned. No dramatic appearances, not even a word. One moment they looked up and the twisted crone was seated on a log, watching The Living mend a net. She was leaning on her cane and watching them with intent, rheumy eyes. The tribe stared for a moment, and then, collectively, appeared to accept her presence and return to their duties. There were no words of welcome or greeting. Nor any questions as to where she went to this time. They merely accepted it. Moriaka was gone, now she has returned. No doubt she would leave again. That was the way of the wise woman.

Moraika licked her dry lips and reached for the water gourd by her feet. After taking in a small quaff, she watched her people. Simple, but necessary beings. True servants of Supay and Allpa. The jungle dwellers were the only others in this region who possessed the same importance. They were protectors of this land, known by the outsiders as the Dark Heart. And this piece of the world must remain as it had since the time before the

Ancients had come to this land. Moraika did not know why this was so, only that Supay and Allpa asserted as much. If this natural piece of the greater world were to fall victim to the depredations of mankind, all was lost. The wise woman also knew this to be a fact, having seen in her visions the results. The pain of those other worlds, domains of gray dead earth, skies filled with choking clouds of chemicals and steel and stone buildings filled her with dread. The grievous disrespect these provinces of metal and pollution inflicted upon creation was an offense to life itself. The Living must never waver in their mission.

But in this contemplation, Moraika realized she needed to perform one act before embracing her end. She needed to secure the future of The Living, ensure their duties as the obedient followers of Allpa and Supay would not waver. There would be another Moraika after she was taken from life. Her memories and wisdom would continue. But the powers of the ancient crone were not infallible. If she could help the one who followed her, she would do a service to her tribe.

She did not make this choice lightly. The spirits she served, her masters, were not kindly figures. They possessed minds far different from that of mankind. There was an alien method to their thinking, one both terrible and wonderful. For they viewed all life at the same time, humanity merely being one tiny facet of their creation. To beg the aid of these beings was to invite anger and retribution. The fish did not ask for visions of their future. Nor did the birds, insects, jaguars or any other form of life. Only humans entreated these higher powers for aid, rather than accepting the natural course of life. To ask was to invite disaster.

But ask Moraika did this day. Clearing her mind, she repeated the words, the formula of petition. The words were of a lost tongue, one not suited for the human mouth. But they were clear in her mind, a simple procedure despite the extreme complexity of the framing portions. As always, her head ached and her lungs seemed incapable of getting enough air as she begged for assistance. The physical toll was always massive. But that was the price one paid for power.

Oddly, this time only one request had to be made for the visions to appear. Usually, hours were needed, with blood spilling from her nose and eyes as she begged for a glimpse to confirm her inner fears. This time, the first time in her extended life, Allpa and Supay responded with astonishing alacrity. Perhaps they wished to convey this information. Or perhaps this was a final gift from the spirits for her long years of service in their name. Moraika did not know. Would never know. And she knew better than to ask. The ways of the beings from beyond are dark and mysterious. One learned quickly that questioning their wisdom and ways was an error with appalling consequences.

Moraika was suddenly in the future, seeing through the eyes of the Moraika to come after her death. She knew her last duty was completed and the future was not in danger from the ones in the house on the hill. But then, outsiders came. They arrived in their oversized boats which belched black smoke into the air. The men carried weapons and were violent and abusive. They questioned The Living, treating them with no respect. Many were killed, their ends without any respect for their life. Some of her tribe were dragged off, slaves to these men. Others were forced to move and live and obey men who worshipped in different ways. Men who whipped and harmed anyone who venerated Allpa and Supay. The land became as dust, a lifeless husk on a world slowly dying.

And the others in The Living? They ran and hid in the jungle. The jungle dwellers ignored them, knowing they were mere remnants of a tribe with some importance to the world. But The Living would be no more. The fragment that survived would no longer venerate the spirits. They would simply exist, their beliefs mere echoes of the ancient ways. Perhaps their duties to Allpa and Supay would pass to another, perhaps not. Moraika would not, could not, know. The spirits blocked that path, a dark wall covering that direction as she attempted to discover that possible future. But another path lay before her, an unexplored possible direction for the future.

Moraika saw The Living packing their few goods on boats and rafts and leaving. They moved along the coast of the lake for a full day, even sleeping on the waters. The tribe stopped before a thick growth of trees and vegetation and then, one group at a time, pushed through the thicket. It was soon revealed that this was an outgrowth of the lake, hidden by the undergrowth so that it was invisible to the outside eye. The stream grew wider and more powerful as they proceeded, becoming a mighty river. It was there that The Living would make their new home. And their current land, as well as the new place, would thrive and survive.

They would no longer be lake people, but would be a tribe of the river. The Living were excellent at adapting. Many generations before the outsiders arrived, they lived in caves surrounded by dreadful giant lizards. Part of the tribe had stayed behind, on that plateau far away.

But others had moved to this place and continued the way of life dictated by the spirits of life and death.

The decision was easy enough. Moraika would remain. But The Living, they would leave. And she would join them, in her own fashion, in time. To do anything else would be to risk their duty, their promise, as a tribe, to the beings from beyond. And the twisted, ancient crone would no more allow that to happen than she would give up breathing. At least not until her time in this world was complete.

"Rebuild the rafts," Moraika's thin voice travelled to every ear. "The time of change is here."

The Living stared at their wise woman, surprised by her words. The change in their life was always something discussed around the fire. But in their hearts, they never believed this would happen. The last time this had happened was when their current wise woman was still a babe. The possibility always felt more like a tale about the creation of all life or the story of how The Living came to these lands.

But in the end, nobody spoke. It was futile. Moraika said they would leave this place. They would obey. There was nothing else for The Living t do. None could defy her will; none would try.

Moraika stared at the lake as the tribe decided on the best method to prepare for the move. The Living would survive, if she completed her last duty to the spirits. If she failed, the whole world would be reduced to the dust…

CHAPTER XXVIII

Elizabeth was in a filthy mood. The trip on the boat, a method of travel she always despised, was difficult. A heavy rain storm swept over the lake and tossed their small craft about violently for over two hours. She was violently ill several times and needed to be helped off the vessel when they arrived in Santa Lucia.

Then their rooms were dusty, musty and filled with many insects. The creatures scurried away when the gas lamps were turned on. But the skitterish, scattering sounds were unmistakable each time they entered the room. Elizabeth lapsed into a sullen fury, her monosyllabic responses to all questions casting an even greater pall upon their trip to Santa Lucia.

Fortunately their factor was only interested in the money they provided, as well as the teenage servant in the cafe where they met. His round, gray-bearded face and dark, hard eyes regarded the saturnine Elizabeth and addressed all his inquiries to Hugh. It was simple enough to provide him with their requirements and see him off. At Elizabeth's demands, their connection was merely business.

"Three locations. One belongs to the ruling family. According to this," Hugh held up the information they received moments earlier. "The family of the late Tiger of San Pedro built him a massive memorial in the center, displacing several family crypts. His wife was buried alongside him as were two of his children."

"No." Elizabeth took a sip of the wine she'd ordered, made a face of disgust and pushed the drink aside.

Hugh was undaunted. "There are family mausoleums for members of the twelve ruling families in that graveyard. And the second one. Many prominent ladies were interred in these elaborate marble tombs. Apparently there was a craze, following that of the Victorians, for elaborate burials."

"No." Elizabeth stared at the passing men and woman, almost oblivious to Hugh's presence. This was a habit of hers, an extreme response to not working. Elizabeth Frankenstein despised sitting still or waiting, she wished to spend her every waking moment in the lab. When unable to do so, a despondency as well as a morose anger filled her very being. Her words became short, clipped and rude. And she ignored most entreaties for more information. Usually a greater length of time was required before this behavior became apparent. But the brief boat journey appeared to have increased her angry responses.

"The third cemetery is one used by the prisons as well as the junta's secret police. Unmarked and occasionally, according to what I am reading here, made up of large charnel pits. Mass graves. But not unsanctified. The cousin of the vice-president is a bishop. His lesser priests apparently perform the burial rites as part of their duties. Imagine trying to do that in London or Edinburgh. The ministers would revolt and begin making speeches on the streets." Hugh tried to lighten the mood, but saw immediately he failed. There was no moving Elizabeth at this time. This was something he comprehended after all their years together.

But Hugh didn't mind. He was completely satisfied. Though his wrists and backside ached, and there was blood in his britches, he was very satiated. Elizabeth had been more ardent that he'd seen her in some time. In fact, she was so incredible that night, Hugh hadn't even contemplated going to one of the many brothels in the capital city. This was probably a good thing in the end. The madames who ran the houses charged quite a lot of money for Hugh's... esoteric interests in sexual matters. These prices were becoming ruinous, which was why he rarely asked to go to Santa Lucia anymore. Now, after a night with the only woman he was capable of loving, Hugh Larkin was only focused on their work.

"Names." Elizabeth's voice was a garbled whisper, a barely recognizable sound. But she extended her hand for the lists of names in the graveyard. It was at this time that her movements also changed. Usually she was bursting with energy, barely contained under her extreme focus on her latest experiment. But when she was placed in a state of enforced inaction, her anger also brought about an extreme lassitude. Elizabeth would move with the sluggish clumsiness of a drunken oaf.

Dutifully, Hugh placed in her hands the small sheaf of papers. With lethargic fumbling fingers, Elizabeth pushed through the pages. Her eyes slowly scanned the printed words, sometimes returning to read a second time. Normally she would absorb this information in a glance, but not today. It was as if her mighty mind was reduced to a sad state of bare functionality. The Elizabeth Hugh followed through the world, working on research that, in minds of the religious, would damn their souls for all eternity, was gone. What remained as a shell of her former self, a pathetic remnant, a shadow of the true Elizabeth Frankenstein.

"Here." Elizabeth turned Hugh's direction and pushed a page his direction. Her finger was next to a name, a woman interred in the third cemetery. "This one."

Hugh read the name and his breath was caught by what he read. He knew the name, a young woman whose scandals were still in the news at the time of their arrival in this country. This young woman, a wealthy heiress from a good family, possessed a bad habit. She enjoyed watching people die from poison. Apparently the idea came to her from a famous play and she tested the results on her own nanny... the girl had been a mere ten years-old at the time. Enjoying the results, she had studied various methods and tested the many poisonous chemicals and plants upon family members, servants, schoolmates, teachers and several members of the clergy. These illnesses and deaths were attributed to outside forces or accidents.

But all that had changed when she turned nineteen. An arranged marriage was brokered between her family and that of another of the twelve, this one devoted to railroads and banking. But her intended husband had not been interested in marriage. His sexual interests were buxom maids, preferably ones with long wild curled hair. The young woman he was obligated to marry was tall, thin, with short hair and a small bust, which led this reckless young fool to publicly humiliate her, knowing his family would forgive him his transgressions.

But the young woman was of a disposition closer to that of Lucrecia Borgia than that of the fictional Mrs. Havesham. Angered by her terrible treatment, she had paid a maid to fill the wine carafes in the family library was a particularly noxious and painful toxicant. The maid was amenable; the family in question paid poorly and treated their pets better than their servants. A simple lie, that the poison was in fact a powerful laxative, had caused the servant to agree to the mission.

The results were catastrophic. The young man, both of his parents, an uncle, a maiden aunt, three visiting business contacts, and the nephew of the vice-president's wife, had all died from the poison. The maid, tearful, confessed to everything and accepted her conviction and sentence to the gallows.

But the young woman was of a stronger disposition. She had claimed innocence and declared herself a victim of a conspiracy. It appeared likely she would be sent to a sanitarium in Hidalgo or somewhere distant. But then her poison books, diary and collections were discovered. Her family had disowned her and spread rumors that she was, in fact, an adopted child from a foundling home. A sentence of death by hanging was demanded by the many victims' families. The judge ordered her hanged before the next sunset.

The sentence was carried out immediately, with no lawyer willing to appeal the judgment. And so the young woman had died a fast death and had been buried in the pauper's cemetery, row twelve, location forty-two. Her name was rapidly becoming synonymous with a grim specter of death, a nightmare to frighten naughty children.

"Her?" Hugh was shocked by this revelation. But he was happy to see some signs of the old Elizabeth emerging. "This woman was a crazed killer. She reputedly exterminated humans for pleasure. Why her out of all these choices?"

Elizabeth smiled slightly, something of the old energy visible in her eyes. "Can you think of another being more suited for Gouroull? Insane, yes. But murderous and strong in her own manner. Hugh, a normal woman would not survive long with my ancestor's creation."

"Perhaps not," Hugh admitted, knowing Gouroull's alien mind alone would terrify any average male or female in this world.

"Not perhaps!" Elizabeth slapped the table, her anger and fierce mind almost releasing an electrical charge within the air. "Gouroull is not human. To behave as if he were such was a mistake made by others who promised him a mate. They sought to use this creature, not realizing this was an impossibility. The only coin of value to him is the creation of one of his species, a mate. My ancestor mentioned the need for a strong, powerful corpse. Perhaps that was sophistry, perhaps not. But any chance of success lies in a two-fold approach."

"Creation of his mate..." Hugh supplied, not following Elizabeth's reasoning beyond this simple fact.

Elizabeth nodded, her movements suddenly more graceful. "Correct. He prizes my genius and my work."

"And the second part? I fail to see anything beyond that which Gouroull demanded." Hugh took a long sip of the sweet wine, fascinated by this discussion. But then all talks with Elizabeth interested him in truth.

Elizabeth shook her head and chuckled. "You fail to realize an area of equal important. Acceptance. This mate must be of the same inhuman mind as his, the same lethal genius. Otherwise she will reject him and we will be viewed by Gouroull in an unfavorable light. I think you fully comprehend the terrifying nature of that situation. Death would be a mercy compared to an enraged, rejected Gouroull."

Hugh nodded quickly, feeling a cold sweat break out across his back at the very thought of Gouroull at his most infuriated. They had received a small glimpse of such fate the other night. And Hugh knew that moment would be the stuff of his greatest nightmares until his dying days.

"A female as monstrous as himself. I see your meaning better. But would that remain within the corpse? Would not death remove the stain and memory of her crimes?" Hugh knew he was venturing into metaphysical questions, but did feel he had to ask.

Elizabeth waved a hand in a gesture of disinterest. "That is beyond my control. We are merely attempting to limit the risk of an unpleasant response. Imagine if we took the body of a normal young woman. Then place a trace of her prior personality into her remade form. What would be the result?"

"Possibly nothing. But also this hypothetical female might hiss and scream in terror at the very sight of Gouroull." Hugh pictured such a scene, the remade woman looking upon her intended mate in abject terror. Gouroull's response would be terrible, to say the least.

"Correct, Hugh. This would then rid the world of my future accomplishments. Therefore I must allow my ancestor's accomplishments as my guide in this area. Gouroull's mate shall be one well-acquainted with killing other humans for pleasure. Tonight. Do you have all we require?" Elizabeth was closer to her true self now, the torpidity and smoldering rage vanishing away before Hugh's eyes.

"Two shovels, block and tackle, wagon, horses and a large packing crate marked medical supplies. Have I missed anything?" Hugh knew all too well what was required for a bit of grave robbing.

Elizabeth shook her head. "Take me back to the inn. I want to eat and sleep until we leave. Two o'clock. Make sure you can find the way in the dark."

Hugh didn't answer. Instead, he paid the bill and escorted Elizabeth back to the accommodations. He still had a great deal of work to do before the night approached.

The cemetery was the biggest they'd viewed since they lived in London. There, they made regular use of Blackgate, the English graveyard filled with hundreds and thousands of the dead interred for over a century. While not quite that extensive, it appeared likely that over fifty thousand corpses lay beneath their feet. Impressive considering the small size of San Pedro. But there were a lot of civil wars in the last century. That did make for a higher than average death rate.

To many, a lonely, dark, foggy graveyard would be a source of terror. Childhood nightmares of ghouls and ghosts would come to mind, especially in so silent a location. This cemetery was distant from the main city, a district dominated by the Santo Leonardo Prison. The high stone walls loomed off in the distance, a beacon of illumination in the stygian darkness. According to legend, the prison shipped their oldest prisoners to this graveyard, burying them alive to save on the cost of medicine and food. The story was probably merely a legend to demonstrate the sinister nature of the penitentiary. But the tales did cause locals to avoid the location at all cost.

Elizabeth consulted the map several times as well as her compass while searching for the grave. Hugh discovered the location ten minutes earlier by counting the rows and numbers of graves. But he knew better than to mention that fact to Elizabeth. To do so would be to invite a long lecture on the exact method of performing every action. Best to merely keep the comments to himself and get the shovels.

The earth was loose and wet, difficult to move. Digging in such soil quickly tired them out, forcing them to take frequent water breaks for well over an hour. Finally Hugh's shovel struck a solid object. The sound was familiar, that of a poorly made wooden box substituted as a coffin. They discovered these caskets in graveyards throughout the world. It didn't matter the wealth of the individual buried. There were many wealthy men and women in this world who were fortune enough to be fully placed in the ground. The relatives of these deceased persons were more interested in their inheritance than memorializing the dead.

Unearthing the coffin, the attached the block and tackle to their borrowed wagon. With a few short pulls, the casket was raised and pushed into the wagon. They were about to begin covering the coffin with boxes and blankets when a light suddenly appeared a short distance away.

"Who are you? What are you doing? What are you doing? Are you medical students?" the voice was cracked and high-pitched, growing louder as a harsh yellow light suddenly broke through the murk.

"A guard?" Elizabeth looked to Hugh. She appeared unconcerned as the illumination grew.

Hugh shook his head. "A verger. He lives in a hut near the grounds."

A man appeared a moment later. He was tall and painfully thin with hunched shoulders and watery brown eyes. His nose was long, wide and possessed long, thick hair protruding from the nostrils. The verger was carrying a large lantern in one hand and a small battered shovel in the other.

"You're not medical students. What are you doing? What are you doing? What are you doing?" The verger's voice grew higher pitched and louder each time he asked the question.

"Will he be missed?" Elizabeth asked in English, ignoring the man.

Hugh shook his head. "Doubtful. Lives alone and said to be nearly deaf."

"Acceptable." Elizabeth smiled and lifted her shovel. With a hard swing, she struck the verger in the face. His jaw was shattered and he fell backwards, stunned. Elizabeth swung three more times at the fallen man's skull. The sound of wet meat being slapped grew louder with each strike of the shovel. By the time she stepped back, very little of the verger's skull remained. Elizabeth shattered the facial bones and a red, granulated mass remained.

"Get rid of that." Elizabeth turned away and began covering the casket. More than once in the past a verger or guard interrupted their grave robbing. The results were always the same. Hugh and Elizabeth murdered the guardians of the dead and used the desecrated hole in the ground or tomb and went about their business. The time it took the authorities to discover the body helped their work and often was attributed to professional body thieves.

Hugh pushed the body into the ground and began refilling the hole. Elizabeth joined him a moment later, work that was far faster and more satisfying than the labor of unearthing the grave. Neither spoke as they rapidly completed the replacing of the soil in the cemetery. Though it would easier, and probably safer, to merely leave at this time, in the long view this would be a foolish lapse. By recovering the funerary grounds, there would be little evidence of their passage. This slowed the search for grave robbers, always a preferred path for their less than legal scientific research.

A half hour later, they were riding out of the grave-yard, the only sound audible the soft clip-clopping of the young draft horse pulling the wagon. A few miles away from the cemetery, Elizabeth tossed the shovels off a bridge and into fast moving stream. Useless equipment was always disposed of in that manner by her, a habit acquired after an ax was discovered by a nosy neighbor on their property in New Jersey. That was a bad time, one of their worst moments in their many years of travel.

The woman's name was Mavis and she had spent the majority of her time looking out the window of her home. Elizabeth and Hugh were living in a home of a deceased doctor. The location was perfect. They bought the residence and all of the doctor's equipment from the inheriting nephew. The man, a pharmacy student named Clarke, was delighted by the money and left without looking back.

But they didn't know about Mavis and her young daughters, Gladys and Harriet. They appeared to spend the majority of their time peeking out from beneath her drawing room curtains. And then, when anything hap-pened of even the slightest interest, her piercing voice would call out.

"Henry! Henry! Look and see what those Franck's are doing! Henry! Henry!" the piercing voice would shriek. Her two daughters, especially Gladys, would be huddled by the window, staring out with wide eyes.

For his part, Mavis's husband Henry was disinter-ested in any of the proceedings. He rarely stirred from his seat, spending his time reading the newspaper or reading a book. The rare times he did get up and walk over to the window were amusing. By that time Hugh or Elizabeth heard the shrieks and would get out of sight. Henry's irritated response was almost always the same.

"There is nothing there, Mavis. Come away from the window," followed by a written or a verbal apology. He appeared to love his wife and daughters, but was incapable of comprehending their obsession with gossip.

Hoping to embarrass the woman and end her bizarre behavior, Elizabeth conceived of a plan. One night, an evening with a very bright moon, they went out dressed all in black. They returned hours later, lugging a barely concealed body. They even allowed an arm to be visible as they attempted to stealthily return to their home. They appeared to even peek out of their closed curtains. Their gestures were ridiculous, even theatrical. But, as expected, Mavis believed everything and her voice floated across the street.

"Henry! Henry! Those Francks! They're hiding dead bodies! Call the police! Call them! Call them now!" Mavis's voice was a shriek and several other homes in the neighborhood heard her words clearly.

"Father! Father! I saw it too! Father! Come look! Father!" The older daughter, Gladys was almost as loud as her mother. But even the Jones family at number twelve down the street heard her shouts.

As expected, the local constables were summonsed and knocked upon the door within the hour. Mavis and Gladys watched from behind a phalanx of officers, Henry stood at their side looking very apologetic.

"Mister and Missus Franck?" the oldest of the five officers asked as he stepped closer to the door.

"Yes, sir?" Hugh asked; his accent was plummy, sounding closer to that of a stage actor attempting to sound like royalty. He knew the Yanks loved the sound of the British dialect, believing it made the speaker more intelligent and related to the nobility. Despite all their love for independence, there was an envy of people with titles. It was an odd dichotomy that he was unable to fathom.

The older officer straightened slightly. "My name is Deputy Sheriff Macintosh. We apologize for disturbing you at this late hour. But we received a report from your neighbor that you transported a body into your home. We are sure there is a reasonable explanation, but we must search your home."

"No need, my good sir. Allow us to show you what this good lady viewed." Hugh stepped aside and bowed them all inside. He even waved in Henry, Mavis and Gladys. Harriet was nowhere in sight; no doubt this was past her bed time.

Elizabeth led the small party down the hallway and into the late doctor's surgery. There, on the iron operating table, was a large form, covered in a heavy white sheet. The police stared in shock, staring at Elizabeth and Hugh, hands reaching for their belted revolvers.

"Henry! Henry! I told you! I told you! I told you! A body! It's a body!" Mavis's voice pierced through the walls of the house and floated out throughout the neighborhood. Soon doors in the nearby houses could be heard opening, with the owners filing outside and into the street near Hugh and Elizabeth's home.

"Perhaps you had best explain." Sheriff Macintosh was holding his gun in hand, pointing the weapon at the ground. But his body was tense and his eyes narrowed as he stared at Elizabeth and Hugh.

Hugh nodded and smiled. "I believe you will understand momentarily." He and Elizabeth approached the table, ignoring the rising handguns and pulled off the sheet. The tension in the room was thick and Mavis was biting her knuckles while gripping Henry's hand. Even the normally insouciant Henry was white faced and staring with wide eyes.

There, lying on the table was the body of a man. He was about six feet tall and completely hairless. His chest was open and the organs within were visible for all to see.

Mavis screamed in terror and buried her face in Henry's chest. Several police officers leaped backwards and raised the guns in shaking hands.

"Lower those guns you danged idiots!" Macintosh's voice sliced through the rising tension and he slapped down the extended guns. Holstering his, he stepped over the body and knocked with a large fist on the leg. A hollow sound filled the air, causing even Mavis to gaze with a confused expression on her narrow, pinched face.

"Hollow? Sheriff, bodies aren't hollow." One of the officers, the youngest of the group was the first to speak. He looked like he was about to become sick, but his bewilderment was overcoming his forthcoming nausea.

Sheriff Macintosh looked angry and rolled his narrow eyes. "Bodies aren't hollow? My, oh my, what a brilliant observation! Tell me Eddie, will the sun rise from the east or the wet? Is water wet?"

"Um, the sun..." the young officer named Eddie stammered, looking a little scared now. "Sheriff? I...um..."

"Shut up!" Macintosh looked exasperated and shot Mavis a venomous look. "A dead body? Get over here and look, you pack of foolish flatfoots! And you nosy bodies. Get over here and look!"

The officers, Henry, Mavis and little Gladys crept slowly towards the table. Their every move was slow and filled with tension. Hugh was tempted to drop a bedpan or similar metal object which would cause a loud clatter. He bet Eddie and at least one other present would wet their pants in fright. But he held back, choosing to ignore a possibly very amusing moment.

Everyone present stared down at the dead body. And it was obvious immediately that, while looking human from top to bottom, Hugh and Elizabeth had nothing to be concerned about at this time.

"My husband and I are doctors, sir." Elizabeth's accent was also an affected English which sounded musical to an American ear. To Hugh, her articulation was bordering on mockery of the upper crust Surrey intonations. But to those present, Elizabeth was a great lady of importance and breeding.

"Yes," Hugh drew the word out in the manner of an over-bred ass named Wooster he'd met once in London. The man was wealthy and as silly a fool as one would ever meet. But kindly and friendly at least. Hugh was actually glad they hadn't been forced to kill him, a rare bit of sentiment. "We are designing artificial bodies for medical students and science classes. A business to assist science."

Macintosh tapped on the leg again. "Made of wood and rubber. Saw it immediately. Unlike these dopes!"

He shot his men an angry look. For their part, they holstered their sidearms and looked ashamed at the revelation. But Macintosh's ire grew as he stared at Mavis. She looked suspiciously upon the false corpse, ignoring the acerbic expression that was spreading upon the faces of the lawmen.

"But I'm telling you, I saw a body! A dead one!" Her voice rose again and she looked at Elizabeth with angry, mistrustful eyes.

"Maybe you should spend more time minding your own business, lady." Macintosh's snarling words were accompanied by a mocking sneer. "Or take up knitting. But keep your big bony snoot out of other people's business."

Mavis was about to retort, when Henry clamped a hand over her mouth. He muttered a brief apology and dragged his wife and child out. The police officers soon followed. All muttering their apologies before leaving the house. But the tale spread fast throughout the neighborhood and soon the town. Mavis was discredited and Elizabeth and Hugh were able to continue their work without interruption.

Until the day Hugh accidentally left a bloody ax in the tool shed. They were forced to destroy a failed experiment earlier that day. Elizabeth and Hugh were obtaining corpses from a pauper's graveyard in Newark, a small city not far from their house. Their work was somewhat successful at that time. They succeeded in resurrecting three corpses. But all three were useless. The revenants were crazed, mad, murderous cannibalistic creatures. Little more than brain consuming shambling corpses. The best and only means of destroying these failures was to decapitate them with an ax. The remains were then disposed of with acid.

But one escaped and was captured and killed while consuming a tramp outside town. Hugh tracked the undead beast down and sliced it into pieces. He then buried the remains of their failed work and the dead hobo in an abandoned field. Exhausted, he tossed the soiled ax into the tool shed, deciding to clean the tool after a brief rest.

A strong hand shook him awake several hours later. Elizabeth was by the side of his bed, her face white with fury. "What did you leave in the tool shed?"

Still foggy with sleep, Hugh shook his head several times before understanding her inquiry. "The ax! The one I used to destroy the escaping creature."

Elizabeth slapped him hard across the mouth. "Idiot! Mavis was sneaking about and ran back home with a bundle in hands. She will reveal everything!"

Hugh gasped, the full weight of this mistake filling him with dread. "What can we do?"

Elizabeth frowned and glanced at the wall. That was the direction of Mavis and Henry's home. "We do not have time to fool her a second time. Direct action is required. Do we have any mnophka remaining in our stores?"

Hugh nodded quickly having inventoried the store earlier that week. The horrifyingly powerful hallucinogen was one they used on live subjects to keep them from struggling during vivisection. It was rare and Hugh still didn't know how it was created. Only that a small pharmacy in Innsmouth supplied the drug to Elizabeth for a high price. "Three doses."

"Place all three in saline solution along with a mixture of black lotus. Mavis shall disturb us no longer after this night." Elizabeth smiled, a ghastly sight to behold.

"But Henry and their children?" Hugh had few compunctions about killing others. But he felt sorry for their neighbor. And he'd never stooped to murdering children.

"They left an hour earlier. I believe there is a church function or some other pagan nonsense. They will not be involved this day. Now go!" Elizabeth shooed him away and continued to stare at the wall as he left the room.

Moments later, Hugh knocked on the front door of Mavis's home. As Elizabeth predicted, the gossipy hag spied him through her curtains and fled into the house. While reaching for her telephone, no doubt to call the police, Elizabeth clamped a soaked pad over her nose and mouth. She struggled for a moment before falling limp.

Elizabeth lowered Mavis to the floor, smiling at the euphoric expression across her face. The fact that her eyes were moving in two separate directions was slightly concerning for the woman's health. But in truth, Elizabeth didn't care. She gathered up the ax, left through the back and sneaked back into her home. There she burned the bloody tool as well as a small diary Mavis used to record her observations.

By the time Henry, Gladys and Harriet returned from the church bazaar, they found an astonishing sight in the kitchen. A naked Mavis was dancing with the mop while tossing vegetables on the floor. The family doctor was summonsed and a diagnosis of some type of brain fever was determined. Mavis was transported to a nearby hospital, not returning for two months. And when she did, her memory was irregular. Mavis, formerly a gossipy, observant woman was a shell of her former self. She was a silent ghost of a woman, shuffling from place to place like a sleepwalker, eyes low and shoulders perpetually hunched.

This was a genius form of attack by Elizabeth. Murdering Mavis would have brought far too much scrutiny. But by reducing the woman to a sad, pathetic wreck, the gossip was perpetually discredited. The use of obscure ingredients guaranteed there would be no detection of the drugs which had driven Mavis mad. A perfect plan, and a lucky one. Had Elizabeth not reacted quickly, they might have been captured by the authorities. As it was, they left New Jersey for Boston, when a revenant escaped and began terrorizing the New Jersey swamps.

This was why all tools used in killings were destroyed quickly. Elizabeth wished she could destroy the boat and seamen bringing them back home, but that would invite too many questions. But they were an issue that would have to be confronted in the future.

"The ship will leave at dawn." Hugh knew the question was on Elizabeth's mind. Then the true work would begin. The creation of the mate for Victor Frankenstein's terrible creation, the monster known as Gouroull.

CHAPTER XXIX

"Who are we meeting tonight? Who are we meeting tonight?" Martin Mars straightened his white tie in the mirror. Hans stood to his left, carefully brushing Mars's coat, ensuring that there were no visible blemishes in any way.

"The minister of finance, his family. Also present will be his younger brother, the third ranking general in the army. The others present will be members of the powerful families which rule the country." Hans knew an explosion of anger was coming. This was inevitable, but he was prepared for the coming storm.

"Not the president? Not even the vice-president? Not the president? Not even the vice-president? Am I so unimportant? Am I so unimportant?" Mars's voice was low and hard, his anger unleashed and about to become violent. His hands were balling into fists and his eyes glittered.

"We could meet the president and vice-president. But I believed you wished to meet someone of importance." Hans continued to brush Martin Mars's coat, pretending to be oblivious to the growing rage in his master. That was an important facet of his job, ignoring his employer's unsavory habits. Mars released rage on a regular schedule, at least twice a day. To behave with fright would later cause the man to become embarrassed and overly effusive in his praise. And that would be even more awkward for both Mars and Hans. Best to just let the fury pass without comment.

"Explain what you mean. Explain what you mean." Mars stepped away Hans and leaned down to force the latter to meet his eyes. Confusion was written all over the monster killer's face and his hands were quickly balling into fists and releasing each second.

Hans looked at his master with a careful planned placid expression. He knew the more pathetic and non-threatening he looked, the more seriously Martin Mars would take his statements. This was a method of dealing with the man Hans perfected over their years together.

Clearing his throat, Hans explained: "The president and vice-president are powerful men. The junta that returned the family of the president to power are popular with the masses. But their true power comes from a group of wealthy families. These clans are happy to allow others to sit in the seat. But they control the finances in San Pedro. The president's power is based on that of the army. But if those in charge of trade, banking and finance, were to challenge the military, the army would execute the president. The minister of finance is the most powerful man in San Pedro."

Mars pursed his lips and absorbed the information. He always wished to be favored by the dominant members of any society he encountered. Partially because it would allow him to hunt with impunity. But more importantly, it allowed him the right to claim friendship with legendary figures throughout the world. Like when he was in China and met the dynamic military leader, Chiang Kai-Chek. They enjoyed each other's company immensely and the great man even awarded Mars a medal after the latter killed a goblin who was haunting a river. A great man, Chiang. No doubt he would rule China for decades to come.

"Acceptable, acceptable. But make sure I meet the president at least once before I leave. A photograph of us together is necessary for the records. While you and I know who truly rules this land, others are not so well-read as we, eh, Hans?" Mars chuckled and returned to the mirror, straightening his cuffs with theatrical motions.

"You always know best, master." Hans walked across the room and picked up the invitation. He would attend as his master's servant, an accepted arrangement in this and many other countries. He and others would hover near the great men in the room, whispering names in their ears and ensuring they did not commit any social blunders.

"What else do I need to know? What else do I need to know?" Mars checked to make sure he had his cigarette case, monogrammed lighter and gold-plated fountain pen in his pockets. These were his favorite tools in social situations. The case was filled with an obscure French cigarette prized by the former Emperors of France as well as the former archduke of Austria. The lighter was specially made for him in London and released a soft blue flame that was a sure method of getting attention. And the pen was a gift of a Prussian prince. Martin Mars never smoked and rarely wrote anything other than his name on contracts. But he did like toys which gained him attention from others.

"Avoid all discussion on cats. The former leader of San Pedro, the ancestor of the current president, was known as the 'Tiger of San Pedro.' He is well despised by these men and woman since he executed members of their family in his period as master of this country. Cats of any type, other than the gentle house pet variety, receive angry scorn. Tales of vampires and ghosts are popular in this country. The American film, *London After Midnight*, from some years ago, remains a popular viewing subject." Hans always hired researchers in ad-

211

vance to coming to a country. Preparation was always the best method of success in the world-wide quest Martin Mars conducted. Not killing monsters, but acceptance as a great man in the world.

"I'll tell them of our hunt for the vampire countess of Andalusia. The vampire countess of Andalusia." Mars turned back to the mere and checked the positioning of his cufflinks. They were gold and once belonged to an Italian prince whose family were rumored to practitioners of witchcraft and devil worship. The young man may have come from a dark lineage, but he possessed far different interests. The young prince was more concerned with writing a *magnum opus* about a peasant girl who served as maid servant to a pope who may have been Jesus Christ in disguise. The novel was already over one thousand pages long and the young lass was still cleaning the floor for a minor bishop. No end was in sight, but it did take all his time day and night. To sponsor his "art," he'd taken to selling personal possessions. The family already prevented his sale of the family villa and artwork and were deciding whether to force him into a marriage or replace him with a younger sibling.

Hans nodded and smiled. "Very good master. The most important families all trace their lineage to Spain. Even the ones with no connection created tales of heroic adventurers coming to these shores. Spanish lineage is very prized, master."

What Hans also knew was that the true story of the vampire woman of southern Spain was far less exciting than the tale Martin Mars would recite. The vampire in question was an ancient being, but stunningly lovely woman, named Luisa. She claimed ancient lineage by birth, having told all that she was one of the infamous Karnstein clan. Both Martin Mars and Hans doubted this to be a fact. The Karnstein clan was more of a myth than reality, based on their studies. Who could believe several dozen women who preferred other women to men? They both agreed that was a myth, all women desired men first and foremost.

This Countess Luisa lived in the stone ruins of an ancient castle she claimed was owned by her noble husband. All knew she resided in these ruins in the district. This was no secret to the locals; they wisely avoided her castle. Actually the parents of the area used evil Luisa as a figure of fear. Disobedient or naughty children were threatened with the notion of being given to evil vampire for food.

Why did the people of the area ignore a monster in the midst? The answer was soon apparent when Martin Mars and Hans visited the location. Luisa rarely ventured past the grounds of her ruin. She fed mostly on the plentiful rats of the district and the occasional traveler. And as recompense for being left alone, she protected the district from other predators. Murderers under the guise of knights, traveling bands of French deserters, members of the Inquisition looking for people to torture... Luisa would consume them all and leave no traces of their passage. A good arrangement.

But Martin Mars found such creatures to be offenses against nature and mankind. Unwilling to allow her to live, he formulate a very simple plan. Spying on her from a distance, they observed her movements for two days. Like all long-lived beings, she was a being whose habits were ingrained in her very being. Twice every evening she walked to a small balcony and stared into the darkness for exactly ten minutes. That was where they would strike.

In the next day, Hans climbed up to the balcony and lowered himself just below the base. There he placed a small, heavily muffled box. Then he retreated they watched the stone edifice from a safe distance. At precisely two o'clock in the morning, an explosion echoed through the area. They rushed to the castle and found the balcony and a good portion of the wall destroyed. Hans's bomb operated exactly as predicted. The clockwork timer set off the bundle of dynamite and black powder and decimated the stone structure instantly.

As to Countess Luisa, she was easy to discover. Her torn and battered body lay beneath a pile of heavy masonry. A human would be dead from the injuries, impact or the pile of stones pinning her chest to the ground. But being an undead creature, Luisa was vainly struggling to free herself and find a mean to continue her extended existence. She hissed at Martin Mars and Hans, the sharp incisors, pale skin and red eyes confirming her inhumanity. But Luisa was unable to free herself or produce more than weak sibilant sounds.

Without a word, Martin Mars chopped off Luisa's head with his heavy, sharp cavalry saber. He watched as the hair and skin slowly vanished from her head, leaving behind a skull with inhuman fangs. The body also deflated and was reduced to mere bones, many of which were shattered.

Hans searched for and found Luisa's coffin. He lugged it up and they interred the broken body within and left the area within the hour. Not a dramatic method of destroying monsters, but effective. Martin Mars was always willing to talk of battling the horrors of the Earth, but his preferred methods were always pragmatic.

This meant that tonight he would tell of a fiendish, beautiful, powerful, bloodsucking vampire queen. She would terrorize the poor and seduce the foolish. Who were the ones she enticed changed depending on his audience. For a group of bankers who were angry at their government for taxing them, the stupider victims were government agents. Other victims included foppish stupid wealthy men, anarchists, journalists and holy men. Martin Mars knew the best method to keep his listeners enthralled.

The story would include a terrible battle, a life or death struggle. But Mars would emerge triumphant, the evil creature dying while cursing all life. Usually these battles were physical affairs, the unholy power of the monster pitted against the brave skills of the modern knight of good, Martin Mars. They were good tales, ripped straight out of the magazines Mars enjoyed reading. Those stories were rather simplistic, the hero always triumphed, the villain was either captured or died screaming. Nothing like reality, but the truth was not their business.

Hans's part of the story varied as well. Usually he was the blundering butler who carried his master's weapons while shaking with fright. Occasionally his duty was to be a prisoner of the monster, rescued from death by the masterful foe of evil, Martin Mars. And at other times, his presence was totally removed. No matter the version, Hans would stand by his master's word. His ultimate duty was to be a faithful hound who was able to speak words of respect and loyalty to his owner.

"Anything else? Anything else?" Mars took the invitation and lead the way out of their suite. A car was waiting for them, taking them to the finance minister's home.

Hans nodded once. "The general, brother to the minister? He recently married a young lady. She attended school with his eldest son. Very beautiful. He is insanely jealous of anyone who pays any attention to her. Called out two men for duels of honor."

"What is the advice of your informant? What is the advice of your informant?" Mars strode through the hallway, heading for the elevator. His walk was based on the triumphant strut of an army commander. They had once observed a man as he had accepted medals from his president. Since that time, Mars based his walk on that warrior's confident march.

"Treat the young woman in question with the same respect you would demonstrate for an elderly matron of society. You'll honor the general and his bride, and he will have no concern for your interest in his wife." Hans explained, grateful that the services they hired in this country were so detailed. Whoever this Clyde Burke was, his information was excellent, no matter where they happened to require intelligence.

Martin Mars didn't reply. He merely walked with his confident air into the elevator, ignoring the operator. The performance had already begun.

CHAPTER XXX

"Master?" the slave asked, approaching the great man. As expected, he was seated on his gold and wooden chair, a seat of importance. The slave dropped to his knees and pressed his head to the ground, waiting for the word that he should rise. He knelt there for a great length of time, the hard stone floor hurting his knees and back.

"You may speak." The Master's voice was barely audible, a soft rustling sound that was quite alien in intonation.

The servant, his head still pressed against the cold stone floor, closed his eyes and began to recite: "Mighty silver hawk, master of the desert wind, the seers greet you and stated that the confluence is imminent. All the players are moving to the positions as predicted."

The Master did not reply. Only silence filled the chamber. Even the flickering flames of the braziers appeared hushed and silent as the time stretched. Finally there was a rustling as the great man rose. His slow footfalls could be heard, vanishing in the distance.

The servant rose and stretched his knees and back. The great one was more silent than usual lately. The events he insisted the seers view appeared unimportant to his eyes. Groups coming together in a distant jungle seemed to be a waste of time. There were so many other events of terrible importance. What of the mad sorcerer and his followers who were controlling the inner circle of the National Socialists of Germany? Or the scientists who wished to execute millions of Russians to support an engine that would bring ancient sleeping gods back to this world? Were they not the most terrible problems the world must face at this time?

But the servant knew it was not his place to question the ways of the great one. The Master possessed a different vision of the world than the common mortals. He was great and ancient. He was not all-knowing, but he did appear to see the world with the clear vision of an outsider. The servant knew better than to question the great one's reasoning.

Backing out of the room, the servant scurried down the corridor and sat on a stool near a doorway. Either the Master would summons him, or the seers would use him to send messages. This was his place in the world. And it was a good one. He served a mere sixteen hours each day. His mate cleaned walls eighteen hours daily; she was not so exalted in the eyes of the Master. Perhaps one day she would rise to a great post such as furniture duster. Then her hours would drop to sixteen. But the Master would know when she was ready.

Until such time, the servant would do as demanded and waited on his stool. Like his father and his father and all throughout the ages, his family dedicated their lives to the great ones. There was no other higher calling.

CHAPTER XXXI

Hugh stared at the corpse lying on the metal table. He was struck immediately by the overwhelming scent that filled the air, overwhelming the chemical odors that permeated the very walls. He knew these stenches all too well, having lived many years surrounded by corpses of the recently executed. They were often Elizabeth's favorite choices for experimentation. Her reasoning was that the majority of those executed by the state were unwanted by society. Few, if any, mourned their passing. Therefore any despoiling of their grave would go unnoticed. Occasionally, a guard attempted to intervene, but they dealt with such nuisances in a simple manner. Kill them and dispose of the body in the same grave.

The first scent was always the same, dried shit and piss. One fact uncovered by writers and journalists present at the executions was this smell. A corpse voided their bowels shortly after death. Not romantic, so often forgotten by those writing of the death of a criminal. In particularly heinous cases, the dead body was merely checked to ensure they were definitely deceased. Then they were simply tossed into a coffin of pine box for burial. No care was given to ensure a peaceful passing. They were dead meat, rotted flesh meant to be disposed of before the foul aroma lingered.

The second scent was always a surprise in each executed corpse. No two were alike and Hugh always found the sensation a surprise. The smell was that of the last meal of the victim, consumed usually shortly before being dragged to their execution. In the case of this woman, the odor was that of spoiled chicken and rice. Unpleasant, yes, but not nearly as bad as the man they had unearthed in Germany. He'd consumed fruit and vegetables prior to being hanged. A disgusting smell, that took weeks to remove from one's clothing.

And the final smell was the one that always took the longest to rise and fill the air. A sweet odor with a terrible tang, a pleasant scent that grew more horrific with each passing second. The smell of rot and corruption. All corpses released this fragrance in time. Hugh knew that, in the end, this was the ultimate fate of life. Unless Elizabeth succeeded. Then, there was the possibility of avoiding such a pathetic passing.

The corpse itself was of some interest. The woman was, despite her blackened face and protruding tongue, somewhat attractive. Tall and angular, almost regal. She might have been a bedmate capable of interesting sexual perversions. That could make up for her tiny breasts and almost non-existent rear end. Elizabeth possessed similar proportions, but no whore could match Elizabeth for creativity in sexual congress.

Still, Hugh considered that a little cold flesh wouldn't bother him much. Elizabeth would be a little longer out of the lab. She was retrieving supplies to begin mixing the compounds they required for the two elixirs. Cutting away and destroying the clothing, he stared at the body. While not his first choice for a bit of fun, beggars couldn't be choosers, as the saying went.

But then a movement to his left caused him to turn. A shadow crossed the window, a mere flash of darkness blocking the streaming sunlight. Hugh immediately comprehended the full import of that simple view. His heart began beating quickly and his breath came in ragged gulps. Gouroull was present, observing the proceedings. The fiend was capable of uncanny stealth. Yet he wished Hugh to know of his presence.

Hugh knew this was the monster's warning. This was Gouroull's method of ensuring that his mate was unsullied by the actions of any, even Elizabeth Frankenstein's assistant. It was easy enough to forget that the monster was a thinking being with a fiendish intelligence. When one read of the terrible acts Gouroull visited upon humanity, it would be easy to simply toss these aside as the deeds of a murderous, non-thinking beast.

Yet there was a sadistic genius behind many of these assaults upon humanity. The assault upon a hobo in Ireland was often viewed in such a manner. Yet Elizabeth's research revealed that the tramp, a disgusting, lustful pig named Vrollo, had sought to control Gouroull as a mindless beast. A foolish move. Anyone who treated him as a brute was a fool. But they were not long-lived fools. Gouroull ensured as much.

But most telling to Hugh was the often repeated tale of the false holy man named Schleger. That Nietszchean obsessed ass wished to use Gouroull to create a race of supermen. Therefore he wished to mate the monster with kidnapped girls. Hugh supposed the ultimate strategy was to birth demi-gods, all under Pastor Schleger's wise guidance. But the kidnapped girls were far too frightened of the monster to be of any use. Each was killed by Gouroull's hand, sad but probably merciful ends to those poor females. But the monster's rage exploded and he had raped Schleger's wife Ingrid, murdered the false prophet and vanished for a time.

These two actions were clearly reported by very reputable sources. The doctor who attempted to treat Ingrid for her remaining days was the first. His notes, stolen by an orderly of the Hallshofen Lunatic Asylum told of a tormented woman, a victim of the violence of the creature known as Gouroull. The doctor himself was killed by the fiend who believed Ingrid had given birth to his child. This was a foolish notion on the part of Gouroull. He could no more mate with a human than a human could with an ape. While similar, they were two distinct species. No crossbreeding was possible.

As to Ingrid, she hanged herself in her cell at the notion of the monster's return into her life. This demonstrated the horrific, malevolent intellect behind that of Gouroull. While he could have simply slaughtered Schleger in his rage, he chose a more monstrous route. Raping poor Ingrid was the creature's means of tormenting the man who failed him in his quest for a mate. Ingrid's horrific treatment by Gouroull was both an assault upon the woman and her husband. This demonstrated the dreadful demonic mentality at the core of the miscreation that was Victor Frankenstein's monster.

Which was why, in the present day, Hugh Larkin stepped away from the still form on the metal table. For him to even consider conflicting with Gouroull would be an act of suicidal madness. He could no more battle the monster than he could empty the ocean with a spoon. The lethal elemental force that was Gouroull would destroy him utterly. And Hugh had little doubt that the death would be one of slowly mounting agonized anguish. That was the message Gouroull sent to Hugh, by allowing his presence to be known.

But Hugh also realized that this afforded him a level of safety as well. Gouroull required him to assist Elizabeth. As long as he fulfilled this position and did not cross the now established rule, Hugh would be safe from the monster's wrath.

Of course, this security was tenuous at best. They were about to attempt to fully recreate the experiment of the legendary Victor Frankenstein. As far as history was concerned, this operation was a single success. Gouroull was created and still existed over a century later. But Victor had not expected the results he'd received. Instead of a docile, decent, dog-like follower, he birthed a demonic apex predator in the form of a human male. And this fiend was a slave to no man, a being unwilling to conform to the whims of the man whose science had brought him to life. Should Elizabeth fail, as so many other scientists had in past days, their lives would be in permanent peril.

And Hugh also comprehended that in success, their lives were also at risk. Could Elizabeth convince Gouroull to allow them to survive after he had his mate? Probably. Her scientific acumen and force of personality persuaded the monster to allow them to survive after Gouroull believed he had witnessed their betrayal. Elizabeth would need to apply such skills in a very short time. If they failed, she could inform Gouroull that they were still committed towards his demands. If they succeeded... Hugh wasn't sure what her point of argument would be to keep them alive. But no doubt, she had something prepared for this eventuality.

Elizabeth appeared a few seconds later, a cart of bottles and a pair of fresh, sterile mortars and pestles in her hands. The cart also possessed eight hypodermic needles, each new, covered and gleaming in the light.

Rolling up her sleeve, Elizabeth produced a needle. She tapped her vein and injected herself with a double dose of ephedrine. She closed her eyes and shook for a moment, then opened and looked to Hugh.

"Dose yourself. We shall work without stopping until the experiment is complete. If it all goes as I believe it will, Gouroull's mate will live." Elizabeth deposited a hypodermic needle filled with the drug on the table.

Hugh pulled up his sleeve and, in a moment, injected himself with the powerful stimulant. His mind suddenly became more active and he forgot all fears regarding Gouroull and their future. All that matter was getting their work done now.

"Begin grinding the Deep One scales and then mix it with ghoul's flesh. Precise measurements, Hugh. I don't want the slightest variation. And ensure no extraneous matter is added. If a fly so much as touches the table, you are to dump it and start over. Is this completely understood?" Elizabeth stepped over to her own table and pulled on gloves, mask and glasses. Hers were the more dangerous and corrosive chemicals, a mixture capable of melting the flesh off your arm in the blink of an eye.

"Yes, Elizabeth." Hugh smiled her way, knowing she would not notice his show of affection. But he still hoped she recognized he was working with such bizarre chemicals in this remote location for her. Always for her. In the end, that was the most important facet in his universe. Friends, colleagues, lovers, reputation, home, they were all temporary parts in the life of Doctor Hugh Larkin. Elizabeth Frankenstein, noble-born doctor and scientist, was all that mattered. Perhaps creating Gouroull's mate would return them to the world they were both born to, and resided in, for the majority of their lives. They could live openly in Edinburgh, London, Paris, and so many other places. No longer keeping to the shadows, residing in half-savage lands most good Europeans never knew existed. Or perhaps not. All that mattered was Elizabeth. All for Elizabeth.

CHAPTER XXXII

The Living were ready to move to their new home. The rafts were packed, the fishing boats were filled, and every member of the tribe was working to finalize the change in their lives. Oddly, they were all excited by the future. Even the grumblers seemed to be looking forward to a new life and direction. They didn't even know if their tribe would remain known as The Living. Could the change in homes also transform the deeper truths of their existence? They didn't know, but were looking forward to learning the new ways.

Old Moraika sat upon a rock, almost forgotten by the tribe. She leaned on her cane and watched their every movement. It was almost as if she was drinking in the sensations of the ordinary lives of The Living. No movement was missed, not Khuno the hunter's jokes of walking on the water, or Pacha's complaints of his probable position on the raft. Every moment appeared important to the twisted crone.

And this was truth. Moraika embraced her coming end. She lived more lives than every member of the tribe combined. Death was just a step to her. She would join in the memory of the Moraika's before her, alive in the mind of the new wise woman. That was her second to last duty.

The passing of her place in the tribe would only occur when she fell. But she needed to choose her successor. A young girl, one who would use the knowledge to make the transition to The Living becoming river-dwellers complete. No matter the age, the new Moraika would be respected as the wise woman of the tribe. The ancient knowledge was respected and would be revered as it had since days long forgotten.

But who? She discounted the older women. They were too set in their ways, too believing they knew the truth. They could not embrace and become one with the memories and lives of the Moraika's from before. No, only a child could accept they were a unique being who lived to serve Allpa and Supay.

Moraika heard that the blancos and other outsiders had ones who learned the ways of the universe from books. Who changed the words of the spirits to fit their personal views of the world? How could any call those beings holy? A wise man or woman served the powers of the universe. That was why she and the jungle shaman were the voices of the spirits among their tribe. They did not rule. They steered their people towards their mission. Serving and protecting the land. To believe otherwise seemed quite insane in the labyrinthine mind of ancient Moraika.

Three girls were possible. They were all of similar ages, all intelligent and hard-working. That set them up as possible successors. But one she soon eliminated. The young girl was too demanding, attempting to woo or bully the other boys and girls. Such a wise woman would become a tyrant in time, a monster who would use her antediluvian knowledge as a weapon to control the tribe. A queen could not serve the spirits. Without humility, her mission would be lost in favor of her own views of how best to protect the lands.

The remaining two were both good children, though one was just a little shier than the other. She waited for others to speak before she joined in conversations and yielded to the demands when battling appeared unimportant. Moraika watched her with investigative eyes.

Was this humility that led her to choose to allow others to have their way? Or fear? If the latter, than she was unsuitable. Allpa and Supay were beings from beyond. They were all life and all death. A fear-filled follower would fail in a short time. They needed one who obeyed their laws and ways, yet walked through the world without terror at the universe's many perils.

And so old Moraika sat and watched. The two girls helped The Living in their final preparations for the great move. The jolly atmosphere caused many to sing as the rafts were checked again, the food wraps examined to ensure they were secure and safe. Their wise woman was almost forgotten, her tiny form as unmoving and disconnected from them as a stone along the sand shore.

But finally, she rose and approached the girl. Though cautious at the first look, there was an inner strength in this child that made her the proper choice. She allowed others to win battles because they were unimportant. When she saw a wrong about to occur, she steered the others towards a better path. Moraika realized this was a willingness to work with others rather than fear. Humility, a rare commodity among the young.

This insight arrived over a toy, a tiny round yellow stone. One of the little boys wanted it, but the one in passion looked reluctant to share. The quiet girl intervened, made the holder of the toy realize he could have more fun if they all made a game involving all. The simple solution prevented angry words and concerns from the adults of selfish behavior, one of the true sins among The Living.

That was the way of the wise, the holy path of the Moraika. She lived for her duty to Allpa, Supay and every life in their lands. The wise woman could, under the wrong hands, become an oppressor, using her knowledge to destroy any who rejected her demands. But then all life would begin to fail, the world would torn apart in favor of humans rather than coexisting with mankind. Metals and stones within the soil would ripped, spoiling the plants and animals and leaving behind a world of dust and ashes. All for the glory of an ancient sovereign who lost their way.

Only a humble advisor could receive the mantle of the Moraika. To allow anyone else was a final failure. And Moraika never miscarried her mission.

Her choice made, she stood and caught the girl's eye. Her name was unimportant. Soon enough, she would use another. Raising a gnarled dark finger, Moraika called the girl to her side.

"Do not speak, child." Moraika pulled a small white saucer from her pouch. This was the head cap of Father Pupo, now a special sacred drinking bowl.

Moraika poured a blue liquid into the saucer and handed the bowl to the girl. The child held the cup in two tiny hands, her large eyes staring the twisted crone. There was both fear and interest in those young orbs and Moraika sensed she had made the correct choice.

Pricking her left pointing finger with a stone blade, the wise woman dripped three drops of blood into the liquid. The fluid darkened slightly, becoming almost black. Moraika waited and watched as the potion slowly transformed back to the original blue shade and nodded to herself. It was time.

"Drink." Moraika did not explain why she issued this command. She knew the child would obey. All obeyed the demands of the wise woman of The Living.

The girl swallowed the potion in three quick, greedy gulps. Moraika still knew the taste of the liquid, an odd but pleasant bitter mixture which slowly turned sweet in your mouth.

Taking the bowl back, Moraika thrust it back in her pouch. She then lifted the ancient skin sack from her waist and placed it around the girl's neck. Moraika then placed her primordial black stone blade in the child's hand and repeated a series of antediluvian eldritch phrases before stepping back. She felt older and even more tired, but the work was complete.

"You will be the Moraika. Soon enough. You will know when." Moraika almost cackled at the confused expression upon the girl's face. It was mirror of her own all so many seasons ago.

Raising a withered claw to silence the child, Moraika shook her head. "All will be as it will be. Worry not. Go now. I will tell them I will join them soon enough. I shall."

With that said, old Moraika, wise woman and crone of the tribe known as The Living, hobbled back to the stone seat. Tonight. Tonight would be her last night. But not now that the choice was made. There would always be a Moraika.

CHAPTER XXXIII

Elizabeth Frankenstein checked the positioning of the needle wheel for the tenth time. She knew this was the tenth time because that was the number she determined was necessary to ensure the perfection of this operation. No elements could be left the chance. Each link of the lowering chains was examined three times in finite detail. The wires leading to the electrical generator performed optimum after five tests. And the amazing generators were also tested ten times to ensure the exact flow of current. The needles were as sharp and strong as the metal allowed. And all the surfaces were free of any contaminating substances.

As to the potions, that took the longest. Each needle was checked with minute fastidiousness, Elizabeth's actions bordered on mania. Hugh was forced to recreate three elixirs because of imagined contamination. But Elizabeth was resolute. Failure, if it occurred, would be caused by science and science alone. Not because of any outside force, such as a short-sighted, if excellent medical man like Spratt forced them to pull her funding. Or because a passing policeman heard the sounds of their machines and investigated at the wrong moment. Or a tramp informed a clergyman who led a mob to their home to destroy all their work. In this desolate villa with nobody nearby, they were safe from such encumbrances. The savages nearby were of no importance. They never approached the house and did not even possess the most rudimentary weapons of war. But to be safe, Hugh spied upon their village. Happily he reported they appeared to be migrating somewhere. Final proof that their venture was to proceed.

If there was any surprise, it was Gouroull. He was spotted by Elizabeth several times. He did not venture within the laboratory. Instead he prowled outside the building, circling at odd intervals like a hunting jungle cat. She'd been positive that her ancestor's creation would wish to be present. But the monster demonstrated no desire to approach the building.

Elizabeth thought of bringing the observation up to Hugh, but decided against the action. Her assistant was frightened of Gouroull. This was a healthy and under-standable response. The monster was frightening, lethal and capable of unexpectedly insightful methods of demonstrating his prowess. Elizabeth needed Hugh fo-cused upon the job at hand, nothing else.

And she did have her own theory of the fiend's lack of interest in approaching the lab. At first, she thought it was fear. The last time a Frankenstein was attempting to create a mate, terror caused by the monster's dreadful visage had frightened Victor to the core of his being. He destroyed the proto-female and refused to assist his mis-creation in mating with another of his kind. To Victor, Gouroull was the embodiment of evil, a demonic ogre whose very presence was a blight upon the Earth. To scientifically birth a metaphorical Eve for the Adam of his labors would be an anathema to his very existence. And this lead to his hunt for Gouroull, who fled in the face of his creator. Perhaps the creature believed Victor possessed the secret of his destruction. The memories of that terrible time could cause Victor's monster to fear entry into a lab of a Frankenstein.

But Elizabeth discounted that belief as folly. Gouroull was unafraid of her or her science. He did not possess the aversions to the past that would plague a normal man, for he was not human. No, fear did not keep the monster at bay this day.

Elizabeth believed the emotion that kept the creature circling and watching was far more basic. Protectiveness. Gouroull was still subject to some basic biological imperative, to exist, to mate, to protect his own. Elizabeth surmised that the fiend believed in the success of this venture and was intent on ensuring none interfered. Gouroull, too, left nothing to chance, knowing that humanity was capable of destroying this process on the eve of success. Far too many times his mate had nearly been within his grasp, only to be destroyed mere moments before awakening.

That in mind, Elizabeth Frankenstein was surer of her imminent success. With the human element removed, all that remained was the science. And she was as visionary as her ancestor, Victor. Once this operation was completed the real work began. Refining the process, increasing the strength of the creature. Could the square cubed law be overcome and the giants of ancient myth emerge from her laboratory? Elizabeth would explore all avenues. For in the end, nature would be the slave of Elizabeth Frankenstein. Only her imagination and time could hold her back from spawning the races which would replace mankind upon this planet. Centuries from now, the myths of creation would have a new name for god: Frankenstein.

The most difficult part would be the substances used in said creation. Victor utilized elements and the flesh and lifeblood of creatures unknown to science. Some were positively strange. The scales of a Deep One. The only hint she possessed of what a Deep One was came from a pamphlet by a psychotic imprisoned in an asylum in the United States. Fishmen? Immortal ones who mated with humans? The tale was cockamamie, to use a Yank term. Yet she possessed a store of such grey-green tissue in her store room.

Additionally some of the elements were positively ridiculous. The black stones from the Vampire City of Selene? How was that necessary in any way? The difficulty was attempting to determine the balance between Victor's spiritual notions and the realities of science.

Completing the final checks, Elizabeth thrust the leads into the body as the whine of the generators climbed in intensity. Her reflexive mood always led her to the same question at these moments. How did Victor produce enough electricity to power his experiment? There were times in the modern world when this was a great struggle for Elizabeth. And this was a time when great minds like Fen-Chu, Tesla, Rukh, Edison and Daka were making strides in the generation of power through various means. But her ancestor managed to somehow, centuries earlier, produce massive power. Electricity at Victor's time was an almost mythical element of the universe. Oh, it was known to exist. One could merely watch a thunderstorm to learn of the substance. And the simple parlor trick of generating static electricity was probably as old as mankind. But to achieve a means of intentionally creating such energy with the crude science of the past was a remarkable achievement unto itself.

Her theory was he utilized the most obvious element, lightning. Through the use of metallic kites and wires the proper amount of electricity would be harnessed. The places he chose for his experiments were storm-battered lands. The winds were perpetually howling and vast powerful tempests raged day and night. It might take several attempts, but Victor Frankenstein, like his modern ancestor, was obsessed with their work. Every difficulty would be overcome, electricity being no exception to the rule.

Hugh's theories were far wilder and odder. At first he believed Victor designed a device which was generated by the power of the human body. Bicycles or walking feet on a moving platform could empower a turbine which would then yield electricity. He abandoned this theory when, through the use of simple arithmetic, that this would require a minimum of twenty turbines, each powered by thirty-five or more adults.

His next theory was far wilder. Hugh held, at that time, that Victor had in his possession dozens of electric eels. Each, when angered, would empower a device. While a slightly better theory than the previous notion, there were serious flaws in the conception. For example, the care and feeding of such beasts would be a major undertaking requiring a staff of assistants. And also another difficulty was obvious to Elizabeth, if not to Hugh. How would one anger and induce dozens of such beasts to assault with their electrical charge at the exact same moment? She humorously suggested that reading the political debates of the period might annoy the creatures. Or possibly the eels were infuriated by the poetry of the times. Elizabeth herself had sympathy, such wastes of time caused her to wish for the power to shock the reader to death. Hugh brooded over the mocking for a short time, but then agreed the cognitive content of his hypothesis was flawed.

Lately he muttered something about a combination of wind power and the tidal movements creating a charge. That was a more sensible solution and Elizabeth told him as much. But she did raise the fact he missed there were no windmills near the two labs Victor Frankenstein used in his experiments. She conceded they may have been destroyed by time, but the remains appeared to be missing as well. Still, at least he was thinking on the subject. Hugh was not a particularly creative scientist, but he was excellent in his own way. Elizabeth prized his dog-like devotion to her and commitment to her work. Once they successfully created Gouroull's mate, she would accept his standing request and marry him in a small ceremony. But Elizabeth would not change her name. She was a Frankenstein and that would be the name that would change the world.

"We are approaching full charges, Elizabeth." Hugh appeared in the lab and moved to his station. He pulled on his mask, goggles and heavy gloves and gripped the metal lever with a shaky hand. "Wheel is ready."

Moving to her place, Elizabeth checked the dials and nodded once, "Lower the wheel. We begin."

Hugh threw the switch. The creation of Gouroull's mate commenced...

CHAPTER XXXIV

Gouroull prowled. He circled the villa containing the Frankenstein laboratory, knowing his very presence kept even the meanest insects from approaching the location. Nature, in all its red fury of tooth and claw, recognized that he was the most dangerous presence in the jungle that day. Instinctively, the animal kingdom recognized danger and did their level best to avoid its passage. On land, he was one of the apex predators, death to anything that crossed his path. Perhaps those leviathans known as elephants were more dangerous on land, but few other animals upon the Earth were his match.

There was a creature had Gouroull learned of who possessed the same place he occupied within this world. They were a species so powerful, so dangerous, that only man's technology were capable of defeating them in battle. They were an ocean predator known as the killer whale. These beasts were massive, immensely strong, and capable of destroying any animal they chose to attack.

One time, while walking on the floor of Arctic Ocean, he had spied a killer whale challenging a shark. He had heard tales of sharks, the creatures who invoked the most fear among humans when speaking of ocean life. Gouroull had heard these sea monsters were the creatures of ancient myths, antediluvian marauders capable of bringing low even the mightiest man. In his mind, the shark was like an oceanic titan of myth, a monstrosity from ancient times, still dwelling within the murky depths of the sea.

But then, he witnessed the killer whale. The beast was monstrous, almost as titanic as his enormous krill-consuming brothers. Yet, this black and white specter moved with a liquid grace within the churning currents. The killer whale, though massive, was far faster than any being that size should be capable. And it attacked with the ferocity that reminded Gouroull of himself. The shark was destroyed after one strike of the killer whale's massive tail fin, and a bit that nearly ripped the dying shark in twain. An impressive, if alacritous demonstration of power.

And that was the moment when Gouroull understood his place in the universe. Though mankind, at times, hunted him in their fear, in the end he was their superior. Their weapons did give them the ability to approach him with some confidence, but in the end, they were weak, soft creatures who possessed few natural gifts. Their power was in their fiendish minds. This terrible innate gift that allowed them to recognize their lesser place in the battle for survival. And as a means of compensating, they designed weapons of such destructive power that they risked to unmake all of creation.

In the last two millennia, humanity had moved from striking each other on the head with rocks and bones to bombs capable of killing whole cities. They stabbed each other with pieces of metal they tore from the Earth and produced gases so poisonous that no life could survive even after the most infinitesimal exposure. They slaughtered each other because of their different appearances or methods of worshiping, and chose to prize colored stones over their fellow man. They were selfish, foolish, short-sighted and destructive. All characteristics that made him their enemy. Not because Gouroull was a paragon of virtue. Not in the least. But because he was the more honest product of their race. Gouroull recognized he was all that they secretly prized within their hearts. But, unlike humanity, he did not pretend to be righteous.

Victor had recognized this truth. He had attempted to reject Gouroull by refusing the creation of his mate. There was a line, torn from Victor's diary, that the monster remembered. It demonstrated a rare insight and perspicacity in the man. He wrote a phrase that confirmed all that Gouroull believed of himself, one he embraced completely since birth. The words were simply this:

"I shuddered to think that future ages might curse me as their pest, whose selfishness had not hesitated to buy its own peace at the price, perhaps, of the existence of the whole human race."

It was then that Gouroull had recognized the danger of his creator. Victor had designed him; he could have a method of unmaking his work. In a real sense, Frankenstein was his God, and the fiend was his Adam. And like the biblical originator of all, Victor became enraged by his genesis. Which led Gouroull to flee before a being he could stamp out with little effort. Because, like his earlier thoughts upon mankind, the endlessly inventive evil of humanity made them almost impressive.

But in the end, Victor Frankenstein had died. Unlike his creation, the Arctic wastes had destroyed the man. One of the finest minds in history, a being capable of creating life from the dust, had died because he was unable to survive in a harsh environment. Gouroull continued, his uniqueness a protection against the planet's worst elements.

Sniffing the air, Gouroull sensed the approach of man. No, not the tangy stench of their sweat or the coppery smell of their blood. Not even the rotted meat or alcohol they consumed that seemed to exude from their very pores. No, this was an aroma that was theirs and theirs alone. The scent was acrid and sour, charcoal-filled with just a hint of burnt metal. Once sensed, it could not be mistaken for anything else in the universe. This was the smell of gunpowder. This was mankind's true cologne, the bouquet that permeated from the very core of their being. For what other substance was utilized for the extermination of millions of their own species, not to mention enormous segments of the animal kingdom?

Gouroull loped into the stygian darkness, approaching the spoor. There were two and they smelled... unusual. They both consumed alcohol, meat and tobacco. But the stench of scorched metal and fire hung about one of the pair. They moved at a moderate pace and were approaching the house from the nearby dock.

This could not be allowed. Gouroull would not permit the approach of any man or beast on this day. Elizabeth Frankenstein must be allowed to complete her work without interruption. This day would not be subject to the extraneous outside forces which had plagued all previous attempts at the creation of his mate. If success eluded him, it would be because of a failure of science, not the intervention of an enemy.

Moving swiftly and silently, a gray specter in the darkness, Gouroull moved towards the approaching men. They were talking in loud unconcerned voices. And one of the pair's movements hit the ground with a heavy, destructive tread he could feel through the soles of his shoes. Very odd.

But even odder was a series of missing scents. The tribe of men and woman who lived a short distance from the Frankenstein villa were gone. There were lingering odors in the air of their recent passage, but they had left the vicinity sometime that morning. Very odd. Why did the savages abandon their homes? Did they recognize that Elizabeth's true work was about to commence? No, that appeared unlikely. They possessed no true technology beyond that of their Stone Age ancestors. The experiment taking place within the villa above was centuries beyond their meanest comprehension.

In the end, it didn't matter. Their lack of presence actually encouraged Gouroull. One fewer human element had been eliminated. But the strangeness of their actions did disturb him to a tiny degree.

"Light a second lantern, Hans. Light a second lantern, Hans. This dark is blacker than a banker's heart. Than a banker's heart." The larger of the two spoke in an excited voice. He was almost as tall Gouroull and far, far heavier. There was an odd metal grinding sound every time he stepped and he was surrounded by the smells of gunpowder, flame, blood and fear.

The smaller of the pair ignited a lantern, filling the air with the harsh tang of kerosene. It was then that Gouroull comprehended the scene far better. The taller of the pair wore a metal and leather harness across his arms, legs and torso. The arms and legs were covered with metal gears and other instruments that whined every time he moved an extremity. But he was carrying, in a pair of metal gauntleted hands, a massive gun and a huge device that smelled of gasoline. This man moved slower than the other, but it was apparent he was able to lug weapons far too heavy and powerful for a single human.

Despite himself, Gouroull was impressed. This man and his follower had created a gimmick capable of producing death and destruction on a monumental scale. An army of such men would exterminate thousands of humans each hour. There was something wonderful about that thought, but it did not deter Frankenstein's creation in the slightest. He would kill these men, despite the fact that he would have been delighted by the spreading of this murderous technology.

"The Frankenstein woman may resist us, Master. May I use my new knives upon her soft skin?" The smaller man possessed a sibilant voice. He almost hissed each word and possessed an undercurrent of whine beneath his statements.

"Yes, of course! Yes, of course! Enjoy! Enjoy! All I want is the monster, Gouroull. Gouroull!" The metal covered man guffawed loudly and continued to head towards the house.

And that was when Gouroull stepped onto the edge of their lantern's illumination. The harsh yellow light cast an odd glare across his chalky gray skin. He stood there for several seconds, his unblinking amber eyes almost glowing as he watched the hunters.

"Master! Master!" The shorter man began to jump up and down and scream. "The monster! Gouroull! The monster is here!"

The taller man spun and stared at Gouroull, who melted back into the void without a sound. "Die, inhuman freak! Die! Die! Die!"

Gouroull just stepped into the tree line when the whole world began to explode...

CHAPTER XXXV

Elizabeth Frankenstein took a long cleansing breath and looked to Hugh. "Lower the wheel," she said.

She knew her voice was shaking as she spoke. But she truly did not care. This was the culmination of her whole life. Once this creation succeeded, all the deprivations of her existence would be worth their price. She had done so much over the years to ensure a constant flow of capital. Though she was wealthy, thanks to her family, she knew that was, in the end, a finite resource. Through the years, she had used her medical skills to add to her coffers.

In Paris, a criminal group paid her to transplant a new heart in their leader. This man, only known as the Colonel, survived and ensured she was well-paid. He even had her smuggled out of the country and into Austria when one of her experiments escaped into the Paris tunnels and began killing people.

In Germany, she had assisted a doctor friend in the creation of an artificial woman. He knew that her creation would be as terrible and as monstrous as Gouroull, in her own way. But that was not her concern. The creation of a life from the spilled sperm of a hanged man was not her mission in life. All treatises on the subject stated the result was a life-form lacking a soul. They died by their own hand or were killed in the end. A waste of time. But the money earned was excellent and in gold.

Perhaps the oddest service was in the United States. A circus performer had come to her, explaining he wished both of his arms amputated. According to the man's tale, he had performed an act in which he threw knives with his feet. She and Hugh went to see his show. An impressive display of muscular control and strength. He smoked cigarettes and ate food with a fork entirely through the use of his feet. His arms were strapped against his body and he impressed the crowds with his skills.

Interested despite herself, Elizabeth had allowed another meeting with the circus man. According to him, he was in love with his partner. But she could not bear the touch of a man's arms. This amused her enough to agree, and Elizabeth took all of his money in payment for the double amputation. The arms were then utilized for her work and, later, the circus man, who died saving his love, became her property. Sadly those experiments were failures, resulting in a fire that killed over one hundred men, women and children. But the money was excellent. Elizabeth had used the majority of it to move their operations to Mexico and later San Pedro.

The wheel lowered slowly, exactly positioned above the corpse of the dead woman. Her body lay upon the metal slab, hovering just above the chemical tank. The led to the electrical generator were pressed deeply within her flesh; no other preparation could be made now. The experiment was commencing, though the slowness was causing an odd feeling of excitement in Elizabeth. She glanced at Hugh. He was watching the wheel while checking his lever. Very committed was her Hugh. A perfect follower.

The hypodermic needles plunged into the corpse simultaneously. The metal structure caused the chemical elixirs to enter the body with exact precision. Within seconds, the barrels of all eight syringes were empty and Elizabeth signaled to Hugh to withdraw the wheel.

Hugh dutifully pulled up the lever and the wheel retracted. He moved the device away from the tank and, after a nod from Elizabeth, pulled the second switch. The corpse was plunged into the chemical vat. According to Victor's notes, these compounds ensured the success of the internal and external transformation of the creation. Elizabeth watched as the changes to the epidermal layer began. It was time for her to enact the final step of the experiment.

"Clear!" Elizabeth's voice was high-pitched and shaky. There was actual fear building within her normally calm inner self. This was the conjunction of all her life, the precipice of a mighty mountain of science.

"Clear!" Hugh stepped back behind the lead shield and watched, his dark goggles in place over his eyes.

With a shaking hand, Elizabeth threw the knife switches and counted backwards. Upon hitting zero, she pulled the levers and watched the generator's charge build once again. Upon touching the red line, she flipped the switches on again. Each time she moved, the corpse shook and moved, a St. Vitus dance within a viscous liquid. Under other circumstances, Elizabeth might be amused by the musical hall quality of the convulsions of the body. But not now, not on this day.

After the fourth transmission of electricity, Elizabeth powered down all of the generators and placed the knife switches into the safety positions. "Retract the slab. Bring her up and remove the wires."

Hugh pulled the lever and retracted the slab. The heavy liquid from the tank spilled across the floor as the metal table emerged. He guided the steel sheet onto a nearby operating table, settling it in place with a light metallic ring. Secured, Hugh ran to the corpse and pulled out the heavy electrical cables, rolling them up and placing them across the room.

Elizabeth was by the side of the body and watched the transformation. The skin color was lighter than their last failure, chalk gray and spreading with uncanny speed. The body was already lengthening, the paroxysms were increasing as she observed. And with each tremor, the figure on the table grew in height. Elizabeth estimated her creation would stand over seven feet in height. But she was far lighter than the massive Gouroull.

The oddest sight of the metamorphosis were the hands. They lengthened, the large middle finger being longer than Elizabeth's hand. And each finger were capped with lengthy, tapering barbed talons. These nails did not resemble that of a human female in any way. In fact, no creature in any epoch of history ever possessed such terrible natural weapon.

Elizabeth was about to remark as such to Hugh, when the body twitched. The arms and legs shuddered and the torso lifted slightly from the table. Then, her eyes opened and amber orbs focused on Elizabeth and Hugh. The head slowly swiveled their direction, the alien eyes focusing on the two doctors.

Elizabeth raised her hands above her head and her voice began to cry: "She's alive! She's alive!"

And then, the outside door flew open...

CHAPTER XXXVI

The bullets decimated a tree to Gouroull's right. The splinters exploded outward, shredding the vegetation within a ten-foot radius. A normal human would have been torn in pieces, but Frankenstein's most lethal creation was unharmed. Still the impact of the heavy lead projectiles tossed him backwards. Another series of explosions rocked the area, causing Gouroull to be tossed aside once again.

Standing, he began to circle away from the villa. There was danger in each of these bullets, even to one with his inhuman skin. But most importantly, this weapon could decimate Elizabeth Frankenstein's lab instantly. He could not allow such an occurrence, not again. There were too many failures in the past and he needed to draw this hunter away.

The man and his servant hated him. Who knew why? Possibly, they were do-gooders. There was that monster-killer, the English warrior who had slain the vampire countess in France. Or that Templar knight, the immortal who wandered the Earth fighting evil in the name of Heaven. Could these two be such heroes? Doubtful by the crazed way the taller one screamed, "Die!" over and over a moment ago.

Possibly he killed one of their families in the past. There were legions of such victims throughout Gouroull's extended life. The survivors were often too terrified to even consider acting. But there were those who took such momentous events as a reason for living. They trained and planned, seeking a means to battle him one day. Gouroull became the very focus of their exist-ence... they usually died quite terrible deaths...

It didn't matter in the end. His duty was to protect Elizabeth Frankenstein, her sad dog of an assistant and, most importantly, his mate. Gouroull ran through the jungle, leading the hunters away from the villa...

"Oww! Damn, shit, fuck, piss!" Martin Mars re-moved his hand from the metal gauntlet and shook it several times. "The damned glove is boiling! The damned glove is boiling!"

"My apologies, master." Hans stepped forward and poured a large flask of water over the machine gun and metal gauntlet. "This particular gun is very, very power-ful. But it heats up quite quickly. After each burst, I shall douse it with water."

Martin Mars chuckled. "No apologies, Hans. No apologies, Hans. This device is wondrous! Wondrous!"

And so it was for Martin Mars. The harness spread the weight of the weapons across his shoulders, legs and back. And the servos increased his relative strength by double. This enabled Mars to carry the heavy machine gun with ease. And, more importantly, he could fire this terrible weapon without the need for a tripod. Because the entire structure was the support. An impressive de-vice, even for the very clever Hans.

For his part, Hans was only armed with a new set of knives and a heavy revolver. But he was almost as load-ed as Martin Mars. Three more belts of bullets were in a box strapped to his back. Such ammunition was often carried by a large soldier who was deemed best at lug-ging heavy gear and little else. In this situation, such duties fell to Hans. Fortunately he had strong legs and a good back.

"I hear him, master. I believe the monster is trying to circle back to our boat!" Hans's voice rose at the thought of being trapped out in the middle of this desolate death zone. The jungle was teeming with unclean creatures, monkeys, lions, tigers, bears, giant apes and tribes of head hunters. This was not a land for a civilized man!

"Well heard, my little friend! Well heard, my little friend!" Mars stepped forward and fired a long arc of fire from the flame thrower ahead of the position Gouroull appeared to be fleeing. The jungle burst into flames, a large fallen tree instantly igniting and sending long tongues of flame up into the sky.

"Oh, isn't it lovely?" Hans stared at the burning jungle. The flames were so beautiful... so intoxicating. Fire was a purifier, something the world needed more and more as vulgarity overtook even the most innocent. Perhaps that was the way to save the children, fire...

Just then, Gouroull leaped from the thicket and grabbed Hans from behind. Mars heard his servant's shriek of shock, but the heavy harness prevented him from turning fast enough to aid his aide.

Gouroull lifted Hans above his head and threw the little man over Martin Mars's head. The tiny German child-killer flailed in the air until he landed in the middle of the inferno. Hans screamed as the flames ignited his clothing and the box on his back. He was about to scream a warning to his master, when the heavy machine gun bullets exploded.

The explosion rocked the very ground they stood on, with after effects being felt all the way to the distant towns. Martin Mars's servant was torn to pieces as heavy lead bullets ripped him apart as they flew in every direction. Gouroull scrambled to his feet, his mission still not complete. The hunter was also rising and turning, his weapons still dangerous enough to imperil Frankenstein's monster. The death of the hunter's helper was a well-timed bit of luck. Gouroull would need to search for another.

Vanishing into the jungle, Gouroull headed towards the abandoned village of The Living. This would be an excellent spot for the battle.

Martin Mars snarled as he slogged after the monster. The loss of Hans angered him to his very core. Where would he find another servant with the little German's skills?

CHAPTER XXXVII

Elizabeth and Hugh spun towards the door as it slammed open. Both imagined Gouroull was making his presence known. But the titanic terror was nowhere to be seen. Instead, the withered crone from the village of savages hobbled in. She leaned heavily upon a cane which, to the eyes of both medical professionals, looked like a human thigh bone. She raised a gnarled finger and began whispering, her words holding the edge and venom of a curse.

And then, she stepped closer and swung her cane in a long arc. A table full of test tubes and flasks exploded into tiny shards of glass which flew about the lab. Chemicals fell to the ground, some smoking as they hit the stone floor or mixed together. Moraika screamed again and a bottle full of vampire blood fell to the floor. The heavy stone container did not break, but the precious liquid dribbled to the floor.

Elizabeth snarled with rage as she picked up a heavy, newly sharpened bone saw. She swung the instrument straight for the throat of the elderly wise woman, who surprisingly did not back up or even attempt to fend off the assault. Instead, she smiled and waited, allowing the surgical tool to nearly decapitated her ancient neck.

Moraika died as she fell to floor. But she would never truly die. Her way was prepared by Allpa and Supay.

Elizabeth tossed the bloody bone saw aside and sighed: "Savages."

Then a low growl filled the air...

The Living sat huddled around a large cooking fire. Normally they would be singing and dancing, celebrating the end of the day. But not tonight. Their wise woman was still not here. She said she would join them and she was still missing.

"Moraika will come," sour old Pacha the Lame insisted when one of the tribe grumbled. He might be the most unpleasant of The Living. But he never doubted the words of the wise.

"Moraika is here," a small voice piped up. The young one who wore Moraika's bag stepped into the circle of the fire light. She slowly turned, looking each in the eye. All of The Living dropped their eyes in surprise and fear. The child, formerly a young, happy little girl, was no more. Her eyes held the ancient terrible gaze of the wise woman. Moraika lived again. Moraika would always be with The Living.

Elizabeth and Hugh stepped backwards. More dissonance joined the growls. A hiss, buzzing, chirping and howls floated to their ears. The jangle of sounds grew in intensity with each passing second, a cacophony of natural noise. Hugh covered his ears as he backed away, terrified to his core.

Then the doorway appeared to expel the entire contents of the jungle known as the *Corazon Negro* into their lab. A cloud of insects and colorful birds flew in, their passage reducing visibility instantly. They were followed by lizards of all sizes, alligators, monkeys and odd animals whose taxonomy was unknown to man's science. Then came the serpents. Two enormous snakes, each longer than five men and enormously thick. And smaller ones, their hissing joining the rising discord.

Hugh turned and noticed their creation was nowhere to be seen. He screamed Elizabeth's name and reached to grab her and pull her from the attacking beasts. Just as he touched her hand, a savage shriek filled the air. A yellow and black blur had struck Elizabeth and slammed her to the ground. A jaguar, larger than Hugh, bit down on her throat, killing her instantly. This was the final act of ancient Moraika, destroying the woman who Allpa and Supay held was the true danger in this stone house.

Hugh Larkin wept as he fled through the house. Climbing out a window, he was surprised none of the monstrous jungle creatures pursued him through the villa. But they were dumb animals; perhaps something in the lab frightened them and they were fleeing back the way they came. Who knew what creatures from this misbegotten land would do?

The vanishing of their creation was also bizarre. Perhaps she was hiding in the closet in the lab. If so, she would be destroyed as fast as poor Elizabeth. Those giant snakes and jaguars were as deadly creatures as could be found on the planet. No matter how strong Elizabeth's revenant was, the sheer volume of predators would drag her down. No matter. Hugh would create another.

Hugh ran into the jungle. His plan was simple. Walk in a long circle to the shore of the lake. Then he would walk along the shore until he found that mining town. He could hire a boat there, return and salvage Elizabeth's journals and scientific equipment. Then he would reproduce the results before a board of reputable medical men. Elizabeth's genius would never die. By this time next year, all would know the name Elizabeth Frankenstein!

Looking back over his shoulder to take one final look at his former home, Hugh tripped over a fallen root or a loose stone. He tumbled forward, the air exploding from his lungs, causing him to moan with pain and feel slightly dizzy. Opening his eyes, Hugh was surprised to see a pair of feet mere inches from his face. They were large and dark in the darkness, not that of Gouroull or his mate. Rescue was here!

Rising, Hugh stared up into the fast of a tall, sturdily built native carrying a black wooden spear. His face and body were covered with a rainbow of colors and he examined Hugh with ancient, dark eyes.

"Oh, thank Heaven! Please help me!" Hugh practically fell back at the man's feet. Even a savage was better than those terrible animals back in the lab.

The tall man pointed his spear at Hugh, not uttering a sound. Two men appeared from the darkness, twisting Hugh's arms behind his back in a painful manner. A third stepped into view and tied a rope around the European's mouth as he began to protest. They then dragged Hugh Larkin into the darkness, never to be seen again. The jungle shaman's promise to the spirits was complete...

CHAPTER XXXVIII

Martin Mars slowly stumped after Gouroull, spotting glimpses of the monster, but never long enough to take aim. They were soon in a village, one that reminded him of the Indian long houses he'd viewed in museums. Perfect. If a bunch of Indians were huddling inside, they would just be more victims of the monster Gouroull.

Stepping forward, Mars fired the flame throw onto the roof and nearby wall of the long house. The wood and grass structure ignited instantly, filling the air with the harsh, hot flames. Day became night as Martin Mars laughed and searched for Gouroull. He was winning; he would destroy this monster and be recognized as the world's foremost expert on the unusual. All would bow when he walked in the room, knowing they were in the presence of greatness.

Just then, a hand seized his neck and he heard the sound of ripping paper in his ears. A flow of red liquid sprayed across the ground and Martin Mars narrowed his eyes in confusion. Rain wasn't red. Why was there red water on the ground? And what was the world spinning? And he couldn't seem to breathe. What was happening?

Martin Mars died face down before the burning long house once belonging to the tribe known as The Living. A tall figure stood over him, gazing down at the expiring form with alien amber eyes.

A second figure stepped into view, hidden mere moments ago by the burning building. The giant approached, the light illuminating horrific yellow eyes, chalk gray skin, black lips, tangled back hair and razor-sharp teeth. His face was a twisted parody of humanity, terrifying to view, a gargoyle brought to life. This was Gouroull, Frankenstein's terrible monster, the mythical fiend who was a nightmare to mankind.

The second figure was a head shorter than Gouroull, possessing the same inhuman yellow eyes and chaotic mass of black hair. But this hair was longer, falling past narrower shoulders. This being was female, with flared hips and large breasts that did not appear oversized on her seven-foot form. Her face was frightful, a sharply angular demon with an extended pointed chin and a long, twisted dagger of a nose.

"Gouroull," he said, breathing his name, his first word upon gaining life, as he peered down at the only other of his kind.

"Basheer," the woman hissed back, her black lips twisting into a bizarre parody of a smile.

"Basheer," he replied, extending one massive hand towards her.

"Gouroull," she breathed back, entwining her finger within his and moving closer to her mate.

They were mated; they knew this instinctively. This was the start of a new race. This was truly the triumph of Frankenstein.

CHAPTER XXXIX

The Master stepped away from the seer pool and smiled. All went as he predicted. Turning to his slave, he issued his orders: "Summons all. Bring those two to me. I have... plans for them..."

The slave bowed deeply and backed from the room. The Master sat down on his lesser throne and stared into space. He, the mighty Nephren-Ka, greatest of Egypt's priest kings, unliving being for over four thousand years, smiled. This new race would serve his needs well. His father, the Black Pharaoh, would rise once again to rule the Earth. These two were the gateway...

Afterword

Gouroull returns and, after almost two centuries of looking for her through eight novels, finds his mate. A troublesome journey, to say the least. It is still mind-blowing to me that I'm following in the footsteps of the legendary Jean-Claude Carrière. The man is one of the greats of modern cinema, writing films that are spoken about by fans and critics alike. Not too much pressure, eh?

This book had an interesting history. When my friend/editor/mentor/publisher Jean-Marc Lofficier let me know he'd like another Gouroull tale, I thought long and hard about what to produce. Originally, I was think-ing of something similar to the present tale, a small, tight novel with a group of characters dealing with the horror that was Frankenstein's monster.

But I thought I needed to go bigger, a huge tale complete with battle scenes and terrible menaces. This idea was something akin to *The Horror of Frankenstein* meets a World War II film, with a side order of a Holly-wood epic. Jean-Marc, whom I prize for his amazing writing and editing skills, as well as his total honesty with his writers, shot the idea down. He made it clear to me that my idea might work for a Marvel Cinematic Universe film, but for a book, not so much.

And of course, he was right. But he almost always is under these circumstances. Going back to my original idea, I was forced to step up as a writer and produce a true novel. I hope it worked, but it was a learning expe-rience for me. Despite being published about thirty or so times by the time I write this afterword, I still consider myself very much a beginner in the literary world. Happily, I have guides like Jean-Marc, and others, to help show me the path.

Triumph has a far smaller cast than *The Quest of Frankenstein*. That novel was a sprawling epic, one that took place in many areas of the horror universe. Still, you should know something of the characters who appear throughout. Some chapters use the same characters, so I won't detail them further here.

Chapter 1: Moraika and the tribe known as The Living emerge from one of my favorite places in the world, the American Museum of Natural History. Every year, sometimes twice a year, I travel into Manhattan and visit this incredible collection, which covers all facets of our amazing planet. The collections I spend the longest in are the North American animals, the dinosaurs and the North and South American native peoples. From the latter, I learned of the many unique ways the natives view our world. Their religion connects deeper with the natural world and possesses depths that rival any of the better known faiths, such as Christianity, Judaism, Islam and Buddhism. Allpa, Supay, and the names of the Living, were derived from ancient Incan spirits and proper names. Their views of the Earth were a combination of several Central and South American belief systems, with just a touch of my strange ideas, thanks to a lifetime of reading H. Rider Haggard, Robert E. Howard and other amazing scribes.

Chapter 2: Martin Mars is an original character. He's a combination of the legendary oddity showman Robert Ripley of *Ripley's Believe It or Not* fame, the various Hammer Horror monster hunters created after

Peter Cushing moved on, and carnival barkers I've encountered over the years. His habit or repeating himself comes from an interview I once saw with a serial killer. Every time he got excited, he repeated himself. It was odd to watch and I still haven't a clue what it signifies. Hans is based on the infamous Hans Beckert, the child-murdering serial killer of Fritz Lang's masterpiece *M*. That film still moves me, demonstrating the power that a motion picture can have upon a person. Peter Lorre's performance as the pathetic, twisted murderer was one of the great moments of the man's long career. And Hans Beckert is one of the truest demonstrations of the soul of a habitual killer. I honestly don't think any film has equaled *M*'s stark sad power.

In mentioning Peter Lorre, I do need to relate a story, since I knew of the man far longer than would be expected. For several years, I lived with my parents in South Orange, NJ. Back then, you knew your neighbors, one of whom happened to be Peter Lorre's brother. And they looked amazingly alike. One day, while watching a horror film program called *Chiller Theater* (best known for a sequence in which a hand rose out of a swamp while an creepy voice intoned, "*Chiller*"), I spotted a familiar face on the screen. I called over my mother.

"Mommy, why is Mister Lorre on TV?" I asked.

My mother laughed and explained that this was our neighbor's older brother, a famous actor named Peter Lorre. I don't remember how I reacted, but I never forgot that little fact. And it made me a lifelong fan of the great actor.

Chapter 3: Elizabeth Frankenstein comes out of the great tradition of Frankenstein family members who went into monster creation. Her lineage is based on

Mary Shelley's details of Victor Frankenstein's family, only embellishing in subsequent generations. Her insanity comes from my having spent over forty years reading and watching various mad scientists who were attempting to follow Victor's legacy.

Hugh Larkin comes from an odd place in my psyche. One series of films I've always enjoyed were the Richard Gordon *Doctor* movies. Most starred a young Dirk Bogarde, who played Simon Sparrow, a talented medical man who was always in search of love. The true star was actually James Robertson-Justice as the irascible, loud but secretly kind surgeon, Sir Lancelot Spratt. Bogarde and his doctor pals went through nurses, heiresses and models with astonishing regularity. Usually our young hero would find the love of his life in these films; they weren't complex affairs, although the lady in question almost never appeared or was mentioned in the subsequent movies. Of course, that led my rather twisted mind to transform the virtuous, upright physician into a self-deluding monster who was, if anything, more horrible than Elizabeth Frankenstein. Yes, I'm crazy that way.

Chapter 9: The Master and his followers come from a combination of Egyptology, mummy films and H.P. Lovecraft. I've always wanted to write such a character and Nephren-Ka was a perfect choice. One day, I hope to write more on the infamous Black Pharaoh and his plans for the modern world.

Chapter 10: The jungle shaman comes from the same source as Moraika. While at the American Museum of Natural History, I once viewed a film in the South American hall which showed the elaborate piercings and paints worn by certain tribes. Their rites were impressive and elaborate, and very hard for me to completely comprehend. The rites he and Moraika underwent are all from my own imagination; I don't honestly know where they came from other than that scary place. The location is a combination of many lost empires and cities written by Edgar Rice Burroughs, Haggard, Howard, Lin Carter and Clark Ashton Smith. To this day, those types of tales thrill me and I love to read them, despite their improbability in the modern world.

Chapter 11: A chance to use Jack Woltz was a fun moment. The character is such a pig. While viewing the film, which I saw years before reading the novel, I'd hoped they do something to him rather than the horse. But it was a powerful scene none-the-less.

Chapter 13: San Pedro and the "Tiger of San Pedro" are from the Arthur Conan Doyle's Sherlock Holmes story, *The Adventure of the Wisteria Lodge*—not one of the better Holmes tales overall. But it played into some research I did when people were making a big deal over the play *Evita*. I decided to look into the history of the Peron presidency and found a world of scary politics and thievery worthy of an organized crime family.

Martin Romero and his tale come from rising men I learned of when I was studying that realm of political history, along with that of Mexican history. Scary stuff. Later, I learned of similar history in countries like Liberia, the Central African Republic, and many other countries.

Chapter 16: Colonel Bozzo-Corona is the dreaded and seemingly ageless leader of the Black Coats, a crime cartel introduced by Paul Féval, whose novels have all been translated and published by Black Coat Press.

Chapter 25: Hidalgo was the country from which Lester Dent's pulp hero Doc Savage received regular shipments of gold. According to those amazing books, Doc used much of the gold to help the country, so I tried to show the locale as a pleasant one.

Chapter 26: The scientist mentioned, Fen-Chu, was a villain in *L'Enigmatique Fen-Chu* by George Fronval (1944). He's an Asian mastermind bent on world domination through his super science. Nice and obscure!

Chapter 28: The young woman with a love for poison is derived from the 80-90s American obsession with true crime. There were tons of books on men and women who committed heinous acts towards friends and family, but the ones that stuck in my mind were some of the terrible poisonings performed by wealthy women. There's something really frightening about those stories. Odd stuff, but useful for a horror writer. Mavis is the mother of the infamous Gladys Kravitz, the nosy neighbor in *Bewitched*. I loved that character; she is such a harridan!

Sheriff Macintosh is based on many intelligent police officers I've known over the years. One thing I learned is, if I ever went into crime, these men and women would catch me with ease. Happily, I never possessed any desire to break the law. Oh and getting to mention Bertie Wooster, even in passing, was a joy. I love P.G. Wodehouse's comic novels and stories, especially those featuring Jeeves and Wooster. If you haven't read them, I advise you to do so and enjoy the hysterical world Wodehouse created.

Mnophka was a narcotic discussed by the legendary horror and fantasy writer Clark Ashton Smith in *The Plutonian Drug*.

Chapter 29: Countess Luisa was a character I created for an early short story that was, I'm happy to say, never published. It's a really poorly written work, before I had a clue on how to tell a tale that people actually might enjoy reading. But she lived again, if briefly, in this chapter.

Chapter 31: Vrollo was the tramp who revived Gouroull in *The Tower of Frankenstein* by Jean-Claude Carrière. Pastor Schleger and his wife Ingrid appeared in *The Night of Frankenstein* with a mad Ingrid returning as an inmate in the Hallshofen Lunatic Asylum in *The Seal of Frankenstein*.

Chapter 33: A brief shout-out to the previously-mentioned Sir Lancelot Spratt. Created by Richard Gordon and played by James Robertson Justice, Spratt was a bellowing monster who was a surgical mastermind. And he possessed a decent side hidden beneath his scary, snarling persona. Justice played him as larger than life, taking what could have been a minor character and making him one of the most important facets of the series. His dialogue was always a delight and I think I preferred him to the younger stars of the films.

The fish-men are the Deep Ones from H.P. Lovecraft's works and the vampire city of Selene is the site of Paul Féval's novel *Vampire City*.[1] The latter was written in 1875 a full 24 years before Bram Stoker's *Dracula*.

---

[1] Black Coat Press, ISBN 978-0-9740711-6-9.

Also mentioned were Dr. Daka, the evil Japanese scientist from the *Batman* serial, played by J. Carroll Naish, and Dr. Janos Rukh, played by Boris Karloff, from *The Invisible Ray*. The latter also stars Bela Lugosi, one of these their better pairings, the best being *The Black Cat*.

Not as many shout-outs as *Quest*, but that's not surprising. They are two vastly different books, though I hope this one was an even greater pleasure for you, the reader.

As to the future of Gouroull, no clue here. This does feel like the final act of the monster, but who knows what the future holds? In the world of horror, endings are rarely final.

Special thanks to Jean-Marc Lofficier, Gail Schildiner, Ruth Schildiner, Shihan James Amorosi, Win Scott Eckert, Rick Lai, Tommy Hancock, Chuck Loridans, David Gerrold, Peter Rawlik, Ron Fortier, Tony Isabella and the Wold Newton Meteoric Society members.

Frank Schildiner

SF & FANTASY

Adolphe Alhaiza. *Cybele*
Alphonse Allais. *The Adventures of Captain Cap*
Henri Allorge. *The Great Cataclysm*
Guy d'Armen. *Doc Ardan: The City of Gold and Lepers; The Troglodytes of Mount Everest/The Giants of Black Lake; The Abominable Snowman*
G.-J. Arnaud. *The Ice Company*
André Arnyvelde. *The Ark; The Mutilated Bacchus*
Charles Asselineau. *The Double Life*
Henri Austruy. *The Eupantophone; The Olotelepan; The Petitpaon Era*
Barillet-Lagargousse. *The Final War*
Cyprien Bérard. *The Vampire Lord Ruthwen*
S. Henry Berthoud. *Martyrs of Science*
Aloysius Bertrand. *Gaspard de la Nuit*
Richard Bessière. *The Gardens of the Apocalypse; The Masters of Silence*
Chevalier de Béthune. *The World of Mercury*
Albert Bleunard. *Ever Smaller*
Félix Bodin. *The Novel of the Future*
Pierre Boitard. *Journey to the Sun*
Louis Boussenard. *Monsieur Synthesis*
Alphonse Brown. *City of Glass; The Conquest of the Air*
Émile Calvet. *In a Thousand Years*
André Caroff. *The Terror of Madame Atomos; Miss Atomos; The Return of Madame Atomos; The Mistake of Madame Atomos; The Monsters of Madame Atomos; The Revenge of Madame Atomos; The Resurrection of Madame Atomos; The Mark of Madame Atomos; The Spheres of Madame Atomos; The Wrath of Madame Atomos* (w/M. & Sylvie Stéphan)
Félicien Champsaur. *Homo-Deus; The Human Arrow; Nora, The Ape-Woman; Ouha, King of the Apes; Pharaoh's Wife*
Didier de Chousy. *Ignis*
Jules Clarétie. *Obsession*
Jacques Collin de Plancy. *Voyage to the Center of the Earth*
Michel Corday. *The Eternal Flame; The Lynx* (w/André Couvreur)
André Couvreur. *Caresco, Superman; The Exploits of Professor Tornada* (3 vols.); *The Necessary Evil*

Gaston Danville. *The Perfume of Lust*
Camille Debans. *The Misfortunes of John Bull*
Captain Danrit. *Undersea Odyssey*
C. I. Defontenay. *Star (Psi Cassiopeia)*
Charles Derennes. *The People of the Pole*
Georges Dodds (anthologist). *The Missing Link*
Charles Dodeman. *The Silent Bomb*
Harry Dickson. *The Heir of Dracula; Harry Dickson vs. The Spider*
Jules Dornay. *Lord Ruthven Begins*
Alfred Driou. *The Adventures of a Parisian Aeronaut*
Odette Dulac. *The War of the Sexes*
Alexandre Dumas. *The Return of Lord Ruthven*
Renée Dunan. *Baal; The Ultimate Pleasure*
J.-C. Dunyach. *The Night Orchid; The Thieves of Silence*
Henri Duvernois. *The Man Who Found Himself*
Achille Eyraud. *Voyage to Venus*
Henri Falk. *The Age of Lead*
Paul Féval. *Anne of the Isles; Knightshade; Revenants; Vampire City; The Vampire Countess; The Wandering Jew's Daughter*
Paul Féval, *fils. Felifax, the Tiger-Man*
Charles de Fieux. *Lamékis*
Fernand Fleuret. *Jim Click*
Charles-Marie Flor O'Squarr. *Phantoms*
Louis Forest. *Someone is Stealing Children in Paris*
Arnould Galopin. *Doctor Omega*; *Doctor Omega and the Shadowmen* (anthology)
Judith Gautier. *Isoline and the Serpent-Flower*
H. Gayar. *The Marvelous Adventures of Serge Myrandhal on Mars*
Louis Geoffroy. *The Apocryphal Napoleon*
G.L. Gick. *Harry Dickson and the Werewolf of Rutherford Grange*
Raoul Gineste. *The Second Life of Doctor Albin*
Delphine de Girardin. *Balzac's Cane*
Léon Gozlan. *The Vampire of the Val-de-Grâce*
Jules Gros. *The Fossil Man*
Jimmy Guieu. *The Polarian-Denebian War* (2 vols.)
Edmond Haraucourt. *Daah, the First Human; Illusions of Immortality*
Nathalie Henneberg. *The Green Gods*
Eugène Hennebert. *The Enchanted City*
Jules Hoche. *The Maker of Men and His Formula*
V. Hugo, P. Foucher & P. Meurice. *The Hunchback of Notre-Dame*
Romain d'Huissier. *Hexagon: Dark Matter*

Jules Janin. *The Magnetized Corpse*
Michel Jeury. *Chronolysis*
Gustave Kahn. *The Tale of Gold and Silence*
Gérard Klein. *The Mote in Time's Eye*
Fernand Kolney. *Love in 5000 Years*
Paul Lacroix. *Danse Macabre*
Louis-Guillaume de La Follie. *The Unpretentious Philosopher*
Jean de La Hire. *The Fiery Wheel; Enter the Nyctalope; The Nyctalope on Mars; The Nyctalope vs. Lucifer; The Nyctalope Steps In; Night of the Nyctalope; Return of the Nyctalope*
Etienne-Léon de Lamothe-Langon. *The Virgin Vampire*
André Laurie. *Spiridon*
Gabriel de Lautrec. *The Vengeance of the Oval Portrait*
Alain le Drimeur. *The Future City*
Georges Le Faure & Henri de Graffigny. *The Extraordinary Adventures of a Russian Scientist Across the Solar System* (2 vols.)
Gustave Le Rouge. *The Dominion of the World* (w/Gustave Guitton) (4 vols.); *The Mysterious Doctor Cornelius* (3 vols.); *The Vampires of Mars*
Jules Lermina. *The Battle of Strasbourg; Mysteryville; Panic in Paris; The Secret of Zippelius; To-Ho and the Gold Destroyers*
Maurice Level. *The Gates of Hell*
André Lichtenberger. *The Centaurs; The Children of the Crab*
Maurice Limat. *Mephista*
Listonai. *The Philosophical Voyager*
Jean-Marc & Randy Lofficier. *Edgar Allan Poe on Mars; The Katrina Protocol; Pacifica 1, 2; Robonocchio; Return of the Nyctalope;* (anthologists) *Tales of the Shadowmen 1-13; The Vampire Almanac* (2 vols.)
Ch. Lomon & P.-B. Gheuzi. *The Last Days of Atlantis*
Camille Mauclair. *The Virgin Orient*
Xavier Mauméjean. *The League of Heroes*
Joseph Méry. *The Tower of Destiny*
Hippolyte Mettais. *Paris Before the Deluge; The Year 5865*
Louise Michel. *The Human Microbes; The New World*
Tony Moilin. *Paris in the Year 2000*
José Moselli. *Illa's End*
John-Antoine Nau. *Enemy Force*
Marie Nizet. *Captain Vampire*
Charles Nodier. *Trilby and The Crumb Fairy*
C. Nodier, A. Beraud & Toussaint-Merle. *Frankenstein*

Henri de Parville. *An Inhabitant of the Planet Mars*

Gaston de Pawlowski. *Journey to the Land of the 4th Dimension*

Georges Pellerin. *The World in 2000 Years*

Ernest Pérochon. *The Frenetic People*

Pierre Pelot. *The Child Who Walked on the Sky*

Jean Petithuguenin. *An International Mission to the Moon*

J. Polidori, C. Nodier, E. Scribe. *Lord Ruthven the Vampire*

P.-A. Ponson du Terrail. *The Immortal Woman; The Vampire and the Devil's Son; The Police Agent*

Georges Price. *The Missing Men of the* Sirius

René Pujol. *The Chimerical Quest*

Edgar Quinet. *Ahasuerus; The Enchanter Merlin*

Henri de Régnier. *A Surfeit of Mirrors*

Maurice Renard. *The Blue Peril; Doctor Lerne; The Doctored Man; A Man Among the Microbes; The Master of Light*

Restif de la Bretonne. *The Discovery of the Austral Continent by a Flying Man; Posthumous Correspondence* (3 vols.)

Jean Richepin. *The Crazy Corner; The Wing*

Albert Robida. *The Adventures of Saturnin Farandoul; Chalet in the Sky; The Clock of the Centuries; The Electric Life; The Engineer Von Satanas*

J.-H. Rosny Aîné. *Helgvor of the Blue River; The Givreuse Enigma; The Mysterious Force; The Navigators of Space; Vamireh; The World of the Variants; The Young Vampire*

Marcel Rouff. *Journey to the Inverted World*

Marie-Anne de Roumier-Robert. *The Voyage of Lord Seaton to the Seven Planets*

Léonie Rouzade. *The World Turned Upside Down*

Han Ryner. *The Human Ant; The Superhumans*

Louis-Claude de Saint-Martin. *The Crocodile*

Frank Schildiner. *The Quest of Frankenstein*

Pierre de Selenes: *An Unknown World*

Norbert Sevestre. *Sâr Dubnotal: Vs. Jack the Ripper; The Astral Trail*

Angelo de Sorr. *The Vampires of London*

Brian Stableford. *The Empire of the Necromancers (1. The Shadow of Frankenstein; 2. Frankenstein and the Vampire Countess; 3. Frankenstein in London); The Wayward Muse; Eurydice's Lament; The Mirror of Dionysius; The New Faust at the Tragicomique; Sherlock Holmes and The Vampires of Eternity; The Stones of Camelot* (anthologist) *News from the Moon; The Germans on Venus; The Su-*

preme Progress; The World Above the World; Nemoville; Investigations of the Future; The Conqueror of Death; The Revolt of the Machines; The Man With the Blue Face; The Aerial Valley; The New Moon; The Nickel Man; On the Brink of the World's End; The Mirror of Present Events; The Humanishere
Jacques Spitz. *The Eye of Purgatory*
Kurt Steiner. *Ortog*
Eugène Thébault. *Radio-Terror*
C.-F. Tiphaigne de La Roche. *Amilec*
Simon Tyssot de Patot. *The Strange Voyages of Jacques Massé and Pierre de Mésange*
Louis Ulbach. *Prince Bonifacio*
Théo Varlet. *The Castaways of Eros; The Golden Rock.; The Martian Epic* (w/Octave Joncquel); *Timeslip Troopers* (w/André Blandin); *The Xenobiotic Invasion*
Pierre Véron. *The Merchants of Health*
Paul Vibert. *The Mysterious Fluid*
Villiers de l'Isle-Adam. *The Scaffold; The Vampire Soul*
Gaston de Wailly. *The Murderer of the World*
Philippe Ward. *Artahe; Manhattan Ghost* (w/Mickael Laguerre); *The Song of Montségur* (w/Sylvie Miller)

Victor Margueritte. *The Bacheloress; The Companion; The Couple*

NON-FICTION

Stephen R. Bissette. *Blur 1-5. Green Mountain Cinema 1; Teen Angels*
Win Scott Eckert. *Crossovers* (2 vols.)
Georges Grison. *The Heads that Fell in Paris*
Jean-Marc & Randy Lofficier. *Shadowmen* (2 vols.)
Randy Lofficier. *Over Here*
Brian Stableford. *The Plurality of Imaginary Worlds*

www.ingramcontent.com/pod-product-compliance
Lightning Source LLC
Chambersburg PA
CBHW030359020726
47493CB00003B/887